# A Natural Order

greenhill

Copyright © 2024 Tyson Lait

All rights reserved. No part of this publication may be reproduced, distributed, or transmitted in any form or by any means, including photocopying, recording, or other electronic or mechanical methods, without the prior written permission of the publisher, except in the case of brief quotations embodied in critical reviews and certain other non-commercial uses permitted by copyright law.

(*) greenhill

https://greenhillpublishing.com.au/

Lait, Tyson (author)
*A Natural Order*
ISBN 978-1-923214-78-1
FICTION | FANTASY

Typesetting Calluna Regular 11/18pt
Cover Image by AI generated (Adobe Firefly)
Cover and book design by Green Hill Publishing

# A Natural Order

**TYSON LAIT**

# Prologue

THE LIGHT WIELDERS came into being at the end of the first war between the Spirits and the humans, around two thousand years ago. The war had been raging for some time when an Anomaly emerged and claimed to have a staff that had been made from a branch freely given to him by the Spirit tree. The story went that the staff had a sliver of the Spirit's soul within. The two god-like beings and creators of the human race, Freom and Muefrede, also sang a portion of their souls into it. This act condemned the Spirits and the humans to the same fate, as the staff could now destroy them both.

The Anomaly forced the two warring sides into signing a treaty, and the terms of it had to be enforced. The problem was solved by the Anomaly who, for lack of a nicer term, 'convinced' Freom and Muefrede to create a race capable of doing so. The race was created and its members were called Light Wielders, since they were able to absorb the land's natural energy that flowed within all things, and to form the raw energy into castable spheres. The earth's energy also endowed them with incredible strength, and with this combination of abilities they kept the Spirits and humans in check. The Light Wielders called themselves the Jelery.

The Light Wielders that followed the initial emergence did not come from other Light Wielders, as was the case with humans and Spirits; they were born into the the entire land from within every social order of the humans, from the rich to the poor. It was the job of the Ravers to announce their arrival, and an infant Light Wielder would be collected from the mother after he had been weaned. It was deemed a great honour for the family to have a Light Wielder born into it. They gained prestige from it, and were held in high regard in their respective communities.

Things flowed smoothly for the first fifteen hundred years as the Spirits and the humans followed the rules of the treaty, and the land flourished. But there came a time when one of those amongst the Jelery sought more than the mundane existence he was living. He experimented with the forbidden technique and found, much to his delight, that his power surpassed all in the order. However, for dabbling with the forbidden, he was expelled from the order. As his power grew, so did his legend, and soon several other Jelery sought him out in order to learn his ways. He openly defied the teachings of the Jelery, and took another name designed to reflect the opposite values and rules, calling himself and his band of followers the Telirian. Those in the Jelery order scoffed at the young upstart, but did nothing to quell his slow rise to power. They later lamented their decision to sit idly by as his ranks grew in number. He eventually died, as do all Light Wielders, albeit after living four times the life span of a normal man. They hoped that with his death the order would fizzle out, but it endured and produced many an influential leader, and their power became greater still. Eventually, as the Telirian influence started to weaken the treaty's rules and regulations, things were heading for the inevitable outcome.

Once again the Spirits grew hateful of the human race, but humans paid no heed to the warning signals the Spirits provided. And once again the Anomaly had to act, but he found his body was too weary to respond. So the Earthbound Spirits had to search for another. They whispered to the mad men called the Ravers that the time was at hand for a second reckoning, to quell the uprising of the Spirits and enchain the humans back to the rules, so that the equality that once flowed throughout the land might be restored. Yet a number of the Spirits did not want a second reckoning. They felt that the time for revenge upon humans was at hand, and sought to actively thwart the rise of the new Anomaly and the forced subjection he brought.

But the Earthbound Spirits were talking more frequently, and excitement was running through them. They whispered to all who could hear them that the time of the new Anomaly was almost at hand. *Beware his coming*, they warned, *lest you be destroyed.*

# 1

'SHUT UP, SHUT up!' screamed Crawley.

He lay back down on the hard straw mattress and squeezed his temples between the palms of his hands, until flashes of pain shot across his forehead and bored into the back of his eyes. He began to cry softly and curled himself into a foetal position, trying to gain comfort from the heat his body emitted.

'Soon he will come, soon,' whispered the voice.

'Soon, soon, soon,' joined in the other voices in an even quieter tone.

'You know what you must do,' said another in a commanding tone.

'You know, you know, you know,' echoed the other voices in unison.

'Yes, yes, now let me be!' screamed Crawley. He began to weep and the tears streamed down his face. Then he suddenly smiled, and a heavy wave of drowsiness overcame him and dragged him into a deep sleep. At last the voices had ceased.

'Wake up, Crawley. Much to do'.

Crawley's eyes sprang open, and a strong ray of sunlight struck them. After a moment of temporary blindness, he scanned the living area of his small, cluttered hut for the speaker of the voice. In his sleep-weary state, it took him a few minutes to realise that as always, he was alone. He squeezed his eyes shut, and of its own accord his tongue ran at a feverish pace over his bottom lip. Oddly enough, it had a calming effect on him, and he remained in his bed, pondering the voices in his head until a crow's shrill cries urged him to rise. He threw back his featherdown quilt and was transfixed as the disturbed lint and dust sparkled like diamonds in the sunlight filtering through his only window.

'Enough daydreaming. Things to do,' he muttered to himself.

He swung his legs over the side of the bed and stood up slowly. The hard dirt underfoot sent a shrill lance of pain up his withered legs, and he pulled on his dirt-caked boots with speed surprising for his age. As warmth slowly filled his aching feet, a low rumbling in the pit of his stomach hinted at its lack of food.

'Yes, food. I will need to build my strength,' he stated, looking at his stomach.

He shuffled over to the furthest wall and opened the door of his pantry. A large rat let out a squeal and disappeared into a hole at the back. Crawley seemed not to notice, and he began to rummage around in the bottom shelf. His fingers clasped something soft and slightly squishy and he slowly withdrew his hand to see what he had grabbed. He let out a cry, and flung his quarry to the ground. The rotting, half-chewed carcass of a rat lay there. He painfully kneeled down, and lightly ran his fingertips over the hard-crusted hair of the rat.

'Hmmm, it would seem as if you were the only food in the house,' he said sadly. He rose to his feet with the dead rat cradled carefully in the palm of his hand. 'I cannot eat you, but I know someone who can.' He quickly placed the rat into the top pocket of his grey, long-sleeved tunic. 'But first things first. I must get some food.'

He hurriedly shuffled over to a large wooden chest that lay between his bed and the hard-packed mud wall. He bent down and grabbed the lid, and with a groan from the hinges, it reluctantly opened. It made a dull thud as it met the wall. In the dim gloom of the chest it was hard to distinguish what lay within, but after a short and erratic search, he found what he sought. He rose to his feet and closed the lid carefully. The small leather pouch that hung from his wrist by its cord swayed with his movements. He expectantly shook it, and was somewhat relieved to hear the dull metallic clash of coins.

'Let us see what we have, then,' he said, emptying the contents into his hand. An frown formed on his forehead as he counted. 'Four coppers. What happened to my gold coins?' Suddenly, the answer came to him. It had to be, there was no other explanation. It was the crows. The crows had stolen his money. He charged toward the door, hell bent on revenge, but halted as he reached it. Something was not quite right. He felt as if he had forgotten something important. It took several minutes to realise that he was looking directly at it, and with an annoyed growl, he reached up and removed his hat from its peg on the wall.

The sunlight filtered down through the trees. The brightness was in stark contrast to the dimly lit hut, and he forcefully pulled his hat down until it sat flush with his ears. Crawley tapped the brim of his hat affectionately, thankful for the shade it cast over his eyes.

'Now to get my money back,' he said to himself as he set off toward town; it would be at least midday before he reached it. 'Much too far for an old man,' he muttered.

It was not by choice that he lived so far away. He once lived in the middle of town and was a welcome member of the community; but that was before the voices started. Alas, the past cannot be changed. Crawley had become a Raver and he had come to cherish his solitary life. Even the somewhat small task of going to town made him sweat with uncertainty. It was not that he didn't like people, it was that people didn't like him. If some of the townsfolk had their way, he wouldn't be alive.

'It is madness, a disease that could be contracted by everyone in town.' Crawley remembered the harsh words of the Mayor. Oh yes, he was pronounced a danger to their lives and a danger to the lives of their children, a cancer on their fair town that must be neutralised. The townsfolk were baying for blood, his blood, and they would have had their way if not for his niece Kieam. Crawley fondly remembered the snub-nosed girl with the mousey brown hair and keen green eyes, as she wormed her way through the crowd to firmly attach herself to his leg like a leech. Then in a voice that should have come from a large man, she screamed for his life and pleaded until sobs of emotion contorted her throat and forced her into silence. A child's tears of sorrow have an effect on even the harshest and most hate-filled man, and it was with great reluctance that he was set free, but on the condition that he live far away from the townsfolk and only come into town out of necessity.

As he stopped dead in his tracks and pondered his need to venture into town, his stomach squelched and rumbled in hunger. 'Yes,' he thought to himself, 'food is a necessity.' And he continued forth.

He was quietly enjoying the feel of the warm breeze caressing his wrinkled face, so much so that he didn't notice a group of boys who had been following him for a good mile or so, until he felt a sharp stinging pain in the middle of his back. He swung around with a pain-filled grimace on his face.

'Crawley Crowcatcher, turn back now. No one wants the likes of you in town,' jeered one of the boys. The other boys laughed along in agreement.

Crawley turned back around, thinking it best to ignore them. He had walked no more than a few paces when another sharp pain erupted in his back. He swung around again, but with more purpose this time.

'Boys, I bid you no wrong. I only have to go to town for a short while. My stomach... I mean, I need to buy some food. I will be no more than a few heartbeats of time,' he stated nervously.

'A few heartbeats too long,' replied one of the boys, launching a rock.

Crawley tried in vain to move; the rock struck him below the eye and a small trickle of blood ran down the crevices of his face. It was only a split second before it was followed by a barrage. With his arm covering his face, he turned and ran down the road like a scalded dog, all the while being pummelled by well-aimed rocks. He began to cry softly. He knew there was no way of outrunning the boys. He only hoped they would soon tire of their game. A particularly large rock found the top of his head and sent him sprawling to the ground. His first concern was not for himself, but for his hat.

As he raised himself on his forearms and worriedly scanned the area, the taxidermied eyes of the crow stared back at him from a foot away, and he reached out and gently caressed its head.

'Well, what do you know – it's not a real bird,' jeered one of the boys.

'Don't tell him that or he'll stop feeding it,' laughed another.

The boys were getting restless with their game, and when Crawley offered no more resistance, they moved off. But not before first giving Crawley a few kicks to the ribs.

The air eventually returned to his lungs and he got to his feet despite the arguments of his aching body. He replaced his hat on his blood-soaked head and continued on. His new injuries meant it was well after midday before he reached the outskirts of town. The dirt track he had been treading for half the day had abruptly stopped, and given way to a slightly uneven cobbled road.

A thick, pungent smog hovered stagnantly over the entire town. 'They have forgotten. They think they can exploit what we have offered them,' whispered the voices in a sultry tone.

'It has been a long time since then, and the minds of most men are fickle and more likely to forget, especially if, by doing so, it will improve their own lot,' he replied. He waited for an answer from the voices, but they remained silent.

Crawley slowly opened the soot-covered door of the grocer's wide enough to allow himself to slip in sideways, in an attempt to remain inconspicuous. He had been trying hard not to be noticed as he walked the streets, but for someone who is covered in blood and dirt, curiosity follows like a faithful dog, and when you have a stuffed crow for a hat, you might as well be banging a drum to announce your arrival. On the upside, at least no one had stopped him this time.

'Crawley!'

Crawley jumped and let out a small cry of alarm. 'I am sorry, Miss Talmon. I didn't notice you there,' muttered Crawley.

'Well, I certainly noticed you. Now, what will it be?' she asked spitefully.

Crawley thought for a moment before replying, 'I have but four coppers left because of the crows. The little thieves stole what gold coins I had, but I will get them back, for you see—'

'Crawley, I care not for what money you don't have. The four coppers you have will buy you naught more than a loaf of bread,' interrupted Miss Talmon.

Crawley's brows creased together in frustration. 'Four coppers for a loaf of bread?'

'You heard me,' snapped Miss Talmon.

'But your sign out front told me that they were half that price,' protested Crawley.

'Well, perhaps if you had been listening more closely, you would have heard the doormat tell you to wipe your feet.'

Crawley followed Miss Talmon's accusing stare to the doorway, and to the thick mud trail he had inadvertently brought in, before looking back at Miss Talmon. Crawley fished around in his pocket and brought out the four coppers and, unknowingly, the dead half-eaten rat. He slapped them down on the counter. Miss Talmon recoiled as the stench of the dead rat invaded her nostrils.

'Truly sorry, Miss Talmon. I forgot that he was in there,' apologised Crawley as he placed the rat back in his pocket.

'Just take your bread, Crawley, and hopefully I can forget that you were ever here,' she replied venomously.

Crawley grabbed the bread and made for the front door. 'Once again, I am truly sorry,' he repeated.

'Get out of my shop, Crawley, before I call the city guard to remove you,' she threatened.

Crawley hastily retreated from the counter and exited the shop. Once again, the putrid smell of the town clung to his nostrils as he walked. 'The crows will pay for humiliating me,' he thought as he subconsciously stroked his hat.

Miss Talmon waited for Crawley to leave before she scooped up the four coppers and placed them in her till. 'Damn old fool,' she spat out as she looked at the mud he had dragged in. 'If I were a whole woman, I probably wouldn't have even let him in,' she thought to herself. 'You're lucky, Crawley, for I know ridicule,' she said, rubbing the stump of her arm where her hand used to be. Deciding not to put off the inevitable any longer, she walked over to lock the door so as not to be interrupted while she cleaned up the mud Crawley had dragged in. She was reaching up to latch the door on her tippy toes, when she slipped on the mud under foot. She let out a cry of alarm, which was cut short as the back of her head hit the countertop and bounced sickly as it hit the floor.

Earl Penetty, the town's illustrious mayor, watched with a scowl as Crawley left the store, and spat in disgust. 'It's a shame I didn't hang him when I had the chance,' he lamented. He waited a good five minutes before he approached the store. The last thing he wanted was to come face-to-face with the old git. 'I would probably end up strangling him,' he thought to himself. 'And that wouldn't be good for my public image,' he muttered as he eased the door open. 'Good afternoon, Miss Talmon,' he bellowed in his best mayoral voice.

Not waiting for an answer, he swung the door completely open, and the sickening smell of human faeces mixed with fresh blood hit him. He let out a cry of alarm when he spotted Miss Talmon crumpled in a heap on the floor with a growing pool of blood encircling her head. Within minutes, half a dozen or so people were crowded around the door, trying to get a good look.

'Out of my way, you nosey bunch of gits!' roared a giant of a man, as he pushed his way through the growing crowd. He halted when he got to the doorway. 'What happened here?' he asked as he studied the corpse.

'I know not what happened in the shop, but I saw that mad man Crawley Crowcatcher leave no more than ten minutes ago,' stated Earl.

The large man declined to reply, and instead carefully inspected the entire shop before he tuned to face Earl. 'It would appear that Miss Talmon has succumbed to an untimely death. You can see right here in the mud that she was near the doorway, and see how the mud in two places has been smoothed down. That to me indicates a slip. She was probably trying to latch the door when she slipped, consequently hitting the back of her head on the counter.'

Earl Penetty carefully stepped over the corpse and closed the door, much to the disappointment of the crowd. 'So tell me, Ethan. You have been part of the city guard now for what, five... ten years?'

'Eight,' replied Ethan suspiciously.

'Hmm, eight years, you say. Now tell me, Ethan, do you wish to be there for a ninth?'

'I intend to serve out the full fifteen years of service,' he replied slowly.

'Good, good. The city guard needs a man like you.' He paused for effect. 'But it would get along just fine without you,' threatened Earl.

'Go on,' implored Ethan nervously.

'Now, we all know that mad man Crawley is a nuisance to the town and its people, and we would all be better off if he just... disappeared. Now, if people ask me questions about what happened here, which they most certainly will, do you have any idea what I will tell them?'

'No, sir,' replied Ethan, wiping a bead of sweat from his brow.

'I will tell them that this was no accident. I will tell them that I heard a squabble coming from Miss Talmon's store, and as I was drawing near, I saw that low life Crawley fleeing the shop like a dog that had just stolen the roast off someone's table, and then I hurried to the shop and found this,' he said, gesturing to the corpse of Miss Talmon. 'I hope by now you are getting the message?' implored Earl with a raised brow.

'Yes, sir, loud and clear.'

'Well, what are you waiting for? There is a murderer walking the streets.'

Crawley left Miss Talmon's store with the loaf of bread tucked under his arm and made a purposeful beeline for the nearest cornfield. 'There is nothing more that crows like to eat than rodents and my gold,' he thought.

As he walked, he pulled chunks from the loaf and stuffed them in his mouth. The bread was salty and poorly made, and the only way to swallow it was to allow his saliva to soak the bread. Only then did he attempt to swallow. His actions reminded him of the way a duck would dip its bread in water before scoffing it down. Crawley had devoured half the loaf by the time he got to the fence that indicated the start of the cornfield. His stomach had stopped aching a short while before, and he thought it best to leave the bread on top of one of the split posts. He ducked between the two parallel planks that joined the split posts at either end. A fence made in this way was useless for keeping animals in or out; it was more or less just a fancy border to indicate whose property was whose. It had proved a very effective way to stop arguments between farmers over a few feet of land.

Once inside the fence, Crawley cautiously removed his hat and cradled it in one arm. Using his free hand, he reached into his pocket and pulled out the dead rat, then proceeded to wedge it firmly between the slightly agape beaks of the taxidermy crow. When he was utterly satisfied that it would remain there, he placed the hat back on his head. Over the years, Crawley had perfected the art of crowcatching. If anyone had asked him about his peculiar skill, he would have answered, 'In order to catch a crow, one must first act like a crow.' And that is what he proceeded to do.

He crept on all fours through the cornfields. This was the most deceptive part of the whole procedure (for if any crow was to see that a human was attached to another crow, it would instantly arouse suspicion). He suddenly stopped and rose to his feet, allowing only the top of the hat to break the surface of the cornfield and, with almost too much ease, imitated the crow call which roughly translated to: 'I have some food. I thought I'd let you know because you are not getting any.' The response was instantaneous. Two crows simultaneously diving for the stuffed crow on his hat. Crawley timed his movements to perfection, and as the first crow struck the hat, his hand shot up and plucked the somewhat startled crow out of the sky. It began to caw wildly. 'Be quiet,' he whispered, carefully clamping its beak shut.

Crawley looked around until he found a patch of dirt that looked more comfortable than the rest, and sat down with his legs straight out in front of himself.

'Now listen up, my little, black-feathered friend,' said Crawley, staring into the crow's eyes. 'You or one of your little friends has something of mine, and I really, really need it back.'

The crow blinked slowly and stared back.

'Okay, we can do this the easy way, or we can do it the hard way,' threatened Crawley. 'Now, if I let your beak go, I expect to be told the answer, and no funny business.' He cautiously released his hold on the bird's beak.

The crow slowly opened and closed its beak, checking if everything was still operational. Satisfied that everything was, it viciously pecked Crawley on the end of the nose.

'You ignorant little sod!' yelled Crawley, roughly shaking the bird.

The bird began to caw uncontrollably, and in return Crawley shook the bird with more force. Who knows how long this would have continued, if not for the bolt that cleanly plucked the crow from his hands. Crawley stood up and quickly glanced around.

No more than twenty paces to his left, a man was busy reloading his crossbow. 'Don't run, Crawley. It would be a waste of time,' said Ethan, calmly winding the windlass as he walked over.

'I was talking to that crow,' Crawley said, a little dumbfounded.

'I wouldn't call it talking,' replied Ethan, raising his crossbow.

'It was a minor interspecies misunderstanding,' defended Crawley.

'Looked to me as if you were trying to kill it,' accused Ethan.

'I would never kill an animal unless it was for food,' replied Crawley defensively.

'Oh, I see. Then how about Miss Talmon?' asked Ethan.

Crawley's mouth dropped open in utter disgust. 'I would never eat Miss Talmon. How could you think such a thing?'

Ethan had a sudden urge to let his finger slip on the trigger. 'I meant kill her, you old fool,' he said.

'I'm offended by such a question. What would lead you to ask it?'

'The fact that she has been murdered,' replied Ethan, a little hesitantly.

'How unfortunate! I only spoke with her this afternoon,' Crawley said sadly. 'Anyway it was very thoughtful of you to come out here and tell me this, but just because you're grieving it does not give you the right to go out and shoot crows, especially the ones I'm talking to.'

'Shut up, you old fool!' yelled Ethan. 'Do you not comprehend what I am out here for?'

'No, not exactly,' replied Crawley thoughtfully.

'I'm here to arrest you for the murder of Miss Talmon. Now just come along quietly, and please don't resist.'

'How dare you accuse me of murder, you snivelling pile of horse–'

The stock of the crossbow hit Crawley on the top of his skull and knocked him out cold. 'Sorry, old timer, but I do have a family to support,' apologised Ethan as he swung Crawley's limp body onto his shoulder. 'The only good thing to come out of this, is that I won't have to listen to him raving all the way back to town,' he mused, as he moved through the cornfield.

# 2

CRAWLEY OPENED HIS eyes slowly and tried to examine his surroundings through a watery haze, but to no avail. He violently rubbed his eyes with the back of his hands in a desperate attempt to clear the haze.

'You're better off keeping those eyes closed, Crawley,' came the voice of Earl Penetty.

'It makes no difference. I can't see a thing anyway,' growled Crawley.

'You'll see just fine in the morning. I expect that you have a slight concussion, but you have no one to blame for your predicament except yourself.'

'I did not hit myself in the head!' yelled Crawley. He instantly regretted his outburst, as the pain in his head flared.

Earl laughed loudly at the sight of Crawley thrashing around the floor of his cell. 'You know, you might –

I stress the word *might* – be more comfortable on the bed,' stated Earl.

Crawley struggled to a sitting position and faced in the direction of Earl's voice. 'I would be more comfortable in my own bed,' croaked Crawley.

'You most likely would be, but I've got a feeling that you're not going to find out. But don't worry,' replied Earl, walking toward the exit. 'Soon you'll have all the rest you could possibly want!' he added as he departed. Crawley blindly felt his way to the foul-smelling excuse of a mattress, and painfully eased his protesting body onto it and tried to sleep.

'You do realise that this compromises his safety,' whispered a voice.

'Indeed, but who can predict humans?' replied the other.

'So do we turn to another to do our bidding?' queried the first.

'It might be feasible if we could find another with strength. But that could take quite a while,' answered the second solemnly.

'Time is not something we can spare,' argued the first.

'Then we haven't really a choice in the matter,' replied the second.

'No, unfortunately, we do not. Let us hope his mind is not faulty.'

'His mind is strong,' said the second.

'So is a twig if you bend it slowly. But with one rushed movement, it can break just as easily.'

'To be slow is to be patient. To be patient takes time, and as you stated before, time is something that we just don't have.'

'Then we must do it now.'

'No, let him sleep a little longer. It's the least we could do for him.'

Crawley woke up early in the morning. He was shivering violently, but despite all his wounds, he strangely felt quite good. That was until he tried to move, and found he could not.

'Well then, I must be dead,' he thought.

That thought, however, was soon dashed when he involuntarily sat up and looked around. Crawley realised that his body was not under his control, and he begun to panic.

Then a voice in his head began to speak to him a lot louder and closer than he was accustomed to. 'You will have control of yourself once we complete a certain task.'

'I don't understand,' replied Crawley. 'I thought I was to do this on my own.'

'In case you haven't noticed, the circumstances have changed; and we are growing desperate,' replied the other voice.

'Enough to turn me into a puppet?' asked Crawley heatedly.

'You are more of a vessel. It may be your body, but we are firmly in control of it,' explained one of the voices.

'I will have no part in this. I must insist you leave my body immediately or else–' threatened Crawley.

'Or else what?' challenged the voices.

'Or else I will scream and alert the guards, and they will come running and shackle me up, so we won't be able to go anywhere,' threatened Crawley.

'If that's what you think is best, then go ahead if you can, but you may find that you've been muted somewhat,' replied one of the voices.

'Rubbish! I'm speaking to you right now,' said Crawley dismissively.

'Are you? If you are so sure, then go ahead and call out to them,' challenged the voices.

'Fine, I will do just that. Guards, guards! I need to speak to you,' yelled Crawley. The minutes ticked by, and it became apparent that no guards were coming. Crawley cursed the voices severely.

'As you can see, we are running the show now, so just relax and enjoy the ride,' dictated the voices.

'Relax and enjoy the ride? I think not. I am not going anywhere,' replied Crawley.

'We shall see.' The voices laughed.

Crawley's overcrowded body rose to its feet and began to walk towards the iron bars of the cell. With each step, however, the movements became slower, until his body froze and he began to laugh. 'Did you honestly think that you could control my body so easily after just a couple of minutes? You seem to be forgetting, I have been in this body for over sixty years, and in that amount of time, you get to know it.'

The two would-be pilots growled in annoyance. 'We underestimated you, Crawley Crowcatcher, but you in turn have underestimated us.' Crawley's legs began to rise, but just as quickly it rejoined the stone floor. With the opposing forces struggling for control, Crawley's body began to quiver. Muscles strained to snapping point, and a trickle of blood began to flow out of Crawley's ears. 'If you don't stop fighting us, your body will be destroyed,' warned the voices.

'You cannot trick me that easily,' replied Crawley triumphantly.

'We were hoping that it wouldn't have to come to this, but you leave us no choice.' The voices released their hold on Crawley's body, and all his aches and pains came rushing back. He let out a hair-raising scream as the pain drove him into the blackness, and he collapsed to the floor.

'Well, there is no doubt that we picked the right one. I wasn't totally convinced, but now I think that his mind is a little too strong,' spoke the first.

'I think it's more stubbornness than strength,' replied the second.

'A little sleep will calm him down,' said the first hopefully.

'If not, he'll be doing quite a lot more of it,' predicted the second.

Lidden woke abruptly as a hair-raising scream echoed off the walls of the dimly lit watch house. He had been on guard duty for the last fifteen hours. Earl Penetty was not taking the risk of leaving Crawley unwatched. He had slipped by before and Lidden was not about to let the same thing happen twice.

'I had better go and check on the old fool,' he said, rising from behind his desk.

He walked the five paces to the door that led to the cells. After a short search through his key ring, he unlocked the door, and on second thought, grabbed his favourite baton. After making sure the door was locked behind him, he casually walked down the narrow hallway that housed the cells, rapping his baton on the bars as he passed.

'Well, well, Crawley. Screamed yourself back to sleep, have we?' derided Lidden, as he came across the crumpled body on the floor. Lidden bashed his bat on the iron bars in an attempt to wake him up. 'Get up, you old git!' Lidden ordered when Crawley did not move. 'Crawley?' implored Lidden with concern. 'Are you all right?' He dropped to his haunches and examined Crawley through the bars. His eyes fell upon the trickle of blood that still issued from Crawley's ears, and his heart froze. 'Oh no, no,' Lidden exclaimed loudly. 'You had better not be dead,' he added, fumbling for the cell keys.

Lidden was sweating profusely as his trembling hands unlocked the door. He swung the door open, rushed over to Crawley, and gently rolled him onto his back. He hesitantly placed an open palm above Crawley's mouth, fearful of what he'd find, then let out a sigh of relief as Crawley's hot breath swept over his palm. He sat back heavily against the wall and ran his fingers through his damp hair.

'That was a close one, Crawley. If you'd died before your trial, it would have been my neck in the noose.'

He was rising to his feet when Crawley's hand shot out and grabbed him by the wrist with devastating force. Lidden heard his wrist snap, and as the pain registered, he screamed. With his free hand, Lidden grabbed the baton resting by his side and swung it with pain-driven force at Crawley's head. The baton struck true, and a river of blood burst from Crawley's forehead, but his grip did not waver.

Lidden raised his arm for another strike, but Crawley casually caught it when the baton was inches from his head. With a violent twist, Lidden's shoulder was dislocated and he began to sob loudly in fear and pain. Through his tear-blurred vision, he watched as Crawley rose slowly to his feet. He didn't fight back, or even try to move as Crawley bent down toward him and placed an open palm on his forehead; and he didn't move anymore after a blinding golden light propelled him into the darkness of death.

# 3

'THERE HAS TO be something wrong with him.'

'You heard the doctor, Earl. He is completely normal, and very healthy.'

'I don't need a doctor to tell me he's healthy, Erika. Any halfwit could see that. There's something wrong up here,' said Earl, tapping his forehead.

'Oh, Earl, that's nonsense. He's just a little slow and nothing more.'

'A little slow,' replied Earl sarcastically. 'Atiol is nearly a year and a half old, and is yet to utter anything close to a word.'

'Maybe he doesn't want to speak yet; and perhaps you will remember this little conversation when we are trying in vain to keep him quiet,' replied Erika, in a slightly raised tone.

'If he ever talks, which I seriously doubt. You can see the lack of intelligence in his eyes. He'll grow up to be nothing more than a lousy farmer, and even that may be beyond him.'

If a look could kill, the penetrating stare from Erika would have killed Earl five times over. 'If you speak and think so highly of your firstborn son, whom you should love unconditionally,' she said, 'I can't help but feel that the love you supposedly show me is as changing as the seasons, and is only a show to enhance your public image.'

'Oh, Erika, don't speak such nonsense,' soothed Earl. He rose from his chair and walked over to Erika, who was standing beside the fireplace. 'I do love you,' he crooned, as he embraced her small body and pulled it close to his own.

'Well, it wouldn't hurt to show it once in a while. And I do wish for you to love your son no matter what he'll grow up to be,' she replied emotionally, returning the embrace.

'I did not say that I don't love him, Erika,' he consoled, holding her at arm's length.

'It gladdens my heart to hear those words directly,' replied Erika, running her hands up and down his forearms. A baby's demanding cry broke the silence. 'I have to go and see what our little prince requires,' she said, turning to leave.

Earl grabbed her gently by the crook of her elbow. 'No Erika, you have done enough today. I'll go and see what he wants.'

Without waiting for a reply, Earl walked away from the fireplace. He had barely taken three paces down the hall, when the sound of cracking timber and his wife's fearful screams engulfed his ears.

'Erika!' he yelled, and rushed back to the sitting quarters. His first concern was for the welfare of his wife, who was huddled beside the fireplace, still screaming like a banshee. 'What is it, Erika?' he asked fretfully as he went toward her.

She opened her mouth to speak but found she had no voice and could only point with a shaky finger. Earl snapped his gaze in the direction indicated by his wife's trembling finger. A scraggly, blood-splattered arm had squeezed through a jagged hole in his front door and was methodically searching for the handle.

Earl quietly manoeuvred to the front of the fireplace and picked up a fire poker and tested its weight, which he found to be to his liking. He walked carefully toward the door, brandishing the poker in both his hands like a shortened spear.

'Try to break into my house will you, you low-life thief!' he spat out, charging at the door.

Summoning all his strength, he drove his substitute spear straight through the protruding arm and into the door. In a fit of rage, Earl was far from satisfied with only one strike, and he removed his weapon, which was harder than he had first anticipated. He had just succeeded in freeing it from the wood when the arm's twin exploded through the door. The hand clasped onto the iron poker that was still embedded in flesh, and with one sharp pull freed it.

Poker in hand, Earl fell back and hit the wooden floor with a thud, but before he could attempt another blow, both arms retreated from sight. He let out a heavy sigh of relief.

'It's all right, sweetheart,' he assured Erika, full of bravado. 'No one will get into this house while I still draw breath.'

The next thing Earl remembered was being thrown across the into the adjacent wall, then being temporarily blinded by a golden flash of light, which was slowly being replaced by thin wisps of smoke. When his swimming mind slowly recovered from the battering, he raised his head off the floorboards and stared in astonishment at the place where his door used to be, and now small, hungry flames danced slowly up the walls.

'Erika, grab Atiol! The house is on fire. We have to get out,' bellowed Earl.

'I wouldn't even attempt it. I will take the child,' commanded the figure that emerged in the doorway.

The voice sounded contorted, as if it had been forced, and try as he might, Earl could not quite place it until the voice's owner walked through the smoke haze.

'Crawley, you swine!' roared Earl. At the sight of the frail old man, Earl's fear disintegrated and he charged at Crawley, brandishing the poker above his head. 'I am going to kill you,' he growled as he swung his weapon at Crawley's temple.

Crawley stepped into the attack and tilted his head just enough to ensure that the poker sailed harmlessly overhead. He brought his fist straight up into Earl's stomach and sent him flying through the air, to land in an undignified heap on the floor. He walked across the room and glanced casually at Earl, who was struggling for breath.

'It would be wise if you stayed where you were – that is, if you wish to remain amongst the living,' threatened Crawley.

Earl craned his neck and was contemplating another swing at Crawley, when a bright green sheen swept over Crawley's eyes. The hair on the back of Earl's neck prickled, and for the first time in a long while, he was deathly afraid. He remained perfectly still as Crawley disappeared down the hall.

Crawley walked through the house, using the baby's cries as a beacon to its whereabouts. As soon as he entered the baby's nursery, the shrill cries ceased, and when Crawley stood over the cot the baby began to coo and squeal in delight. Crawley bent over the cot and gently wrapped the little bundle into a blanket, before tucking him into the crook of his arm for safety.

Earl had not moved a muscle, but when Crawley reappeared clutching his son, he summoned the courage to speak. 'Crawley, you don't have to do this. If you leave Atiol, you can go as a free man and I will admit to all that you are innocent and did not murder the shopkeeper.'

Crawley talked as he walked. 'This has no bearing on my actions. I do not do this to spite you. I do this in order to save you all,' he said as he carefully covered the baby in his tattered tunic and jumped through the growing wall of flames.

The other townsfolk had noticed the flames and smoke rising into the sky, and every available person rushed forth to try and quell the fire. They were so intent on their task that they scarcely took any notice of an old man carrying a bundle, and walking casually along the street. A chain gang has been formed and brimming buckets of water were passed in a continuous stream until they reached the front of the line, where they were unceremoniously dumped onto the flames with a protesting hiss of steam. The fire eventually gave in to the onslaught and a cheer went up from the smoke-blackened conquerors. A more deafening cheer went up when a coughing and spluttering Earl Penetty emerged from the house, carrying his unconscious wife on his shoulders. Several people rushed forward as Earl swayed alarmingly on his feet, and steadied him before taking his wife from his shoulders.

'What happened, Earl?' asked one of the concerned onlookers.

Earl tried to speak but instead was plagued by racking coughs.

'Get him a drink of water!' yelled another.

An old lady shuffled to where Earl sat and offered him a drink. He snatched the tin cup from her hand and drank it down, caring not that the majority spilled down his shirt. The cold water soothed the burn in his throat, and he attempted to talk again.

'Crawley set fire to my house and has stolen my son,' he croaked, as he fell into another fit of coughing.

'Crawley is in jail, Earl. I put him there myself,' said Ethan, appearing from the crowd.

'No, it was him. I will wager my life on it,' replied Earl.

Ethan was about to question him again when a member of the city guard came sprinting forward. 'He has escaped! Crawley has murdered Lidden and escaped,' informed the guard.

'Any further proof required?' asked Earl as he stared at Ethan.

'No, I think not,' replied Ethan. 'We have a double murderer on the loose, and he has the mayor's son,' announced Ethan. 'I will gather four of my best men and drag him back here, dead or alive,' he added.

'Be careful, Ethan. He is a lot more dangerous than he looks. He has already killed one of the guards, and he threw me around rather easily,' warned Earl.

'Fear not. He shall be apprehended,' said Ethan.

Earl stood up and held up his hand to silence the crowd. 'As you know, he has stolen my son. Bring the child back to me unharmed, and you shall receive ten gold pieces. Bring me Crawley's head, and you will get twice that amount,' he announced.

The promise of gold had the required effect, and several more than the four men with Ethan were soon on the hunt for Crawley. Those who were not involved cheered as the enthusiastic posse rode down the street, spurred on by the lure of gold.

The crow perched on top of a soot-covered chimney, unmoving except for its head. For weeks it had watched the comings and goings of the population, but none of that was its concern. It had been waiting for Crawley to make his move. It had watched as Crawley entered the house. It had watched more closely when he emerged through the flames, and now it watched very intently as Crawley removed a bundle from beneath his tunic. The child. The crow watched no more. It had no need, for it had the information it sought.

# 4

SEKER LAY ON HIS side staring lazily into the fire. Every so often he would throw a twig into the flames to alleviate the boredom. For the last few weeks this had been the extent of his activities. His fellow companions had the same dull expressions of boredom, and he knew that he couldn't keep them in this state of inactivity for much longer.

*Caw, caw.*

Seker snapped his eyes toward the sound, and his lips curled slightly into a smile when he spotted the crow. The crow flew around in ever tightening circles as it slowly descended to perch on Seker's outstretched forearm.

'Well, does the Raver speak the truth?' enquired Seker.

'The chosen Raver Crawley has in his possession a child, and as we speak he is making for Galteone,' replied the crow.

'Excellent! Now fly to Arama and inform Lord Delrain that his captive Raver speaks the truth, and that soon we will have a very powerful Light Wielder to aid in our cause.'

With these latest instructions stored safely in its head, the crow took off into the sky, letting out shrill cries as it departed the small band. Seker's men, who had listened intently to his conversation with the crow, had already doused the fire and were hurriedly saddling their mounts with enthusiasm.

Seker spoke as he saddled his horse. 'Remember, men, the Raver we seek has newly inherited abilities and will certainly not hesitate in removing your head from your shoulders, so don't give him the chance.'

'Just lead the way, Seker, and we will remain whole,' replied one of his men.

'For your sake, let us hope so,' said Seker, riding off.

His men scrambled into their saddles and took off after their leader, thankful that finally they would see some action after their long period of inactivity.

Crawley ran, taking long, steady strides along the cobbled road leading out of town. He knew that very soon Earl

Penetty's hounds would be snapping at his heals. He stopped a short while later to allow his burning lungs a brief respite. 'Why do we stop so soon?' questioned one of the voices.

'Because he is already half dead, and we can't push him much more,' replied the other.

'We will have to push him if we are to reach Galteone,' argued the first voice.

'Then we will have to find other means of transport,' replied the second.

'And where exactly will this other transport come from?' questioned the first.

'Why, as we speak we are being pursued by all the transport we could possibly need. All we have to do is persuade them to part with it!'

'And we are going to persuade them, even though we are not the best of speakers,' said the first.

'Yes. And besides, if that fails, there's always a Plan B,' replied the second.

'You always have a Plan B.'

'Yes, I'm rather fond of them,' stated the second.

'I would never have guessed,' mumbled the first in reply.

Crawley made his way down the road for a little while longer, then veered sharply off the road as the first sounds of pursuit reached his ears. From the edge of the road, it was a short dash to the protected cover of the heavily scented pine forest. It took him only a moment to find a suitable hiding place for the child. Then, taking great care to remain undetected, Crawley obliterated signs of his presence by sweeping the ground with a fallen branch, and casually discarded his makeshift broom as he neared the road.

'All right. Now what?' asked the voice in Crawley's head.

'Now we make a trail that even a blind man can follow,' came the reply. Crawley crept to the edge of the tree line, less than twenty metres away, as the chattering mob of pursuers came into view. He aggressively snapped a low-hanging branch on the nearest tree, ensuring the sound would reach those it was intended for.

Instantaneously, all sets of eyes pivoted toward the sound. 'He's over there!' one of them hollered.

'Careful, men, he's a wily one,' advised Ethan.

'Wily or not, I am going after him. I won't get my gold just standing around,' declared one of the men. None of his companions argued with him, and they all sat transfixed as he dismounted and casually walked in the direction of the sound with his crossbow drawn. The other men took the opportunity to do the same with their weapons.

'All right, Crawley, I'll give you a chance to end this peacefully,' he said as he drew near. He waited in the slim hope that Crawley would accept the offer, but was in no way surprised when a reply was not to be heard. He let out a sigh and disappeared into the undergrowth. He returned a short while later and popped his head clear of the undergrowth to report his findings.

'He's running like a frightened rabbit and is taking no care to cover his trail. If we hurry, we'll have our gold before the day is through,' he said.

A beaming smile showed his confidence, and his companions returned it for a brief second. Then their faces turned into masks of horror as a skinny arm burst through the undergrowth, wrapped itself around the top of his head, and with seemingly little effort crushed his skull like a rotten watermelon. Before the body had flopped to the ground, every single man had brought up the contents of their stomach at the repulsive sight. It took some time to recover their composure and settle their stomachs, and they just about jumped out of their saddles when they noticed Crawley standing no more than ten metres away.

'Gentlemen, a moment of your time,' said Crawley casually.

Instead of their time, they offered Crawley a volley of crossbow bolts, which he was anticipating. He threw up a wall of red light that incinerated the projectiles upon contact. He allowed the shield of light to fade, then he walked slowly towards them.

'That was rather hostile when all I wanted to do was offer you a proposal,' said Crawley. 'Now, I'm not much of a speaker, so I'll cut straight to the chase. Excuse the pun. Get it? Chase? No? No one? Well, you're not a very cheery bunch of fellows, are you?'

The group remained quiet and wide-eyed.

'All right, then,' continued Crawley. 'It so happens that you now have a spare horse, and it so happens that I need one. So here is my proposal – hand over the horse, and no one else will get hurt.' No one spoke. 'Okay, I'll take your silence as a yes,' said Crawley.

One of the group, who had a little more backbone than the rest, had slowly eased his dagger out. As Crawley cautiously walked towards the chestnut mare that stood a little away from the group eating grass, out of the corner of his eye he caught a flash of steel. With lightning speed, he unleashed a golden sphere of pure energy from his left hand. The would-be attacker's dagger dropped to the ground, his hands went to the smoking fist-sized hole in his chest, and he slid silently from the saddle. His body produced a small puff of dust as it hit the dirt.

As his companions looked at his still smoking corpse, any thought of capturing Crawley quickly disappeared. Leaving their fallen comrades where they lay, they made a hasty retreat, back towards the relative safety of the city, and the relatively safer task of facing Earl Penetty.

'Well, that was a lot less violent than I thought it was going to be,' remarked the first voice to the other.

Seker and his men heard the retreating posse from a fair distance away, and waited patiently in the middle of the road for them to arrive. Seker had a good idea who was coming toward him. He had forewarned his men to appear helpful and full of concern, and above all else to 'show your distaste for the appalling atrocities that you are bound to hear about'. He would take care of the rest. They only had to wait a short while before the posse, riding sweat-lathered mounts, came into view. They were riding hard, and pulled up a short distance from Seker.

Seker scrutinised the men carefully. They were clearly shaken from their ordeal. 'Hail, good men.

What are you fleeing from that warrants such speed? Is someone chasing you?' he asked, knowing full well why they were fleeing.

'We are fleeing from the mad man Crawley, except it wasn't Crawley as we all know him. All of a sudden he somehow has the same powers as a Light Wielder,' replied Ethan shakily.

'Are you sure? A Light Wielder? There hasn't been a Light Wielder in these parts for nigh on twenty years,' said Seker with a small smile.

'No, I'm not sure. Come to think of it, I am only going on what I have heard about them in idle gossip,' replied Ethan.

'I know a little about the Light Wielders and what they can do, and he certainly fits that description,' remarked another slowly, as he tried to process the previous events. 'But I have known Crawley all my life, and yes, he may be a little strange, but he is definitely no Light Wielder,' he added.

'Well, I have heard that a man can be possessed by certain Spirits that govern all others, which would give him similar traits to a Light Wielder – but only if he is a Raver,' replied Seker.

'What is a Raver?' asked Ethan, glancing warily behind him.

'A Raver is a somewhat mad man who can hear voices in his head constantly. They are the voices of the earth's Spirits that live in the trees, the rocks, the mountains, the streams. They talk to him, give him messages, tell him the whereabouts of Light Wielders that are yet to be born into the land. But, unfortunately, the messages are hard to decipher in the first place, so when the Raver tries to pass them on, they come out as gibberish. Does that sound like your man?' asked Seker.

'That certainly sounds like Crawley,' agreed Ethan suspiciously.

'Ah, if you don't mind me asking... how do you know all of this?' asked another, fearing the answer.

'You seem to be a perceptive man. Why don't you tell me?' replied Seker smugly. The man chewed at his bottom lip as his eyes darted between Seker and his men, who were smiling openly. Fear caused him to sweat. Fear urged him to draw his sword and relieve the smiling strangers of their heads, but his common sense commanded him to reply as calmly as he could.

'You yourself are a Light Wielder?' he replied in a barely audible whisper.

'Indeed I am,' answered Seker.

Everyone in Ethan's group looked around, frantically searching for a viable means of escape. Seker noted the panic and spoke quickly. 'There is no need for flight, gentlemen. I and my men mean you no harm. In fact, we're out here hunting the same man'.

'Well, you can have him. Just let us go on our way,' pleaded one of the men.

'You can go on your way if you wish, but I was hoping you would join us. I am willing to pay for your services.' To emphasise his point, Seker produced a small coin pouch and threw it casually to Ethan.

Ethan caught it just as casually and untied the leather thong. His heartbeat quickened as he peered into the pouch. Gingerly, he reached in with his forefinger and thumb, and removed a blood red ruby the same size and shape as a sparrow's egg.

'They are pure and extremely rare. You will each receive one just like it, if you choose to aid me and my companions,' explained Seker.

The fear that had enveloped the men such a short time ago vanished as they stared at the small jewel and the wealth it promised. 'I will have to confer with my men before we decide on the matter,' said Ethan, clutching the jewel protectively. He looked questioningly at each of them, but none could refuse what the stranger was offering, and they all nodded. 'It would seem that we have a deal... ?'

'Seker. My name is Seker.'

'I am Ethan, and I am, or was, in charge of this group of men. They are loyal and trustworthy and will not let you down. We await your instructions,' replied Ethan.

'I am sure they are, but first things first – I will need that pouch back,' ordered Seker. Ethan replaced the ruby in the pouch, retied the leather thong, and tossed it back.

'Trustworthy indeed,' smiled Seker as he caught the small fortune. 'Well, since you know where the Raver is, you can ride beside me and direct us in our pursuit. I will instruct you further when we catch up to him,' he stated. He did not wait for a reply but continued down the road, and as required, they all followed.

Crawley had watched smugly as his would-be captors made a less-than-gallant retreat.

'If I am not mistaken, which I rarely am, you just enjoyed yourself, didn't you?' accused one of the voices.

'Once again you have proved yourself right, but that is enough fun for now. We still have a long way to go,' replied the other.

Crawley led the horse to the edge of the tree line and secured it to a branch with the reins. He disappeared into the forest and returned a short while later with the baby in the crook of his arm. With his free hand, he untied the reins and threw them over the horse's neck. His knee popped and cracked in protest as he used the stirrup to mount the horse, then he swung the animal around and rejoined the road. He controlled the pace of his mount to ensure its longevity, and to gain as much distance between himself and any pursuers.

'Highly unlikely the fools would try again,' thought the voices.

He rode on for several more hours but was soon forced to stop, as the heat of the afternoon sun had all but sucked the remaining strength out of his withered old body. He halted at a small, inviting creek that ran unhindered across the poorly maintained road. His rubbery legs barely managed the thirst-driven walk to the edge of the creek. He lay the baby on the soft grass by the creek, walked into the stream and plunged his head into the cool, refreshing water, surfaced, and gulped down several mouthfuls. Then he scooped up a handful of water and went to where the child lay. Being as careful as he could, he began to drip water onto the child's mouth; as soon as it hit the baby's dry lips, his mouth snapped open. Greedily, he gulped down another cupped handful then he closed his mouth; his thirst had been quenched. Crawley splashed more cold water on his face before he retrieved the horse from the middle of the creek.

A tingling sensation washed over him. 'Light Wielders!' exclaimed one of the voices.

'Yes, and they come from behind us, which can only mean one thing,' replied the other voice.

'Telirians!' said the first voice. 'We cannot tell how many there are. If we knew, we might be able to stand and fight.'

'No, we have had enough of fighting today. This body is almost spent. We must flee, and *flee now*,' advised the second voice.

Crawley turned to retrieve Atiol from the soft grass, and a smile spread over his wrinkled face. Atiol was surrounded by a miniature forest of wildflowers that had not been there before, and he was squealing and chuckling as he tried to grab at the brightly coloured petals that moved with the breeze.

'Well, it's good to see that you're not concerned with our current predicament,' said Crawley, as he bent down and scooped Atiol up from the fragrant blooms. He pulled himself onto the horse, which was coated white with dry perspiration. 'I'm sorry about this. I wouldn't do this to you if it wasn't necessary,' he said in apology to the weary animal as he nudged it into a walk.

When the horse faltered, Crawley silently prayed; but it was in vain. The horse slowed, and after a short distance stopped with its head down. Crawley kicked at its flanks, but the animal was spent and would not budge.

'Well, it looks like we are back on foot,' sighed one of the voices as Crawley dismounted.

'We won't be going very far before this body begins to falter as well,' pointed out the other voice.

'Then we have a very big decision to make. We can make a run for it and see how far the body can go, or we can find some ground that offers us an advantage, and fight them,' proposed the other voice.

'Despite my views on the excessive use of violence, I am afraid that standing and fighting may be our only chance. After all, it is his body that is faltering, not his mind.'

'I agree, but first things first – we have to find a place to hide the child.'

Crawley walked into the dense undergrowth until he was a fair distance from the road, and stashed the child in a moss-coated hollow log that lay in the leaf litter. Satisfied with the hiding spot, he barged back out onto the road, and the horse nickered in recognition. He walked up to it, removed the saddle and bridle, and urged the horse on its way with a sharp smack on its rump. The sound of cantering hooves filled his ears, and he cocked his head in the direction of the noise, then threw the horse's tack to the ground and charged at the oncoming riders.

Crawley unleashed a flurry of energy spheres from both hands, attempting to take down at least a few of his pursuers. But Seker had sensed the nearness of Crawley and had forewarned the men about the possibility of such an attack. As the first energy spheres flew overhead, Earl Penetty's men jumped from their horses and made for the cover of the woods. Seker and the three other Telirians formed a wedge and rode straight at Crawley. Seker took point and when an energy sphere came too close, he deflected it with a well-aimed energy sphere of his own. Several landed amongst the surrounding trees, and they exploded on impact with a shower of sparks and flame. As the fight continued, the initial flurry from Crawley began to slow. His body was in decline. All his fingertips were blackened from the energy spheres, and blood flowed freely from them, dripping onto the hard-packed dirt of the road. Sweat drenched his body, and his clothes were dark with it. The sweat ran into his eyes, blinding him and greatly diminishing his accuracy. Such was the body's rapid descent that it didn't even register the crossbow bolt that pierced his side, until he crumpled to the ground.

'That will do, men. He is a threat no more,' said Seker.

Ethan and his men lowered their weapons as they gathered over the old man. 'Your plan worked like a charm,' replied Ethan, full of praise.

'It was never going to fail,' reassured Seker as he dismounted and crouched beside Crawley. 'Well, well, well, to think that I and a few men have been able to subdue the raging Freom and his wise brother Muefrede,' he chuckled as he rolled Crawley's prostrate form onto his back.

Crawley's eyes pivoted slowly to look upon Seker; they lingered briefly then averted their gaze to the swaying treetops.

'Too humbled to speak, are we? Well, I know you're not going anywhere. Leaving that body is your only means of human contact. If you left it, there would be no possible way of delivering the child to Galteone. Speaking of the child, where is he?' asked Seker casually.

'Would you put your head into the jaws of a wolf, knowing it would crush your skull?' croaked Crawley in reply.

'What a stupid question! Which one of you asked it? No, let me guess – it was a little too intellectual for Freom, so you have to be Muefrede,' replied Seker.

'You guess right, you Telirian fool, but you still have not answered me.'

'A fool I am not, and that alone should answer your question,' defended Seker.

'Then surely you can see the bind I am in. I will not cut my own throat,' stated Crawley, smiling wearily to himself.

Seker fully understood and rose slowly to his feet, shaking his head. 'Spread out. The child cannot be far. This old fool can't tell us the whereabouts, so keep an open mind,' ordered Seker as he ran his fingers through his jet-black hair.

They searched in the obvious hiding places on the edge of the road, before they moved into the trees and thick undergrowth that bound the forest together in one green mass. The child's hiding spot was proving to be a good one. After half an hour, with no results, Seker widened the search area, and the men spread out further.

Ethan had the furthest position up the road toward Galteone and was muttering curses as he swung his blade into the unyielding undergrowth. 'The old man could not have got this far,' he thought. 'Damn it! I am not a land clearer,' he swore as another branch raked at his unprotected face.

'You are best off staying that way,' advised a voice in his ear. Ethan thought clearing the undergrowth had made him sweat, but the cold steel pressed into his neck encouraged copious amounts to well up from his brow, and it flowed down his neck in little rivulets.

'I don't want to kill you, but I will not be heartbroken if the need arises. Hopefully, you can cooperate,' said the stranger. 'Can you cooperate?'

'Yes,' replied Ethan, swallowing noisily.

'Good. Now tell me how many Light Wielders and how many men are out there, and remember not to lie. I have a knack for telling if you are,' warned the stranger, applying more pressure to the blade at Ethan's throat.

'There are four Light Wielders and twelve men, including myself,' replied Ethan shakily.

'Should I believe you? Hmm. Let's say I do, but for insurance you're going to come with me, and no, you don't have a choice,' stated the stranger, kicking the limply held sword out of Ethan's hand.

The two of them marched through the undergrowth with Ethan being used as a battering ram to clear the path on numerous occasions. They soon found themselves back out on the road in the company of twenty mounted men. Ethan's assailant threw him to the ground. 'I found this one about two hundred metres down the road. He says there are four Telirians and now only eleven men,' he reported.

'Excellent work, Baieta. But what of Crawley and the child?' replied one of the mounted men.

'Forgive me, Mek. I have not asked the captive,' apologised Baieta.

'Do not worry yourself. I will ask him directly,' assured Mek. He looked at the cowering figure of Ethan and raised a questioning eyebrow. 'Well?' he enquired.

'Crawley is near death and the child is hidden in the undergrowth. They are still searching as we speak,' blurted out Ethan nervously.

'Thank you for your time. Baieta, take ten men and as before +, and capture at least another ten of them; and take your time so you don't stumble upon a Telirian,' instructed Mek. 'I trust that Crawley has hidden the child well enough for us to do so?'

Baieta nodded his head in acknowledgment and he set off back into the undergrowth with the men. It took no less than fifteen minutes for Baieta to return with the required number of captives. All had been taken by complete surprise, and they still trembled with fear as they were roughly shoved to the ground to join Ethan.

'Believe me when I tell you all that you are far better off being held captive here than getting killed back there,' Mek informed them, pointing down the road.

'All right, Baieta, it's up to you to keep these men quiet. The rest of you follow me. Have your crossbows at the ready but do not fire unless directed,' instructed Mek.

With his band of horsemen, Mek set off down the road at a steady pace. All of them apart from five had crossbows cradled across their chest ready for use, just as Mek instructed.

Seker sensed Mek before he had rounded the bend in the road. It was only after Seker had summoned his men away from the search that he realised he was several short.

'Damn it!' he grumbled, spitting on the ground in annoyance.

Despite the sudden decline of numbers in his force, against his better judgment Seker decided to stand and face the threat that now loomed less than one hundred metres away. 'They want me to run but I will not give them the satisfaction. I will have to be forced,' he thought defiantly as he remounted his horse.

Seker began firing energy spheres indiscriminately into the oncoming group. However, his attack was quickly forgotten when a retaliatory hail of crossbow bolts threatened to puncture his hide several times over. The other Telirians summoned a red wall of energy to protect themselves but the remaining man fell, riddled with the deadly projectiles. Seker contemplated the situation and snarled in frustration. The only reasonable option left to him was flight, but he wasn't about to leave without first letting fly a few well-directed insults.

'You and your Jelery swine are nothing to my order! There is only one reason we still allow you to exist, and that's because we want you to suffer before we extinguish the Jelery!' he screamed, spraying the back of his horse's neck with flecks of spittle.

'And tell your sister not to wait up for me tonight,' chimed in another.

'Do you think that a sole Light Wielder will swing the tide of power? If you do, then you're more pathetic than you look,' hollered Seker.

He wheeled his horse around and they disappeared down the road in a swirl of dead leaves and dust.

'Do you think he realises how few in number we are?' enquired Terstane once they halted.

'There is no way he can know that,' replied Mek.

'Let us hope not, or the Telirians will surely strike. They attack only when they have the advantage of numbers, such is their cowardice,' added Yolstan.

'Gentlemen, there are more pressing issues to take care of – like the whereabouts of the child,' interrupted Kayden.

'And the fact that Crawley's life is fading, and he must be helped,' yelled Xaryn as he dismounted and rushed to the crumpled form by the side of the road. A mass of bodies soon surrounded Crawley like a pack of wolves waiting for their wounded prey to die. 'Crawley, are you still with us?' asked Xaryn, cradling his head.

'It would take a mighty effort to knock that old bird off his perch,' gargled the voice of Muefrede through Crawley's mouth.

The five Light Wielders looked questioningly at one another as the strange reply bounced around in their heads. 'That is not Crawley. The Spirits still dwell within,' said Mek as the realisation dawned on him.

'Well, it would be senseless to leave without first telling you where the child is now, wouldn't it?' growled Freom as he forced the eyes open on Crawley's head.

'Indeed, it would. Forgive our ignorance,' apologised Mek.

'Ignorance, indeed. The child's name is Atiol, and you will find him inside a hollowed-out log about thirty paces in that direction. He is well concealed but I believe the earthbound spirits would have left a calling card,' instructed Muefrede, pointing a shaky finger into the woods.

'Thank you, wise ones. We shall do our best with him,' promised Mek.

'Terstane, do you want to retrieve the child while I see what I can do for Crawley?' asked Xaryn.

Terstane nodded his head and hurried off into the woods. They were all watching him go, so Mek got a sudden fright when Crawley's claw-like hand clamped down on his forearm.

'I warn you now, Light Wielder, if you allow this Raver Crawley to perish, then I will make it my personal duty to ensure you suffer. He is worth ten times more than any one of you, and he will be treated as such, in the comfort of your own quarters if necessary. Do you understand?' threatened Freom.

The crushing pain in Mek's forearm caused him to gasp, and he had to fight through the pain in order to reply. 'Your wishes will be fully honoured,' he replied through clenched teeth.

'Good,' said Freom, releasing the grip.

Mek let out a sigh of relief and stared in fascination

as a bright green sheen passed over Crawley's grey eyes. His gaze was abruptly interrupted when an anguished scream of pain erupted from Crawley, who thrashed around as the pain in his tortured body began to rise.

'Hold him down,' said Mek.

'Worthless Spirits, thieves, murderers! I will kill them. Do you hear me, Spirits, all of you? Look at what you've done,' cried Crawley as he held up his burnt and bloodied hands. He let out another anguished cry as the pain rendered him unconscious.

'I need something to bandage the wounds up, but what I really need is a proper healer,' said Xaryn.

'Here, use this,' said Kayden, offering him his faded green shirt.

Mek took it silently and began tearing the shirt into bandages so Xaryn could bandage up Crawley's wounds. He wavered when he came to the crossbow bolt that protruded from Crawley's side.

Terstane returned with the child, who was busily trying to rip out his long white beard. 'Here, take him, Mek. He may not be as fascinated with a short-cropped brown beard as he is with mine,' said Terstane, handing over the infant. 'He was well concealed – when I got there he was enthusiastically ripping out, and chewing, the flowers that covered the hollow in the log.'

'Well, that was a stroke of luck,' stated Mek, he passed Atiol to Yolstane.

'I don't believe it was. Flowers don't tend to bloom where there is no sunlight,' retorted Terstane. He walked over to Xaryn. 'I think I will handle that wound, Xaryn. You look a bit lost,' offered Terstane as he crouched down beside him.

'Fine with me,' replied Xaryn.

Terstane was a little more versed in the healing arts. Crawley's remaining wounds were bound tightly and at least for the time being, the blood stopped flowing.

'I have done all that I can for him. He won't last long unless he gets to a proper healer,' announced Terstane as he sluiced the blood from his hands with his water skin. 'That bolt must be removed quickly. The tip is tearing at his insides,' he added.

'There is a small village about half a day's ride on the way to Galteone, and I am pretty sure they have a healer,' said Mek.

'Even if we leave now, we won't get there until well after nightfall, and folks around there are a little hesitant to open their doors after dark. It has something to do with the animals that roam their woods at night,' explained Kayden.

'It matters not. We will go there all the same. It is his only hope for survival,' replied Terstane.

'Then what are we doing milling around here like old men?' asked Yolstane.

'We are old men, Yolstane, very old,' replied Xaryn as he picked up Crawley. Xaryn was a slender older man with badly greying hair, which was slowly morphing white. He was by no means a tall man, so if any besides those present saw him pick up Crawley and place him in his saddle as if he was a small child, it would have caused their jaws to drop in disbelief. 'Perhaps, if one of us rides ahead and forewarns the village, they may be more accommodating when we arrive,' he speculated as he jumped up behind Crawley, to hold him in place.

'I will go,' volunteered Mek.

'It might be a good idea on the way past to tell your Iron Shadow to let the prisoners go,' added Xaryn.

'I was way ahead of you. Besides, I wasn't going to ride into a strange village after dark without him,' replied Mek as he jumped into the saddle, he turned the horse and cantered away.

It took all Mek's persuasive powers and ten gold pieces, but the youngish healer allowed him entry. Mek promised her another ten to treat Crawley when he arrived.

'You can inform me of my expected patient's condition,' demanded the healer as she moved towards a small fire burning lazily in its hearth.

'I will tell you, but I talk more freely when I know the name of the person I am addressing,' replied Mek with his most charming smile.

The healer blushed slightly, and hid her face with her hands in an attempt to disguise her discomfort. 'My name is Tiarn,' she replied, averting her eyes to a suddenly engrossing crack in the wall.

Mek noted her reaction and smiled inwardly. He stood close to six feet tall and had a strong build, with light brown hair that had begun to grey at the temples. His face was regarded as handsome by most women he met, and his short-cropped beard intensified the colour of his deep blue eyes, which added to his appeal. Over the years, he had become more aware of how women in general behaved when they met him and he shamelessly exploited the situation, when it was required.

'Well then, Tiarn, I am Mek,' he replied. Tiarn nodded her head slightly in acknowledgement, but did not trust herself to speak for fear it would betray her thoughts.

'His major concern is a crossbow bolt embedded deeply in his side above his hip. We bandaged it as best we could and managed to slow the bleeding.'

'Is blood the only discharge from the wound?' enquired Tiarn, now that her thoughts were solely on her forthcoming patient.

'Yes, there was only blood, but we can't say for sure until the bolt is removed,' replied Mek.

'That is true. And what of the other inflictions?' she asked.

'We did not have the time to examine him as closely as we would have liked. The only thing I can say with certainty, is that you're going to earn your gold tonight,' answered Mek.

Tiarn did not have time to reply, as Baieta popped his head through the doorway and announced the arrival of the others. Mek jumped to his feet and rushed outside to welcome Xaryn.

'Quickly, Mek, take him. He is deteriorating rapidly. We may already be too late,' said Xaryn.

Mek fought the knot of fear in his stomach as he lifted Crawley up onto the table inside the hut and could only hope that Tiarn's youth had no bearing on her healing ability. Tiarn waited patiently as Mek lay Crawley down.

'Can you remove his shirt for me?' she asked.

Crawley let out a soft groan as Mek struggled with the dirt-caked and bloodstained shirt. A small dagger placed into Mek's hand, after a polite tap on the shoulder from Xaryn, helped proceedings. 'Is there anything else we can help you with?' asked Mek.

'No, not as this point. But I will require someone to hold him down when I remove the bolt and cauterise the wound,' she advised, as she placed a pot of water over the fire. 'Until then, I would prefer to be left alone. I work better that way,' she added.

'Of course. Just let us know when we are required,' replied Xaryn, and he led Mek out by the shoulders into the crisp night air.

Once outside, Mek realised he still possessed the tattered remnants of the shirt, and threw them forcefully to the ground. 'I am fearful of the ramifications if Crawley perishes in our care,' he said with a sigh, and he slumped down against the wall.

'Freom growls ferociously, but Muefrede will not allow him to bite without a just cause,' reassured Xaryn, crouching beside Mek.

'Crawley was chosen specifically, and he proved his worth. You and I both know that without him this would not have worked out, and Freom certainly knows it,' replied Mek, stroking his beard.

'I do not think Freom is entirely finished with Crawley. I had a little chat with the prisoners, and from what they said, Crawley's body is more than capable of conducting energy, and not just meagre amounts of it. But the thing that has Freom impressed is that the energy expulsions were of the highest level,' said Baieta from his vantage point at the corner edge of the hut.

Mek searched Baieta's face for any sign of jest, and frowned thoughtfully when none was to be found. 'He handled golden energy?' he asked as he struggled with the notion.

'Not only that, they say he summoned a shield wall as well.'

Mek's jaw dropped temporarily at the new information, but he began to shake his head. 'They must have been mistaken,' he said. 'Even though he was inhabited by Freom and Muefrede, it could not have been possible. And a shield wall, damn it! Most Light Wielders can't even fathom the idea.'

'That would explain why Freom values his life above everyone else's. But don't worry about Crawley's health. As Muefrede said, *it takes quite a lot to knock the old bird off his perch*,' mimicked Xaryn as he slapped Mek on the knee.

'The problem with that theory is Crawley is not a bird,' replied Mek.

'I can't argue with that,' agreed Xaryn.

Mek ran his fingers through his sweat-dampened hair and looked around, realising for the first time that besides Baieta, Xaryn and himself were the only ones present.

'Xaryn,' he called.

'Yes.'

'Where are the rest of the men?' asked Mek, scanning the surroundings.

'There was no need for them to linger, so they have taken the child and as we speak, are on their way to Galteone,' explained Xaryn.

'Do you think that was wise, considering that Seker may still be out there? And if not him, then perhaps a certain bunch of men seeking revenge for the deaths of their friends?' said Mek, in a disbelieving matter-of-fact tone of voice.

Xaryn failed to hold back the laughter that swelled within. 'Oh, Mek, you're priceless,' he replied breathlessly between fits of laughter.

'I find nothing amusing about the child's safety being at risk,' responded Mek with growing disdain.

'Rest assured, if your angry, revenge-seeking mob wish to pursue us, they had better be fast runners, for you see...' Xaryn struggled to talk as another wave of laughter swept over him. 'For you see, Terstane desired a few good mounts to add to the stables so he had the riderless horses rounded up and he is taking them back to Galteone.'

'If this was so, then why didn't you just tell me instead of laughing your fool head off!' snapped Mek.

'Well, you just seemed so damn sure that if you didn't arrange it yourself, no one else could have. Do you think that because all the remaining senior Light Wielders are getting up there in years, we are incompetent and senile?'

'I get your point. You can stop laughing now,' said Mek, throwing a small rock at Xaryn's laughing form.

'Believe me, Mek, I am truly trying,' laughed Xaryn.

'You have no idea,' replied Mek, trying to suppress a smile.

'If you gentlemen are both quite finished...' interrupted Tiarn, poking her head through the doorway.

'Ahmm,' emitted Xaryn as he cleared his throat. 'Yes, sorry, we will be right in,' he added sheepishly.

Crawley's body had been cleaned to a certain extent, with only the most stubborn patches of grime still staking a claim on the withered body. Fresh bandages adorned his head and hands, but ominously, the crossbow bolt still stuck out of his side, stubbornly declaring that death was lingering, waiting for its chance.

'He has shown no signs of further decline, but that could quickly change,' sighed Tiarn, wiping the perspiration from her brow. 'All right, this must be done quickly and cleanly. Mek, hold him down as firmly as possible. If he starts to move while the bolt is being removed more damage could be done, and frankly, he cannot take much more,' she explained. 'And you–'

'Do you mean me?' enquired Xaryn.

'No, the person behind you! Of course you! There's a flat-bladed dagger in the fire. Hand it to me when I ask, and be careful as the handle will be hot.'

'Certainly, and thank you for the advice,' muttered Xaryn under his breath.

Mek silently snickered at Tiarn's treatment of Xaryn as a child, and thought fondly of the next time he and Xaryn would be alone to talk, and how it would pop up in the conversation numerous times, accidentally of course.

'Mek!' Tiarn's voice interrupted his daydream.

'Yes,' he replied.

'I'm ready. Are you?' she asked with growing annoyance.

'Yes, of course. Please be careful,' he pleaded, almost pathetically.

'I'm a healer, Mek. Being careful comes naturally,' she assured him in a soothing voice. She took hold of the slippery blood-soaked bolt. 'All right, on the count of three.'

On the third count, Tiarn slowly began to ease out the bolt. Crawley let out an angry cry and futilely attempted to arch his body away from the pain in his side. Finally, the bolt slid free with a sucking noise. Tiarn waited expectantly, then let out a heavy sigh of relief when nothing but a slight trickle of bright red blood pursued the withdrawn bolt. 'I don't think there will be any further complications,' she said, 'but there is still the risk of the wound going bad. I'll cauterise it, apart from a small weep hole, just to be sure.'

Xaryn handed her the glowing hot dagger with a crudely wrapped cloth over the handle. 'Be careful of the handle. It may be hot,' he warned with a smile.

Tiarn took no heed of the intended jest and with as much care as the task allowed, pressed the glowing hot blade to the wound. Crawley let out a growl of pain as the sound and smell of searing flesh filled the small hut. Tiarn removed the blade and carefully examined the sealed flesh that was already beginning to blister. 'I think that will do,' she said, wrinkling her nose at the stench.

'If we're not needed,' began Mek, gagging, 'I think we will wait outside.'

Without waiting for an answer, Mek and Xaryn scrambled to the door, holding their breath. They sucked in a long, noisy and somewhat exaggerated breath of air once they were outside.

'I don't know how she could still be in there. I could hardly breathe,' said Xaryn.

'It's just one of those talents that every healer must possess,' replied Mek, staring back through the doorway.

'Well, I for one am glad I'm not a healer,' said Xaryn.

'I second that notion,' said Mek, flashing a cheeky grin.

Xaryn opened his mouth to reply but instead let out a throaty laugh and slapped Mek on the shoulder. 'When Alourin was training you, he seemed to have missed a couple of lessons.'

'Oh, really!' exclaimed Mek through fits of laughter. 'And what lessons might they have been?' he added.

'Just the important ones like respecting your elders and knowing when to keep quiet. You know, the important ones.'

'No, he never forgot to teach me them. I just forgot to remember them,' provoked Mek.

'How very convenient,' replied Xaryn, rolling his eyes.

Tiarn broke up their conversation. 'If you are to move him tonight, my advice to you would be that you do not hurry, and try to keep him still. The last thing he needs is unnecessary jolting,' advised Tiarn, mopping at her brow.

'Rest assured, the last thing I'd want is for you to have worked so hard and skilfully on him, just so that a couple of incompetent fools could get him killed on the ride home,' assured Mek, flashing her one of his more charming smiles.

Tiarn tried to cover her blushing face with a small portion of rag that she had been using to mop her brow. Realising that her actions were futile, she turned around and disappeared back inside before she had a chance to make more of a fool of herself.

'Whenever you're ready, Mek,' interrupted Xaryn, gesturing to the open doorway.

'Oh yes, sorry,' replied Mek.

With exaggerated care, Crawley was carried out of the hut and placed before Mek on the horse. Not realising how tall Crawley was, Mek found it hard to see and had to rise in his saddle, which he knew meant his legs would be painful in the morning. With one last nod to Tiarn, he urged his horse into a slow walk.

'Mek,' called Tiarn. 'Be careful when you go through the woods. There has been several attacks of late, and even disappearances. Something other than the usual animals have been spotted within its depths.'

'Thank you, Tiarn. I will be careful,' replied Mek as he continued to ride away.

Xaryn waited until he was sure Mek was out of earshot before he turned to address Tiarn. 'Your help has been greatly appreciated. Oh, and just for the record, being a fool and acting inept is something we only do for a hobby.' He chuckled as he followed after Mek.

Tiarn had a little laugh to herself as she cleaned up the soiled clothes and bandages from her hut. 'A hobby indeed,' she said out loud to herself as she continued to laugh.

They rode on through the night, not daring to rest their weary mounts for fear they would not move again.

'Weary horses are like rolling boulders. They are hard to get moving, but once they do, they keep going without much effort, and if they are stopped, then it takes a mighty effort to get them going again,' remarked Xaryn as they plodded along in the grey light of dawn. Mek looked at Xaryn but didn't bother to comment.

It was close to midday before they reached the low stone wall that marked the border of Jelery-held ground, and as they passed by the wall, the land took on a brand-new lustre. The trees were growing close together, like a hedge, and there was barely enough room to squeeze between the thick, rough trunks. The low-hanging branches were full of emerald-coloured leaves that gave the whole place a feeling of purity and had a soothing effect on the mind. The sun held no sway in this forest of giants, and only the most determined rays were able to reach the forest floor, where thick clumps of moss dotted the area. The humidity left behind was like a lame animal, and a cooler breath of wind caressed their bodies, causing a flowing wave of goosebumps to wash over them. It took a little while for their eyes to adjust to the growing gloom of their surrounds.

'I feel as though I can breathe easier already,' said Xaryn cheerfully.

'Yes, I feel a lot safer in the forest as well,' agreed Mek. They stopped a short while later when their path encountered a small crystal-clear stream filled with mossy boulders.

'I don't know about you, Xaryn, but I am going to get a little sleep,' announced Mek as he lay out a bedroll next to Crawley and Baieta, who were already deep in slumber.

'Yes, it doesn't seem fair that Crawley gets to sleep the whole way. I suppose it would be all right for you to get some as well,' agreed Xaryn.

'Aren't you going to catch some shut eye?' questioned Mek as he lay down. '

No, someone has to keep an eye on Crawley in case he wakes up; and besides, I have a sneaking suspicion that someone has been following us since we left Tiarn, and I would really love to find the culprit.'

'Suit yourself,' yawned Mek, closing his eyes.

The crow had been following them from the time they had found Crawley lying on the road. Like a shadow, it had remained close, trying to gather information about Crawley's state of health, and anything about the child that might be useful. It watched them now as Mek and Crawley slept. It waited patiently, and silently hopped to a closer branch. Finally, the other Light Wielder leaned his head against a tree and closed his eyes. Sensing an opportunity to get a closer look at Crawley, it moved to a branch that was no more than twenty feet away. Then without warning the Light Wielder who had his head on the tree opened his eyes, and looking directly at the crow with a triumphant smile, he cast a grey, almost transparent energy sphere straight at it. It missed by a hair's breadth and hit the trunk above, blowing out a chunk of bark. Crows have the highest regard for personal safety, and this one knew its little, black-feathered body was on the line, so it hurriedly left its perch and sought the safety of the open skies. Xaryn cursed his bad aim but chuckled nonetheless.

'Delrain's little spies seem to be growing bolder. I shall have to inform the other members of the Council about this when I return,' thought Xaryn solemnly as he resumed his position against the tree.

Mek awoke in the deepening gloom of dusk and was surprised to see a small cooking fire blazing away, wafting the smell of wood smoke and bacon towards him.

'Good to see you got some sleep,' greeted Baieta.

'Good to see we have some food. By the way, I don't recall any pigs in the vicinity, so where did you get the bacon?' asked Mek.

'Ask him,' replied Baieta, gesturing to Xaryn.

'It was liberated from the horses we acquired. Terstane was good enough to slip it into one of my saddlebags along with several loaves of bread, some jerked meat, and some tea and sugar.'

'And the skillet?' asked Mek.

'Yes, that too, and some cups,' he replied, banging the tin cups together.

'I'm going to give him a big hug when I get back,' said Mek, laughing.

'A pat on the back would be enough, don't you think?' said Xaryn.

'I don't know. I am rather hungry,' he replied.

'If anything, we should be thanking those wonderful men that were travelling with Seker,' said Xaryn, laughing.

'Well, then I say we have a little feast in their honour,' announced Baieta.

'Agreed. To the men who travelled with Seker – they fought badly but came well provisioned,' said Mek, raising a cup of tea. The contents of the skillet disappeared quickly, and after several cups of tea and a large chunk of bread, the trio sat around the fire.

'I think I have overdone it,' said Xaryn, and he let out a loud belch.

'I don't think I can even stand,' agreed Baieta.

'In the future, we should always bring an oversupply of provisions in case of unforeseen delays in our travel schedule. I mean, I can go without food for a couple of days if I have to, but I would prefer not to. That's not being selfish, is it?' asked Mek.

'No. I agree thoroughly,' said Xaryn in support.

They sat in contented silence, allowing their swollen stomachs to digest the massive meal at their own pace, and moving only to feed the fire from the small pile of fallen sticks collected earlier by Xaryn.

Baieta sat forward when he felt the hairs on the back of his neck prickle. 'There's something out there," he whispered.

'Nonsense. I am not sensing anything," replied Xaryn.

Baieta gestured for quiet. 'You sense certain things that I can't, but as a human I am definitely sensing something, and it is scaring the hair off the back of my neck,' he whispered in response.

They remained perfectly still and eventually a huge figure casually stepped into the firelight and appraised them like a hungry man eying a meal. It stood higher than any man and was twice as wide, and it seemed to be made of solid stone. It looked at the fire then back at the four of them, before it spoke in a deep voice that made the air vibrate.

'You are planning to burn the forest with that?' it accused, pointing at the fire with a thick finger.

'No, it is for cooking and nothing more, and will be properly doused when we are finished," replied Xaryn calmly.

It stared at Xaryn with its yellow predatory eyes, and Xaryn stared back steadily. 'I don't think you know who you are dealing with, Earth Spirit,' he said as he rolled up his sleeve.

The Earth Spirit noted the tattoo and turned its gaze to Mek, who held his hand out with the palm facing the sky, and conjured a small red energy sphere.

'Hmm, you may be Jelery; and I know that one is a Raver, but he is definitely a human,' he said, pointing to Baieta.

'He is with me, and falls under my protection,' replied Mek.

The Earth Spirit weighed up the situation before it spoke. 'It would seem to be your lucky day, human,' it said, then turned and disappeared back into the gloom of the forest.

Baieta did not realise that he had been holding his breath, and now he let it out forcefully. 'That is a first for me,' he said a little unsteadily.

'Well, I think we know what has been causing the disappearances that Tiarn was talking about,' reflected Mek.

'Meddling Spirits, I will show 'em,' muttered Crawley in his sleep.

'I couldn't have said it better myself,' said Mek.

'It has been a long time since a Spirit has openly shown itself, and I dare say that if we were all human we would not be having this conversation,' assumed Xaryn.

Crawley began to stir. 'He will wake soon,' advised Xaryn.

'This is a good thing, but it would be best if he woke in a soft bed rather than on the forest floor,' agreed Mek.

'We are no more than a day's ride from Galteone. We will leave in the morning as soon as the light allows us to do so,' instructed Xaryn.

'I will keep a lookout in case our friend decides to reappear, so if you both wish to get some sleep...' offered Mek, knowing that Xaryn also feared that the Earth Spirit might return.

'I'll take you up on that offer,' replied Xaryn thankfully.

'If you get tired, you can always wake me up, Mek,' offered Baieta.

'Thanks, but I don't think I will be sleeping any more this night. Besides, I want to be the one to talk to Crawley if he should wake.'

'Suit yourself. I dislike talking to Ravers at the best of times,' confessed Baieta as he lay down on the bedroll.

'I agree. You're lucky to get a word in edgeways with any Raver. Talking to them requires a little more than a nod here and there,' said Mek.

'It's listening to them jabbering on constantly, almost as irritating as someone talking in your ear when your eyes are closed and you're trying to sleep,' interrupted Xaryn with a growl in his voice.

'Well, there's a subtle hint if ever I did hear one,' chuckled Mek.

'Not subtle enough, Mek. Shut up!'

'I live to serve,' added Mek sarcastically.

Xaryn thought about stretching Mek's ears but decided the effort would be in vain and preferred the warmth and the promise of sleep his bedroll offered. He pulled his cloak up, completely covering his head. Mek leaned against a tree with his hands behind his head to cushion it from the rough bark, and sat staring into the fire with a bemused look on his face. Several times during the remainder of the night, Crawley cried out in his sleep and restlessly tossed his head from side to side, but thankfully they had no unwanted visitors.

Mek was by Crawley's side when he began to thrash around violently, but he could do little more than look on with concern. 'Damn it, Crawley, you scared me half to death that time,' swore Mek when the latest bout of thrashing had ceased.

'My apologies,' croaked Crawley.

Mek let out a startled cry and nearly back-pedalled up the nearest tree. 'How do you feel?' he asked once he had calmed down.

'I'm throbbing with pain all over, and my throat feels as though I have swallowed a handful of sand,' replied Crawley, swallowing noisily.

'I am afraid there is not much I can do about the pain, but I can at least give you a drink of water,' offered Mek.

'That would be paradise,' accepted Crawley. Mek helped him up and he drank deeply from the waterskin. 'Thank you greatly,' said Crawley, smiling and patting Mek's hand when he'd had his fill.

'I truly wish that I could give you something for the pain, but I have no such thing. It will have to wait until we reach Galteone, I'm afraid,' informed Mek.

'I can wait. In fact, I can bear the pain. For the first time in years my head is filled with nothing but my own thoughts, and if the pain is the price to pay for that, I can put up with it,' replied Crawley with a relief-filled smile.

'It would seem as though Muefrede and Freom have had a little word with the Earthbound Spirits about the constant badgering over the last umpteen dozen years,' pointed out Mek.

The smile on Crawley's face changed alarmingly into a ferocious snarl. 'Speak not those names to me. They burn my ears and fill my head with murderous thoughts. Speak not those names to me!' snapped Crawley with all the hate he could muster.

Mek thought feverishly for something to say that might calm the fire still raging in Crawley's eyes, but failed to find anything and instead took to throwing small twigs on the fire to watch the sparks drift overhead. Eventually, Crawley calmed down and was soon asleep again, leaving Mek alone with his thoughts.

The gloom in Strangle Light Woods varies only slightly from night to day. Instead of the deep black gloom of night, a slightly brighter deep grey gloom during the day allows you to see for a couple of metres in any given direction. The subtle change can be missed by those with no knowledge of the woods. Miss it and you will lose all sense of time, as the night will never seem to end.

Mek snapped out of his daydream as the change was occurring. 'Wake up, Xaryn. The day is upon us,' he said.

'I am not asleep, Mek. I was watching to see if for once in your life you would miss the change,' replied Xaryn, sounding a little disappointed.

'As I keep telling everyone, Alourin drilled the lessons into my head so thoroughly that every time

I am in need of remembering them they automatically pop into my head, which is very useful except for the fact it feels as though Alourin is yelling them directly into my ear,' explained Mek.

'Then I am glad I never had a teacher of his calibre. I don't think I could stand being taught every lesson over and over for the rest of my life,' mocked Xaryn.

'It would not do any harm for someone your age to undergo another round of the fundamental lessons you're sure to have forgotten – at least, one of them,' rebuked Mek.

'Ha-ha, once again it's about age. All right, let's call it a truce until we reach Galteone. Then it's open season, agreed?' offered Xaryn.

'Agreed,' replied Mek, smiling like a Cheshire cat.

He gently shook Crawley into wakefulness, and offered him another drink of water from the waterskin before they began to move. By this time Crawley was feeling much better and began to talk excessively.

'I think I will scout ahead,' announced Baieta, trying to escape the old man's range. Xaryn looked on in envy as he galloped ahead.

'I will tell you something. It is a frightening and very frustrating experience. Have you ever been in the same predicament?' asked Crawley.

'No, I can't say that I have,' sighed Xaryn in reply.

'Then you are very lucky indeed.'

'Truly,' agreed Xaryn as enthusiastically as he could.

So the rest of the day went on, the sounds of the forest filling one ear whilst Crawley's excessive chatter assaulted the other. He talked happily about his life up to that minute, and seemed in good spirits until Xaryn made the mistake of mentioning Freom in the general conversation. At that, Crawley stopped chatting happily and cursed both Freom and Muefrede with every available insult and curse he could muster before he grew silent and despondent for several hours. A while later he suddenly started chatting again as though nothing had happened.

Gradually, the gloom lightened as the forest thinned, and the sound of rushing water could be heard faintly up ahead.

'Ah, we are almost there. I can hear the River Marset welcoming me home,' announced Mek cheerfully.

'Not a moment too soon,' acknowledged Xaryn thankfully.

Within half an hour they broke free of Strangle Light Woods and came out into bright, blinding sunlight. One hundred metres ahead, a stone arched bridge spanned the width of the river at its narrowest point, which was about thirty-five metres. This was the first time Crawley had crossed such a large river by other means than a ferry.

'Are you quite sure it will remain standing?' he enquired, glancing nervously at the fast-flowing water as they passed over it.

'I see no reason why not. If it hasn't fallen down in nearly two hundred years, it's not going to fall down now,' replied Xaryn with a mischievous grin.

'I would think that if anything was two hundred years old, it would be more likely to fall down. I know if I were two hundred years old, I would definitely feel like falling down,' reasoned Crawley a little shakily.

'You will just have to ask Alourin how he feels once we reach Galteone. Ask him if he feels like falling down,' instructed Xaryn.

'I'm not sure I understand what you mean,' replied Crawley, feeling a bit confused.

'He means that Alourin is nearly two hundred years old, Crawley,' offered Mek.

'Oh, I see. No, come to think about it, I don't,' he admitted.

'He is a Light Wielder. All Light Wielders live a long time. It just so happens Alourin is bumping up the average considerably. Why, Xaryn himself is not helping matters. He is nearly a century old,' added Mek, trying to explain. Xaryn let the comment slide.

Despite Crawley's fears, the bridge held up, and they made it safely across. After they stepped off the bridge, the city of Galteone loomed large in front of them. The front gates were a mere fifty metres from the bridge. The city was three-tiered. The first tier was flat. Only the second tier followed the natural slope of the plains before levelling out on the top one. The first tier was full of the usual hustle and bustle of markets and traders. The second tier housed the barracks and its men, and the top tier was where the people lived, including the Light Wielders who called themselves the Jelery. The third tier was dominated by a huge three-sided tower that was used by the Council members of the Jelery. It was commonly referred to as the Tri Tower, for obvious reasons.

The outer walls to the left were unassailable as the river rushed past them so close that it almost touched, thanks to a natural bend in the river. The right side faced the plains of Galteone and was the most fortified, as it was the only place an opposing force could attack. The front itself was also rather close to the river and didn't allow a force of any notable size to be assembled, and the rear of the city almost butted against the low foothills that bordered the plains. Attack was impossible from the back as there was no room for enemies to gather.

As they approached the city, several figures appeared atop the wall, and they were all greeted warmly before they even entered.

'Hail, Mek. Hail, Xaryn and Baieta. Better late than never, I suppose.'

'It is easy to never be late when the only travelling one does is from the gate house to the ale house,' replied Baieta.

''Tis true that the only destination I wish to travel to is the bottom of my mug of ale, but there is nothing wrong with that,' argued the voice in response.

'Very true, and I would be happy to help you on your travels. But in order for me to do so, you will have to let us in, Falmore,' said Baieta.

'Certainly.' With a lazy gesture of his arm, the gate of Galteone began to rise, and it was several grinding and squealing moments before they were raised to their full extent.

'Either the gate needs a good greasing or we need a man with more experience in the gate house,' said Mek disapprovingly as they entered.

'Sorry, my lord. I will look into it,' replied Falmore.

'Good. I wouldn't want to have to remove you. After all, it's your turn to buy the ale tonight, and you wouldn't be able to afford it if you lost your rank and position, now would you?' added Mek with a sly smile.

'As my lord requests,' replied Falmore.

'Oh, Falmore, I am going to be rather thirsty tonight,' added Mek as he disappeared.

'Somehow people always are when they're not buying,' muttered Falmore. The gate closed with a louder squeal as it crashed down. 'Although there is some truth in what Mek said,' he thought as he yelled abuse at the men manning the gates.

# 5

SEKER MANOEUVRED HIS horse around with a violent tug on the reins. 'I can't wait for the day when we crush Galteone and every living soul that dwells within its walls,' he said.

'Indeed, that day would be sweet, but I yearn to have my hands wrapped around a Jelery neck and to squeeze it until it snaps.' One of his men agreed, miming the words with his hands.

'Lord Delrain waits only for his forces to grow,' added another.

'We have the numbers. Now we should attack Galteone and reduce it to rubble,' argued the other.

'Lord Delrain is no fool. He knows the Jelery still have a lot of support throughout the land. Most people still believe their laws and will fight for them if required,' stated Seker.

'then why don't we crush those who support them first?' proposed the hot-headed one.

'They only fight for the Jelery because they still believe in their laws and rules. And as we have all seen, if the law is followed, it leads to a boring and very oppressive lifestyle. If we offer them freedom from it and also our protection from reprisals, then several will follow our law and do our bidding,' explained Seker.

'How exactly will this come about, Seker?'

'Well, Learman, it has already begun. Lord Delrain has appointed several of our brothers to all the major cities and towns in the area, and we ourselves shall get the ball rolling here when one of us returns with the survivors to Rubalar without the brat. That alone will cause some sparks and then with a few choice words, I am certain we can kindle the fires of hatred toward the Jelery.'

'We don't even know if there is anyone left alive. The Jelery could have killed them all,' pointed out Learman.

'We are dealing with the Jelery, Learman. I would bet your life on it that they would have left the men alive. They don't have it in their weak hearts to kill unnecessarily,' pointed out Seker.

'Seker is right. All we have to do is wait for the survivors. They should be fleeing our way with their tails between their legs,' said Learman in agreement.

'Well, if we are to wait, I propose that we wait beside a fire, and preferably have something cooking on it,' said the hot-headed one. All nodded in agreement.

They were all soon lounging around comfortably, soaking up the warmth of the fire, when the ten surviving men, still wide-eyed with fear, came ambling up the road toward them.

'Hail, good men. We offer you the warmth of our fire and our deepest condolences at the loss of the men who were brave enough to try and stop the Jelery in their unjust cause,' greeted Seker.

'Yes, they were brave. I never thought in my life that I would have to try and take down a Light Wielder,' replied Ethan.

'If we don't do something to stop their constant meddling, then you may be seeing more of them in your area,' warned Learman.

'We will get to that later, but for now come and share a meal with us,' invited Seker.

The men agreed readily, and none refused the several large chunks of venison that had freshly been killed and roasted.

Seker waited until they had all eaten their fill before he once again spoke. 'My friends, today you have seen and experienced the cold-hearted brutality of my enemies, and you now know the power that they possess. It saddens my heart that you all had to find out about it the hard way,' he began. 'Unfortunately, as Learman pointed out before, it will not be your last encounter with the Jelery, and it certainly will not be mine. The problem is that the next time you encounter them, it could be in your very own city and you will be fighting to save more than just your own lives.'

'I thought the Jelery were a peaceful people despite their power. Or at least that is what I have heard,' mumbled Ethan.

'Do you still believe that after today's little run-in with them?' asked Learman.

'No, I suppose not,' he replied. 'Perhaps they were once upon a time, when all the people in the land were firmly under their control, but finally the people are starting to wake up. They are finding that the shackles placed upon their lives by a set of outdated rules are starting to chafe them and restrain them from reaching a better lot in life. They are casting off the shackles, discovering for themselves a better and more prosperous way of life!' illuminated Seker with a fiery passion that had reddened his face. He paused to allow his blood to cool before he continued. 'This is causing the Jelery some concern, for what use is ruling when there is no one left to rule over? My point is that they are now getting a little worried that perhaps a revolution is in the air; and the way to stop it is to crush those who oppose the law.'

'That is all well and good, but where does Earl Penetty's brat fit into the equation?' asked one of the men.

Seker smiled inwardly, as he had been expecting the question and was pleased with himself for remaining one step ahead in the ruse. 'Tell me, is Earl Penetty a man of spiritual wealth or a man of material wealth?' probed Seker.

'Definitely the latter,' replied Ethan with a laugh.

'Of course he is, but which mayor of any town isn't?' joked Seker, with a huge smile. A ripple of laughter ran through the group of men, and Seker had to silence them all with a gesture of his hand. 'A poor man does not become rich if he follows the law, unless he is extremely lucky and happens to come across a large bag of gold in his flower bed. Not very likely, I know,' explained Seker. 'The Jelery have had a spy and they know that Earl Penetty is far from being a law-abiding citizen, and because he is a mayor, that kind of thing could spread to the citizens.'

'The spy was Crawley, wasn't it?' asked Ethan.

Seker nodded his head. 'Crawley, indeed. As you can

see, everything is becoming clear. Now instead of killing Earl, they intended to manipulate his ways, make him toe the line, and set a good example for the rest of the people so they will follow suit, effectively snuffing out the thought of any rebellion before one had the chance to begin,' explained Seker.

'So they came to his house and stole his son from under his nose, and were going to use him to exert leverage,' said Ethan.

'Precisely. And unfortunately, I could not stop this from happening. But with your help, we can stop the Jelery from crushing your lives, your freedom. If we can convince Earl to free the town from Jelery laws and restrictions, then I will offer the protection of my people, and the Telirian people will take up arms to aid you in your cause,' pledged Seker.

'It may be all well and good for you to pledge your support, but what are our town's meagre forces going to do when the Jelery retaliate? Because retaliate they will!' argued Ethan.

'I do not ask you to gather your forces and storm the walls of Galteone. All I ask is that you cast off their law. This thing can be done secretly and without fuss, but there will come a time when Galteone will become a target, and your help will be called upon. And rest assured, many, many more towns, villages, and even some of the larger cities including Arama, will be right at your side,' said Seker.

'You make it sound as though things are going to happen with or without Rubala's support,' said one of the men.

'That it will,' agreed Seker.

'When the time comes, those who are not with us will fall with the Jelery,' added Seker.

'They will all meet a slow and painful death – those who will try to keep this land and its people under the thumb,' growled the hot-headed Telirian.

'I cannot myself offer you Rubala's support, but I can offer you my full support, and I will be certain to talk to Earl upon my return,' replied Ethan after he had a moment to think things over. The other men, seeing Ethan pledge his support, willingly followed his lead and pledged their allegiance as well.

'Although Rubala as of now still remains steadfast to the law, I am sure that the rest of its occupants like you, good gentlemen, will come to see the freedom we offer; and when that day comes, we shall be valuable allies to each other,' promised Seker.

'We will be sure to spread word of your offer to all that will willingly listen, and to make those who don't see the light suffer in whatever way we can,' promised Ethan.

'Excellent, Ethan, but I am sure if one of my men were to accompany you to Rubala and speak by your side, then the mayor and everyone else will see things from our point of view,' advised Seker.

'That would be a most excellent idea, and it would be an honour to have a Telirian speak on my behalf,' agreed Ethan.

'All is settled then. One of my men will accompany you. Jayder, go with these gentlemen,' ordered Seker.

'As you wish, Seker,' replied Jayder.

'Good luck to you all, until we next meet,' farewelled Ethan as the group of men began the long walk back to Rubala.

'Oh, Ethan,' said Seker. Ethan turned to face him. 'These are for you.' Seker threw him the bag of rubies.

'We did not fulfill what we set out to do. We have not earned these,' stammered Ethan as he clutched the bag.

'Think of it as a gift from Lord Delrain.'

Ethan nodded his head and pocketed the small fortune, then caught up with his men to inform them of their windfall.

Learman waited patiently until Jayder and the group of men had disappeared from sight before he spoke to Seker. 'Ohh, we are smooth today, aren't we?' He laughed.

'It is no different any other day,' replied Seker, joining in on the laughter.

'I swear that if you so commanded, they would cut off their little fingers if they thought it would help the cause,' added Learman.

Seker abruptly stopped chuckling, and his brow creased together in thought. Learman edged away from the fire, unsure about the sudden change in Seker's mood. 'Why do you slink away from me? You have done nothing wrong. In fact, probably for the first time in your life, you have had an inspirational thought, albeit by accident, of course,' murmured Seker.

If Learman had been feeling a little uneasy before, the sound of Seker's honeyed voice mocking his cowardice then praising him for a stupid little comment had him sweating in fear. 'I don't understand,' replied Learman hesitantly.

'You need not worry about it. It may lead to nothing. Then again, it may if Lord Delrain approves of it,' assured Seker.

'Approve what? I have proposed nothing that should go before Lord Delrain. I am not one to change things, especially if I like them the way they are,' argued

Learman, not liking the direction the conversation was heading.

'It will go before him, but he must first see how devoted to the idea we all are,' stated Seker firmly. He slowly drew his dagger from its sheath and watched the flames of the fire reflect off the sharply honed blade, then looked questioningly at Learman. 'The question now is: which hand shall bear the mark? I believe the left – it will not be as noticeable.'

Before Learman had the chance to reply to the question, a splatter of blood hit his cheek. 'Are you insane?' he shrieked.

'No, just committed to the cause,' grunted Seker as he cut though the last piece of skin that had held the top half of his little finger on.

'I did not mean you. It was a joke,' gasped the mortified Learman.

'Come now, it didn't hurt all that much. At least, not as much as this part,' consoled Seker, as he thrust the bloodied stub of his little finger into the bright red coals of the fire.

'You take things too far, Seker,' said Learman as he recoiled from the smell.

'Perhaps you are too docile for this line of work. Yet here you sit and as long as this is so, my word is your law. So here, take this,' growled Seker, thrusting the blade to within inches of his neck.

Learman took the dagger in his trembling hand, pressed the blade against the skin of his little finger on his left hand, and took a few steadying breaths. Seker watched with a cruel smile on his face, but grew agitated when Learman failed to get on with the grisly task.

'Do it, Learman,' he said, leaning closer.

Learman grimaced in pain as he drew the blade across his skin, breaking the top layer only. He could go no further and was about to pull the blade away when Seker latched on to the hand that held the blade and began with too much ease to saw through Learman's finger. Learman cried out in pain and struggled as Seker controlled his movements like a grim puppeteer.

'One last effort,' announced Seker as the blade passed through his finger and scraped against the stone it had been resting on. 'Now the part we all enjoy,' he said jovially as he wrenched Learman's hand toward the fire.

'You are insane,' spat Learman. His legs thrashed around in the dust as he tried to stop Seker.

'Probably,' replied Seker as he jammed Learman's bleeding finger onto the hot coals. 'Now, that wasn't so bad, was it?' he asked as he let Learman slump to the ground at his feet.

The remaining Telirian watched on passively then picked up the bloodied dagger. 'Seker, for you,' he announced as he deftly cut his finger off and threw it into the fire.

'Excellent, my brother, excellent,' praised Seker as he watched the young man cauterise his wound. 'You both are marked as I am, brothers. We are a part of something special. We are the first to bear the mark of the revolution, but we will not be the last. Today is the beginning of the end for the Jelery and the beginning of the glorious Telirian uprising!'

So Lord Delrain's men spread throughout the land and coerced, lied, bribed, and threatened their way into positions of influence within the various governments. And that is when the real work began, of undermining the laws of the land, slowly chipping away at Jelery rule. And the land began to respond. Once fertile patches of land failed to yield crops; streams and rivers began to dry up as the people abused nature and deliberately ignored the ancient law that was set down thousands of years before. Whole acres of forests were cut and milled, but the Spirits were not appeased and no land was set aside to counter the destruction.

The people got rich and took what they wanted, and the Spirits' habitat dwindled. They started to exact revenge. Woodsmen disappeared more frequently whilst they were in the forests, and people who lived near water frequently drowned. Only those who lived by the law remained unmolested by the Spirits, but the lines were beginning to blur, and the Jelery held back the descent into chaos as best they could. It had taken twenty years, but Delrain's plan was working beyond his wildest expectations. The added touch of having all Ravers captured and imprisoned in his dungeons drastically cut the Jelery numbers whilst his own force of Light Wielders grew to ridiculous proportions. The time was upon him to unleash his forces and destroy his enemies once and for all.

# 6

'OPEN THE GATES! We have wounded,' hollered Mek as he drew near the gate of Galteone.

'Open up the bloody gates. Hurry it up,' yelled Falmore to the men in the gate house.

The gate rose with a squeal, and the bloodied and flustered group poured into the city. 'What happened out there?' Falmore asked them, full of concern.

'It was a bloody trap. They lured us to an area of land that supposedly required replenishing, and before we knew it, we were surrounded and set upon.'

'Set upon by whom?' asked Falmore.

'I have no idea. The only thing I do know is that they were definitely human, and there were too many of the dirty murderers to count. We would not have made it back if not for the Iron Shadow escort. They are rather handy in a tight spot,' explained Mek.

'So the Council members were right to increase the number of men that go out with any Jelery party,' shouted Falmore as Mek rode off toward the dominating presence of the Tri Tower.

'Yes, I am on my way to thank them for it right now,' yelled Mek in reply. He increased the pace of his horse with a kick to its flank, but it still took a good ten minutes to weave his way through the lower levels of Galteone and reach the Jelery compound that took up only a small part of the upper tier.

'Mek, Mek.' Mek turned his head toward the speaker.

A young man trotted up to him. He had sandy blonde hair that came down to his thin but toned shoulders, and he had a much too expression for his age. However, his bright green eyes still sparkled with the mischievousness of youth. 'I heard you ran into a little bit of trouble out there, and I came to see if you had been hurt,' he said with genuine concern.

'I am not physically hurt, Atiol. I was hurt here,' replied Mek, tapping his chest.

'Then you know who it was that attacked you?' enquired Atiol.

'No, not exactly. But because of the remote location we were in, the townspeople must have known it was an ambush and they did nothing to warn us. I will tell you more about it later when there are fewer ears around trying to gather fuel for their mouths.'

'Understood,' said Atiol, nodding. He stepped back and allowed a young woman with a basket full of bread to walk by.

'I will meet you in the dining room at supper,' instructed Mek over his shoulder as he walked off.

'He is almost a little too curious, isn't he?' stated Baieta, seemingly materialising out of thin air.

'I thought you were going to brush down your horse and fix those nicks in your sword, that you collected from our little adventure this morning,' replied Mek.

'I got a few of the young men that hang around the Iron Shadow quarters to do it for me,' explained Baieta.

'Ahh, free labour from the hero worshippers,' said Mek.

'Yes, they seem to think it will help me reach the right decision with their applications,' replied Baieta with a smile.

'You are a cruel man, and you must be slipping, because I knew you were there,' accused Mek.

'I allowed you to see me – and can you stop dodging my inquiries about your student? I need to know what his temperament is like, so when the time comes, I can assign him a compatible shadow.'

'I have every faith in your judgement, Baieta. You don't need my input. Now, are there more pressing issues at hand that I must know about before I go and see the Council?' asked Mek.

'Would it matter if I did? You would tell me to wait until after you were finished anyway,' sighed Baieta.

'Baieta, you know me too well. I will talk to you in about an hour, or however long the Council decides to take with me,' replied Mek.

Without a word being spoken, the two heavily armoured guards moved to allow Mek access to the Tri Tower, and when he had passed through the entrance, they once again barred the path to everyone else. Mek made his way up a well-lit stairwell of solid granite. There were precisely thirty steps before he came to an alcove that housed a doorway; the steps, however, continued to ascend the tower. Mek swung the heavy oak doors open and stepped through the doorway almost into the points of two gleaming pikes.

'Sorry, Mek, we have been ordered to be alert to all that enter,' apologised one of the guards as they raised the points of the pikes skyward.

'Yes, well, I wouldn't want to rush in here anyway. I might have tripped and fallen on the stairs,' replied Mek. He walked down the short stairway that led to a circular room which was bordered by columns of white marble. A large semicircular table dominated the room. The members of the Council were seated around it in their respective places, gazing at Mek as he entered.

'You seem to have run into some difficulties, Mek. Would you care to tell us exactly what happened?' asked the head of the Council.

'Ter-hal, as you know, we were called out by a small village several days away, directly northwest of the forest path and almost in the foothills of the western mountains. A fire had burnt through a considerable chunk of land on the outskirts of the village. This was supposedly an important area of land to the villagers as it was used for hunting animals, the gathering of firewood, and for the vast supply of edible roots and plants. Despite the concern that without the woods to support their population, they strangely refused our offer of foodstuffs to see them through.'

'Yes, that would be a bit strange, to refuse aid when their food supply was compromised,' agreed Solat thoughtfully.

'Indeed, it seemed strange. And when we reached the village, it was clear that they had an abundance of food, more than enough to last their small population for months. If I had been more perceptive at the time, I would have realised that for the number of people in the village, most of the food would have perished before they had the chance to consume it, but at the time I failed to add that up,' recalled Mek.

'The question now is where did they get that food from, or who gave it to them?' pondered Kayden out loud.

'I bet I could give you all two guesses, and you wouldn't need the second one,' stated Kennieth with a violent snort of disgust.

'Please, if the Council will allow me to continue!' interrupted Mek with a raised voice.

'I am sorry, Mek. Please continue,' apologised Kennieth.

'Unfortunately, that was not the only thing to get by me that day, for as we came to the area, the smoke hung too thickly in the area, too thickly for a fire that had been reported several days earlier. The area was quite substantial and bordered by a heavily wooded forest on three sides. It was as though that part of the land had been branded. It was too perfect for a supposed out-of-control fire, which it was claimed to be by any of the villagers I asked. Unfortunately for us, we were about to find out that we had stumbled into a well-planned and very deadly trap. I and the other Light Wielders dismounted and were preparing to perform the replenishing, when a volley of well-aimed arrows rained down, taking us by complete surprise,' said Mek, pausing to regain his emotions.

'Take your time, Mek,' consoled Xaryn.

'I was not harmed,' said Mek after he had regained his self-control. 'As you know, I have the ability to conjure a shield wall. But the other Light Wielders were of the Blue and Green Order and had not the ability. They fell under the deadly rain.'

'So what was the contingent of Iron Shadow doing when this happened?' probed Ter-hal, trying to pin the blame.

'They were doing their job, Ter-hal. Several of those who could not defend themselves tried in vain to shield the Jelery. They were using their horses, and in some instances their own bodies, as a barrier. It was a futile attempt to uphold the oaths they had taken, and at the same time it was the noblest and bravest thing I have ever seen,' replied Mek as he wiped at his eyes. 'They are not to blame. They did all that anyone could have done,' he added.

'It was not implied that they were,' replied Ter-hal innocently.

Mek fought down the urge to continue the topic of conversation with Ter-hal, and continued with his briefing. 'As I was saying, the Iron Shadow protected us as best they could whilst the arrows continued to fall. When the arrows stopped, our attackers charged from the cover of the trees, seeking to wipe us out. But they got more than they bargained for when they realised that over half of our force was still able to fight. Despite the fact that they we were outnumbered greatly, the Iron Shadow showed them why they should be feared. It took me only a short while to discover that, as the last remaining Light Wielder, I was their target.'

'Are you saying if they'd finished you they would have fled?' asked Ter-hal.

'Perhaps. All I can say is that they were doing their best to avoid the Iron Shadow. None openly attacked them. It was only if they stood in front of me that the enemy hacked at them,' replied Mek.

'This is deeply disturbing. Our own people, people of the land, are targeting us – we who protect them from the Spirits' wrath,' stated Alourin shaking his head.

'It has to be the work of the Telirian Light Wielders. They dare not openly defy us. Instead they coerce the people into fighting for them, Such is their cowardice,' spat Kayden.

'Enough with all the speculation. We must hear what happened next,' interrupted Ter-hal.

'Thank you, Ter-hal. At this point, it was apparent that we had to get out while we still had the numbers to do so. It seemed Baieta had the same idea, because he had scrambled the men into a wedge and they were effectively clearing a path. Those that were capable followed in their wake. For some reason, Our attackers broke off and fled for the trees. I think they had been taken aback by the ferociousness of the Iron Shadow, and it was clear that if they wanted me, the price would be high,' finished Mek.

'Too high for their liking. I think you were lucky, Mek,' said Xaryn.

'Thankfully so, Xaryn,' replied Mek.

'They allowed survivors although they wanted no Jelery to be amongst them. They wanted their actions reported. They are flexing their muscles, showing us a sample of what is to come,' said Alourin.

'Then you believe that the rumours are more than just rumours?' asked Ter-hal.

'I do believe they have set the wheels in motion. They are starting the final stage of the revolution. At this point, we don't exactly know who our enemies are. Galteone itself could be rife with the enemy, and we need to make preparations,' forewarned Alourin.

'Alourin speaks the truth. I too believe that they have begun their so-called revolution, and any number of the enemy could have infiltrated the city. We must put the Iron Shadow on full alert, and those of the troops that we can trust,' agreed Mek. The members of the Council murmured amongst themselves with many a nodding head accompanying the chatter until they all fell silent in agreement, but for better or for worse, Mek could not tell.

'We think it would be best that for now only the Iron Shadow shall be notified about the situation. We also think that it would not be in our best interests to inform the troops. They cannot all be trusted to keep this information to themselves, and the last thing we need is for unheralded gossip to start a city-wide panic with the talk of war when war may not eventuate,' announced Ter-hal.

'If that is the will of the Council, then it shall be followed,' acknowledged Mek, turning to leave.

'Of course, you yourself, being in the Order of the Light, have had the privilege of hearing our proclamation. I expect it to go no further than you,' warned Ter-hal.

'Of course,' agreed Mek.

'Oh, Mek, that includes Atiol,' added Ter-Hal. Mek thought about arguing with the order. Instead, he nodded his head in agreement before ascending the stairs out of the Council chamber.

'I believe it would be in everyone's best interests if all the Jelery were notified about the possible danger they may be in,' disputed Alourin once Mek had departed.

'I disagree. I believe it would be best to let the other Jelery remain unaware so they can focus on their study, for if war does break out, then we are going to need as many of them from the higher ranks as possible to bolster our overall strength,' argued Ter-hal.

'If war does indeed break out, it will not matter that we are too few in number. It will be the people who shall decide the outcome, not us,' retorted Alourin.

'Perhaps in years gone by, the people would have been the target; but now it is we who are being directly targeted by people, who have been itching to get rid of us for centuries. And we need to be as strong as we can to rebuff them,' countered Ter-hal.

'We still have no clear evidence to support the claims, apart from what the few Ravers tell us, and they are hardly a reliable source,' said Solatt.

'I do not rely on the Ravers as a reliable source myself, though I had a vision two nights ago. In this vision, Jelery were dead; not a great number, but as the vision went on, more and more were dying, until all I could see was a pile of dead bodies. I recognised all the bodies, even my own amongst them,' said Xaryn.

'Visions are not accurate at the best of times, but one that represents so much death cannot be ignored,' stated Alourin.

'It will not be ignored, but this information shall remain within these walls until we have had a better chance to discuss it. Is that understood, gentlemen?' threatened Ter-hal as he eyeballed every member of the Council. 'Good. Then you are free to resume whatever you were doing before this meeting,' said Ter-hal as he took their silence for compliance.

Mek walked into the busy, well-lit dining room and sat directly across from Atiol, who was lost in thought as he chewed on the thigh bone of a chicken. 'You know the meat won't grow back on that,' Mek pointed out.

'Yes, I know it won't,' replied Atiol as he chucked the chicken bone on to his plate.

'All right. Then what is wrong with you?' asked Mek.

'There is something wrong with the air,' replied Atiol.

'The air!' exclaimed Mek with a raised brow.

'Yes, the air,' said Atiol, nodding his head.

'All right. You are starting to worry me, Atiol. The other day you informed me that the trees were in great pain,' said Mek.

'They still are in pain, but now the air is slowing. It wants to stop. It says we don't deserve to feel its gentle caress on our skin or to hear it whisper its song as it flows all around us,' explained Atiol.

'Atiol, the wind doesn't sing,' said Mek.

'Of course it does, Mek. You just choose to ignore the obvious. It sings as it flows through the trees with a deep howling. It sings as it sweeps across the tall grass of the plains, and it whispers its melody as it moves past your ears. Its song used to be full of joy but now it is only full of sorrow and pain, and soon it will cease altogether,' explained Atiol.

'How do you know this?' asked Mek as he leant closer.

Atiol shrugged his shoulders. 'I have always heard it, just as I hear the earth talk and the water chatter. Mek, they are dying slowly. The Spirits cannot survive this drastic change in the humans' behaviour. They feel just as you and I do, and they are starting to feel hate and malice. They are going to retaliate. Some already have,' stated Atiol sadly.

'You are forcing me to start accepting your predictions, Atiol. You are an extremely gifted Light Wielder. You have been right from the start, and you are more perceptive of the land's needs. You can tell if a tree is sick even if it shows no outwards sign of being so. The Council refers to it as a gift,' replied Mek as he let out a deep breath. 'For what it's worth, Atiol, I believe you,' reassured Mek.

'Thank you, Mek. No one else will even entertain the idea except Crawley, which doesn't say a lot about my current state of mind,' replied Atiol with a worried smile.

'Crawley is not all that he seems to be. He is more than just a Raver. He is Freom and Muefrede's reluctant puppet, even though he constantly denies the fact. Freom and Muefrede plant thoughts in his head, which he thinks are his own, so half the time he is not himself,' explained Mek.

'So do you think it is them that are talking to me when I talk to Crawley?' asked Atiol.

'Of that I am almost certain. When did you last have a chat with him?'

'Three days ago at breakfast.'

'Then I think we shall have to go and pay him a visit in the morning. And Atiol, do stop picking at the tattoo,' scolded Mek.

'Sorry, Mek,' said Atiol absently as he placed his arm by his side. 'But it is just so itchy,' he added.

'Well, you should be used to them by now, considering it's your fourth one. Someone of your age should be struggling to obtain the Green Order.'

'I really don't like tattoos. I have been holding back,' said Atiol as he conjured a small golden sphere into the palm of his hand to prove his statement. 'As I said, I really don't like tattoos,' he repeated as the sphere was cast into the burning hearth.

In the Jelery, when a rank is obtained, the one in question must receive a tattoo on their right wrist. The tattoo is rectangular and measures two inches in length by one inch in width, and is coloured according to whatever rank they have achieved. The colours are grey, green, blue, red, and finally, gold, or as it is commonly referred to, the Order of the Light. It takes at least five to ten years to obtain the Order of the Grey. After that it takes another ten or so years to advance to the Order of the Green. Attaining the levels after that depends entirely on the individual. Most only ever reach the Order of the Red, and it takes them until they are well into their seventies. It is from the Order of the Red that one can conjure a shield wall.

The tattoos run on the inside of the forearm.

They remain the same size and shape until the Order of the Light is obtained. That rank is signified by a larger triangular tattoo coloured in gold. The tattoo represents the Tri Tower's three sides. Not only does this show one's rank, it qualifies the bearer for a spot on the Council when the opportunity arises, which is rare.

There is one other rank that can be obtained in the Jelery order, when the Order of the Blue is reached. That is when a Jelery is at his strongest physically, and some may wish to remain at this level to capitalise on it; but in the process, they forego the right to advance in rank, giving up the ability to ever obtain a shield wall or a chance to sit on the Council. If they stay at this rank, they receive a thick black line through the middle of their blue rectangular tattoo, signifying that they are in the Order of the Second Blue, or the Order of the Willing Blue. Jelery of the Second Blue are utilised throughout Galteone as a peace-keeping force to maintain order in the young Light Wielders. However, the decision to remain this way is not reversible, and a Light Wielder can live for a long, long time – up to two hundred and fifty years – so the decision is not taken lightly. But an added benefit is that members of this rank are allowed a certain type of relationship with the fairer gender that a higher-ranking Jelery is forbidden to enter into.

A young Jelery begins their training when they are deemed to be capable by their mentor, and relationships with the fairer gender are strictly forbidden. Mandatory excommunication as the punishment, as such relationships can cloud the mind when the person should be focused on practising their craft; it can be fatal for everyone if someone's emotions get out of control. Once the Order of the Blue has been obtained, it is at a stage in the Jelery's life where their powers are stable, and the emotions involved with relationships cannot destabilise and endanger their lives and the lives of others around them.

Mek walked into the busy, well-lit dining room and sat 'We have to make a move before this impending war begins,' stated Muefrede.

'Why bother? This will thin their numbers down nicely. In fact, if we are lucky, the two opposing forces will wipe each other out completely,' replied Freom.

'You would love that, but we can't let it happen. After all, they are still our creations.'

'They were never mine. You created them behind my back and expected me to embrace them as you had,' snarled Freom.

'I may have created them, but your influence and temperament flow through them just as mine do. I thought that if they displayed some of your traits, then you would accept them.'

'Accept them!' yelled Freom. 'I despise them, and I would wipe them out if I could, but you won't allow that because you cannot admit that in creating them you made a mistake.'

'Mistake, no. The only mistake I made was to allow your traits to poison their minds and judgements,' replied Muefrede with a raised voice.

'You would think that after all this time you have spent together, you both might be sick of arguing with each other about the same old thing!' interrupted Ushwinn.

'Shut up, Ushwinn!' they yelled in unison.

'You are the ones who came to me for a discussion, so don't go telling me to shut up, or I will have to cut this conversation short,' threatened Ushwinn.

'No, don't. I am sorry. We both are. It's just that things are about to explode between the Light Wielders, but this time I'm afraid they're not going to stop until one faction is wiped out,' explained Muefrede.

'This has been brewing for five hundred years. It was inevitable that it would come to this,' sighed Ushwinn.

'It can still be prevented if we act now. We have to subdue the Telirians. It is bad enough that they have become so strong, but now they have obtained the support of the people.'

'We can't wipe them out. What will be, will be, and one way or another, our focus should be on the retaliation of the Spirits, and those of the Hiratan that will use this as a chance to destroy the humans,' replied Ushwinn.

'You speak the truth, Ushwinn. The Jelery have to deal with the Telirians. We have to stop the real war that is about to break out,' agreed Muefrede.

'Is the boy at an acceptable level in his teachings to take on the task?' asked Ushwinn.

'It is borderline, but I think he has the ability to learn anything that is thrown in front of him.'

'Then I will make sure he comes, but for now I grow weary', said Ushwinn breaking the contact.

'We will be in touch,' replied Freom in a fading voice.

'Undoubtedly,' muttered Ushwinn.

Ushwinn slowly opened his eyes and raised himself up on his weary legs to gaze down at the vast expanse of the sea, and to watch as its waves thrashed themselves to death on the cliff face down below. The wind whipped his long grey hair into a swirling frenzy and moulded the tattered brown robe to the shape of his stick-thin body.

He silently inspected his age-beaten hands and smiled to himself. 'Despite my frailty, they still fear this withered old body,' he thought solemnly. 'It needs to rest. I need to rest, but only death can give me the sort of rest I seek,' he sighed. 'Perhaps soon, after I teach the boy, I can rest,' he thought.

With his thoughts as his companion, Ushwinn made his way slowly to the small but spacious dwelling he called home. Ignoring his stomach's request for food, he crawled painfully into his bed and dreamed of the day when he wouldn't have to wake up.

# 7

CRAWLEY WAS RUMMAGING through numerous piles of paper filled with erratic writing, when a knock at the door interrupted his search. 'What do you want?' he grumbled.

'It is Mek and Atiol. We have come to talk to you,' replied Mek.

'Well, I am busy at the moment and you will have to...' Crawley paused briefly, then said, 'Come right in. I would love to have a chat, I think.'

Mek eased the door open and stepped into Crawley's concept of a room. The small gust of air entering through the doorway stirred up thin layers of dust and caused the sheets of paper to rise and flutter about the room as if they were alive.

'Geez, Crawley, this place needs a thorough cleaning. It's just about growing its own life forms,' noted Atiol when he had entered the room.

'That will not happen, lad. Those cleaning girls will rearrange and ruin my perfect filing system,' snorted Crawley as a few dust-covered pieces of paper fell from his desk to the floor.

'Wouldn't want that to happen,' agreed Mek with a hint of sarcasm.

If Crawley picked up on it he failed to show it. He stood with his arms folded across his chest whilst his foot tapped impatiently at the wooden floor. 'Well, what do you two want?' he asked peering suspiciously at the two Light Wielders in front of him.

'We have to talk to you about certain matters,' replied Mek, searching the old man's face.

Crawley's foot ceased its impatient tapping.

'I know what you are here for, and we too have to talk to you.' Crawley's eyes were unmoving and staring straight ahead, and a bright green light glowed from within their depths.

'Muefrede, it is good to speak with you again,' greeted Mek warmly.

'Yes, it has been quite a while since we last talked. I am going to make this as quick as I can, for Crawley's sake,' replied Muefrede.

'A good idea. I shall begin, then. Atiol has not been himself of late. In fact, the things he has been talking to me about are anything but comforting. Wait, I will let him tell you,' said Mek.

'There will be no need for that, Mek. I have a pretty good idea, as I have been hearing these things as well,' said Muefrede.

'You have?' asked Atiol, pushing in front of Mek.

'Yes, Atiol, I hear them all the time, even when they are well and happy, but that is not why I am here. I am here to explain why you are hearing them when nobody else is.'

'And why is that?' asked Atiol eagerly.

'It is because you're an Anomaly. Simply put, you are not supposed to be,' explained Muefrede.

'Well, that is not exactly comforting news. Nor does it make much sense,' replied Atiol.

'It makes no sense to us too, but then neither do you. You are not human, and you're not exactly a Light Wielder even though you possess all their abilities. Yet you have the perception of an Earthbound Spirit,' said Muefrede. 'As you are aware, both myself and Freom created humans and, later on, the Light Wielders, to help govern them. You do not fit into our equation,' he added.

'Great! I am nothing more than a freak, a mistake, a waste of life. So why am I here?' screamed Atiol in anger.

'Come now, there is no need for anger, for your anger is a dangerous thing. You don't understand how powerful you are. There is another that resides within the land that is of the same make as you.'

'The same make! You compare me like a piece of equipment. Is that what I am to you?' asked Atiol with a clenched jaw.

'We are not capable of answering that question without angering you further. If you want answers, you shall have to talk with this other Anomaly,' replied Muefrede.

'Then I must converse with a total stranger to get the answers I seek,' said Atiol, summing up the situation.

'Precisely,' agreed Muefrede.

'Where does this other Anomaly live?' asked Mek.

'He is somewhere to the south-west of here. Truth be told, we don't know exactly where he is,' confessed Muefrede.

'Impossible. Surely you know his whereabouts. After all, you are Muefrede. You are all-seeing, all-powerful,' argued Mek.

'In most cases, yes. Usually, everything can be found – anything living, anyway,' said Muefrede.

'How?' asked Mek.

'Everything living appears to us as the stars in the

night sky does to you. Some burn brighter than others. Some are larger than others. And they all pulse differently. All are unique, just as you are, and we know which light represents each individual and where they are at any given time.'

'So why can't you see this Anomaly?' asked Atiol.

'He conceals himself when he doesn't want to be found. There is nothing we can do to track him when he is in that mood. He occasionally forgets to conceal himself, but that is a very rare occurrence,' explained Muefrede.

'Then how do you know he will show himself to me?' asked Atiol.

'He can hear Freom and myself when he wishes to be receptive, and we have already had a little chat. He talked to us with his thoughts. He is very talented at certain things,' said Muefrede.

'That still does not help me to find him,' pointed out Atiol.

'No, it does not, but he will reveal himself when the appropriate time arises." Atiol nodded his head in acceptance. 'Now I must depart. Freom cannot control Crawley much longer. Farewell,' whispered Muefrede as his presence departed from Crawley.

'Those bloody swines. They did it to me again!' screamed Crawley, brushing frantically at his shirt in an attempt to erase their presence.

'Settle down, Crawley,' instructed Mek. He grabbed Crawley by his thin shoulders and guided him down into his chair. 'They have not harmed you. You are whole. They just needed to talk with Atiol. I will send for a servant to bring you some cold meats and a mug of ale. Then we will leave you to your filing,' soothed Mek.

'Thank you, Mek. Do you think they could bring me some cheese as well?' asked Crawley hopefully.

'Of course, Crawley. It will be sent down to you soon,' replied Mek.

Mek steered Atiol through the door before closing it softly behind them. 'I think he is becoming more accustomed to these little visits from Freom and Muefrede. He took it rather well this time,' he said as he and Atiol walked across the white cobblestones of the Jelery compound.

'I don't think anyone could get used to such a thing,' replied Atiol quietly.

'No, I suppose you wouldn't,' agreed Mek.

'I am going to have to leave in order to find this other Anomaly. And when I do I shall be travelling alone. With the impending war, I do not want the city to be even one soldier short,' announced Atiol.

'How do you know about the war's approach? Only the Council members and a few in the Order of the Light know of such matters,' said Mek with surprise.

'You seem to forget that I have many informants these days. I dare say that I could tell the Council a few things they are yet to know, but seeing how everything is being kept such a secret, I think I shall do the same.'

'Or you could tell me,' proposed Mek hopefully.

'I was always going to tell you, Mek. You are the only one who would believe what I have to say, no matter how outrageous it sounds.'

'Atiol, you may think of yourself as an outsider, but to me, you have been and always will be like a little brother,' comforted Mek, placing his arm across Atiol's shoulders.

'And you will always be like a brother to me,' replied Atiol, stifling a tear.e air what doung wrong with then-hicken bone on to the pile ecently deceasde chance to discuss this, is that understood gentle.

# 8

A HOT BEAD of sweat slid into Toi-mun's eye, momentarily blurring his vision. He ignored the stinging pain as he jogged cautiously through the darkened passageway of the gauntlet. Armed only with a spear and short dagger, he had so far defeated four opponents without killing them and had survived all the booby traps that had been placed to kill him. As he entered a somewhat darker room, he slowed to a walk and scanned the area as best he could, whilst also checking for the odd tripwire or loose patch of dirt that would indicate a pressure plate.

'This seems all too easy,' he growled as he crept onwards. He slid his left foot forward and thought for just a moment that the ground under foot had depressed slightly. He held his breath in anticipation. 'Damn it! Now I am becoming paranoid,' he whispered to himself before expelling his lungful of air.

A tiny sound, out of place and unnerving, snapped his line of sight forward towards the source. He peered ahead through the darkness, and his extraordinary ability to see well in the dark saved his hide. A crossbow bolt ripped through the stagnant air seeking to skewer his heart. A desperate defensive action with the wooden shaft of the spear saved him. Toi-mun rotated the shaft of the spear toward himself and let out a low whistle of surprise when he spotted the crossbow bolt buried deeply into it. However, his thankfulness was short-lived as the now well-known and unwanted sound multiplied all around the room.

'Oh, crap,' he announced as he dived forward on to the hard dirt floor, knocking all the wind out of his lungs.

Several minutes passed before he risked a peek from under his arms, that instinctively protected his head. The wall in front of which he had been standing only a frantic dive ago was pin-cushioned with crossbow bolts. A hurried assessment of the situation brought him to the conclusion that for the time being the floor was the safest place to stay, so after gathering his spear and his nerve, he continued on his stomach. He travelled forward in this manner until he came to a stout wooden wall at the end of a small hallway that led to nowhere.

'Great, now what am I in for?' he thought out loud, fearing he would have to retrace his journey back into the deathtrap of a room he had just exited. Then the wooden wall his forehead was resting on lurched sideways an inch. Toi-mun pushed himself to his knees as the wall was pulled completely to the side, which allowed blinding rays of sunlight to penetrate the deep gloom. He raised his free hand to block the light, and saw four figures charging at him with their weapons swinging wildly around their heads.

Instinct and his years of disciplined training took over his body and mind. The first of the would-be executioners surged ahead of the others, and Toi-mun waited patiently before thrusting his spear through his attacker's wrist, causing him to drop his sword, which Toi-mun caught by the blade. Then with silent efficiency, he slammed the handle down hard between the startled eyes of his foe, knocking him out cold. Just as quickly and just as calculatedly, Toi-mun threw the sword at his closest rival. The butt of the sword hit him squarely in the Adam's apple; choking and gasping for air, he went down weaponless as he clutched at his throat with both hands.

The remaining two attackers spread out on either side of him, dividing his attention. He advanced on the man to his right. With both hands on the handle of his sword, he swung it down at Toi-mun's head, striving to cleave it in two. Toi-mun raised the thick shaft of the spear above his head with both hands and the weapons came together a fraction after Toi-mun's boot met with the other man's family jewels, taking the force out of the swing. He went down with more than a tear in his eye and holding his crotch. Toi-mun snapped the shaft of the spear over his knee, finishing what the sword had started, and threw them both to the ground.

He turned sideways just in time to dodge the blade of a sword that was aimed at his skull. Expecting the sword to strike true, the attacker had put a huge effort into the swing that now cleaved naught but air. He was grossly unbalanced, and Toi-mun took full advantage and kicked him squarely in the back, which sent him sprawling face first into the nearest wall. Before he had a chance to bounce, Toi-mun had drawn and thrown his dagger, which pinned the attacker to the wall by the shoulder.

A ladder appeared over the side of the pit and a singular round of applause accompanied him up the ladder and out of the pit. Baieta came from across the other side of the pit still clapping his hands whilst grinning foolishly. 'I almost missed that final skirmish.

It was a damn fine job, Toi-mun. Nice, quick work,' appraised Baieta.

'It certainly didn't seem that quick when I was in there,' said Toi-mun.

'No, it never does, especially for those poor chaps,' replied Baieta as he watched the bloodied and bruised men climb out of the pit.

'It still amazes me that any sane man would willingly enter the gauntlet, knowing that they would have to try and kill one of the Iron Shadow candidates in the full knowledge that they could just as easily be the ones to end up hurt,' confessed Toi-mun.

'Well, the twenty-five gold pieces we offer and the promise that they will not be killed deliberately, brings a few out of the woodworks. Twenty-five gold pieces for a few injuries seems like a damn good trade-off to most.'

Toi-mun glanced briefly at the wounded men still struggling out of the pit and shook his head in disbelief. 'If you say so,' he replied.

'Cheer up, Toi-mun. Don't feel so bad about hurting them. They would have pocketed another one hundred gold pieces if they had succeeded in removing your head.'

'Is that all my life is worth to you!' exclaimed Toi-mun in jest.

'No, lad, it is worth nothing, just as mine is. You were destined to be part of the Iron Shadow, and tonight it will be known by all after we visit the Council for your induction. So don't be late,' warned Baieta as he departed.

Toi-mun watched in silence as Baieta disappeared into the crowd of soldiers outside the barracks. His head swam as he processed Baieta's words and repressed the doubt that tried to flood his being.

'Toi-mun, are you ready?' The voice snapped him back into reality. 'Toi-mun, the Council is ready for you. You're not having second thoughts, are you?' probed Baieta.

'No, I am just taking in the beauty of the stars,' lied Toi-mun.

'Good. Then you had better hurry up.' Toi-mun drew in a steadying breath and followed Baieta up the stairs to the Council chamber's entrance. It was the first time he had seen inside the Tri Tower, and he tried not to gawk. 'We will wait until we are called,' ordered Baieta.

For Toi-mun, it was an agonising few minutes of waiting before the door was opened from the inside by a member of the Iron Shadow. 'Proceed to the centre of the room,' he instructed with a sly smile.

Ter-Hal and the other Council members waited in the centre of the room. Baieta and Toi-mun walked to within a metre of them and stopped to await further instructions.

'He who has shown himself worthy for the honoured position amongst the ranks of the Iron Shadow, step forward,' ordered Ter-hal. Toi-mun stepped toward him hesitantly and stole a glance at the firelit faces that were staring at him. 'Who is the sponsor of this young man?' asked Ter-hal.

'I am,' answered Baieta, stepping forward to stand beside Toi-mun. 'Very well, Baieta. You know the consequences if he is to break his oath, don't you?' warned Ter-hal.

'I am fully aware, my lord, and will accept the consequences,' acknowledged Baieta. With this reply, Baieta stepped back and allowed the induction to continue. Another two of the Iron Shadow dressed in ceremonial green attire came up behind Toi-mun and stood on either side of him. The one to his left held a large silver bowl filled with water, and the other to his right had a large silver tray covered in a soft green cloth.

'Speak your name,' commanded Ter-hal.

'It is Toi-mun, my lord,' he answered nervously.

'Toi-mun, are you aware of what the oath encompasses and what will befall your sponsor if you break it?' asked Ter-hal.

Toi-mun nodded his head and looked over at Baieta, who calmly returned his gaze.

'Then let us begin,' announced Ter-hal, giving Toi-mun a beaming smile. He walked over to the tray and gently rolled back the cloth to reveal a black iron dagger that gave off an unnatural sheen in the firelight. Ter-hal picked it up and went to stand directly in front of Toi-mun. 'Give me your hand, Toi-mun,' he ordered. Toi-mun held his hand up to Ter-hal. 'You are sworn to protect the Jelery with your life. In any circumstance, it is your blood that shall flow to the ground instead of the Jelery you serve.'

With a lightning quick slash of the dagger, Ter-hal opened a cut on Toi-mun's palm. He seized the wounded hand and let the blood splatter onto the polished floor. 'As it is right now, is as it should be. You are bleeding, and I am whole.' The Iron Shadow with the silver bowl turned and stood between the two. With a small grimace, Ter-hal nicked himself and allowed a drop of blood to fall into the water. 'Even one drop of Jelery blood should be painful for your soul.' Without warning, Ter-hal thrust Toi-mun's bleeding hand into the water. Upon contact, Toi-mun had to suppress a scream. The water was in fact clear vinegar.

'Now you must recite the binding oath of the Iron Shadow,' said Ter-hal as he held Toi-mun's hand in the stinging liquid. 'Silent, unwavering, our wills will never bend. The swing of axe and sword, these blows we will fend. We walk amongst the people who remain unaware. Forever we are vigilant, no one escapes our glare. To protect Jelery life, our blood flows freely to the ground. We do our duty with valour for we are honour bound.' The last line was barely audible as the pain shot up Toi-mun's arm.

'Excellent! You are now a part of the elite Iron Shadow. May you serve us well,' announced Ter-hal as he removed Toi-mun's hand from the bowl. 'Take this dagger as a reminder of your oath. Use it not in battle until all other avenues fail.' Ter-hal handed Toi-mun the dagger, which he had wrapped carefully in the piece of green cloth, and turned away.

'You are free to go now, my brother,' said Baieta placing a hand on Toi-mun's muscular shoulder. Toi-mun turned and walked slowly up the stairway. His face gave no hint of the pain in his wounded hand. As he walked through the doorway, he received a reassuring pat on the back from the Shadow who had admitted him into the chamber, but he hardly felt it. The enormity of the situation had his head swimming in thought as he left the Tri Tower as a Shadow.

# 9

SEKER MASSAGED THE scar tissue where the end of his little finger used to reside, and mumbled to himself as a cold numbing wind swept over his muscular chest. A groan of pain snapped his attention to the group of men in front of him. His eyes scanned slowly from side to side before they settled on their object. He walked over slowly and the gravel crunched under his bare feet as he approached.

'You are not men,' he said. 'You are Light Wielders. You are supposed to be Telirian, but when I hear a groan – be it out of pain or exhaustion – you are worthless. In fact, less than worthless. You remind me of the Jelery scum that you are sworn to destroy, the Jelery scum I have destroyed!' Seker's face was crimson with rage, and every time he spoke, a violent spray of spittle erupted from his mouth and flecked the frightened face of the man he was severely berating. 'Now this man in front of me finds it uncomfortable to maintain such a simple thing as an energy sphere for an extended period of time. How pathetic. He should be able to hold it above his head with only one arm instead of two. Now, if you can do so for... I don't know, let's say ten minutes, I will forgive you for your little outburst of weakness,' said Seker with a deranged smile.

The man looked around him, casting silent pleas for help from the group of men around him, but they all ignored his silent cry for assistance, and their eyes continued to stare blankly in front of them. 'As for the rest of you men, you have all proved yourselves today. You can release your energy spheres and watch the ever-developing show from a safe distance,' instructed Seker.

The men did as they were bid. They were soon talking amongst themselves, but none wanted to miss the drama and kept stealing glances at their leader.

'I am going to join the other men. I will begin the countdown when I turn around and face you, and not a moment before,' instructed Seker. He walked painfully slowly and had a good talk and laugh with the men before he turned to face the solitary figure who was licking his parched lips in fear. Seker nodded his head, and the man slowly withdrew one of his hands from the golden energy sphere, which measured roughly three feet across. The added weight on his arm almost caused it to buckle, but he retained it by sheer force of will. Once he had it under control, he stared defiantly into Seker's yellow eyes. As the minutes ticked by, and with his burden pressing down on him, the man's whole body began to quiver with the effort. Seker stood unmoving with his eyes locked on the other man's challenging gaze. The sweat began to drip from his brow, and finally he averted his gaze as his arm began to spasm with the effort. It eventually became too much, and as his arm began to drop, he released the sphere with a scream of pain before he slumped to his knees. Seker shook his head and tut-tutted in disappointment as he walked over. The man had his head upturned as he searched the sky for salvation.

'Six, not quite seven minutes. That is quite impressive, but not nearly impressive enough.' The man continued to search the sky but remained silent. 'You know what we do to those we cannot rely on. Yes, I am sure that you do, but just because you have failed as a Telirian doesn't mean you have to fail as a man, so let us see if you can take your punishment like one,' mocked Seker.

The man slowly dropped his gaze to Seker's face.

'For being pathetic and weak, I expel you from the Order to roam the land as a useless outcast.' The man moved to alleviate the pain of the rocks digging into his knees, and the realisation that this may be his end forced his survival instinct to kick in. 'However, I feel that such a punishment would be demeaning, so I will grant you a favour, the favour of death,' sneered Seker as he towered over the kneeling man.

'I never asked for a favour from the likes of you. Go to hell, Seker,' growled the man. With the desperation of a condemned man, he grabbed Seker by the knees and drove him backward until he fell heavily on his back. As the man rose, he swung a fist at Seker's face, which drove his head into the ground a good inch. Before Seker had time to react, the other man kicked him squarely in the ribs. With Seker down, the other man loped off, trying to make his escape.

'Delsain, you pig!' screamed Seker as he got to his feet, clutching at his bloodied nose. 'I will give any one here a handsome reward if they bring me back Delsain's head,' he roared.

Before he had the chance to add anything to his statement, forty men streamed past him yelling profanities and threats at the fleeing Delsain. Delsain ran on weakening legs but knew he only had one chance to survive, and that was to get to the white skeletal forests that dotted lord Delrain's land. An explosion of dirt and rock to his left frightened a huge release of adrenaline into his weakening body, and he surged forward. Despite his body's natural boost, his pursuers were close, and gaining rapidly. But with a great sense of euphoria, he made the cover of the sparse dead forest. His pursuers realised that he had now gained a slight advantage, and they all reacted accordingly by spreading out to widen the search area.

'Come out, Delsain. You are just making this harder on yourself. All we want is your head. You can keep the rest,' called one of the pursuers, which received around of laughter.

Delsain stood with his back flat against a large white tree trunk and breathed deeply of the air which had rapidly become acrid. He almost let out a huge sigh of relief as the sound of his pursuers faded and disappeared. He rested his head back against the trunk and closed his eyes in a silent prayer of thanks. He drew a few more deep calming breaths to settle his pounding heart, then opened his eyes slowly and leaned forward with exhaustion.

'Boo!' announced Seker, a second before he smashed his fist into Delsain's head with a huge uppercut that would have crushed an ordinary man's skull to bits. Delsain catapulted through the tree he was resting on and slammed into another tree behind him, halting his backward progress. He was by no means weak, but he knew that if he stood and fought with Seker, he would certainly be killed. So with desperation and a new veneration for his life, he got unsteadily to his feet and ran for his life between the trees.

Seker waited until he had a clean line of sight before he threw a golden energy sphere that struck Delsain in the back, but to Seker's surprise and slight admiration, he remained upright and kept on fleeing. The commotion attracted a lot of unwanted attention, and it was not long before the other men had joined the fray, and soon Delsain had been struck numerous times. The smell of his charred flesh and the burning pain of numerous wounds at last caused him to weaken beyond recovery, and he found himself falling to his knees into the sucking mud of a riverbank. A momentary feeling of fear was soon replaced with relief as the pain in his body caused his vision to blur before he blacked out, and he fell headfirst into the brackish water that was as poisoned as the land around it.

'Do you think he is dead?' asked one of the men as they watched the still body float down river.

'If he is not now, he soon will be. Nothing can live if it drinks that water, and right now I would say his lungs and his belly are slowly filling up with it,' replied another of the men who crowded on the bank.

'It's a shame he had to go and die like that. I was just starting to have some fun,' chuckled another.

'Worry not, men, for soon there will be plenty of fun to be had by all. We just have to be a little patient and our time will come,' replied Seker.

'I cannot wait,' stated one of the men with bloodlust in his voice.

Seker let out a sharp laugh. 'Neither can I, neither can I,' he agreed, as the body of Delsain slipped out of sight around a bend in the river.

# 10

'WAKE UP, ATIOL, the time has come. I have much to teach you, things you must know. You cannot refuse to do what you have been created for, or the consequences will be dire.

Atiol sat bolt upright in bed, and scanned the room for the speaker of the voice. When none was to be seen, he lay back down and closed his eyes to sleep.

Atiol felt his mind leave his body and float through the stone wall of his sleeping chambers. Then like a bird it flew swiftly over the land which was shrouded in a thick mist. The thick veil of mist parted with an unnatural gust of wind. It took several moments for Atiol to realise that the ruin he was looking at was in fact Galteone. The Tri Tower had collapsed and the walls had been destroyed. Piles of corpses littered the streets, and the carrion birds gorged on rotting flesh until they could not fly. And all around, the stench of death, pungent yet sweet, filled the air. But one figure still stood. He was standing outside the front entrance of the city, and a pile of freshly killed bodies surrounded him. His weapons dripped blood and he had a huge gash on his face that had blinded him on one side. Atiol saw dark fluid shapes baying for blood as they came at the man, who went instinctively into the fighter's stance. Then he was whisked away over a festering wasteland that contained no life, only death.

Atiol's eyes flew open and stared up at the ceiling of the room. He glanced out of his window and judged by the stars that it was close to midnight. 'Strange dream,' he murmured. He yawned, and pulled his blankets up to his chin to resume his slumber.

Atiol was walking towards a small hut that was set a little way back from a towering cliff that overlooked the vast ocean. When he got to the hut, an ancient man sat calmly on the rocky ground in front of it, a wide grin spread across his face.

'Who are you?' asked Atiol.

'The answer to that, I think, you know already. Besides, it is not so important at this time. We will have time to exchange pleasantries when we meet. The bigger question right now is, who are you? You know what

I speak of, don't you, Atiol? I warn you again, you must find me: it is your destiny to do so.'

Atiol had not the chance to ask any of the questions that swarmed around in his head before his eyes sprang open, and he realised that he was back in his bed, with a dull headache.

'Good, you're awake. Hurry up and get dressed. Today is going to be important,' advised Mek.

Atiol rolled his head lazily to the side and stared disinterestedly at Mek, who stood in the doorway looking too excited, considering that the sun had only just begun to rise.

'All right. If only to amuse you, I am dying to know – why is today so important?' asked Atiol as he gave in to Mek's impatient gesturing.

'I thought you would never ask,' replied Mek.

'It crossed my mind not to, but I couldn't have you standing there all day just looking expectantly at me,' teased Atiol.

'Today is the day that your Shadow will be appointed,' announced Mek, ignoring Atiol's jest.

'I told you, Mek, I don't want, nor do I need, a Shadow. Let him be appointed to one of the other Light Wielders. I can look after myself better than most of the members on the Council,' argued Atiol.

'We have been through this before, Atiol, and one day you will see the benefit of having a Shadow by your side,' asserted Mek.

'I seriously doubt it, but nonetheless, I shall suffer through it, if only to please you,' said Atiol, resigning himself to his fate.

'Well, at least you are going to give it a chance. Now, as I said before, hurry up and get dressed. Then come immediately down to the courtyard,' ordered Mek, and he departed.

'Certainly, straightaway, your Majesty,' mocked Atiol as flopped back down on to his bed with a sigh. He thought of the night's events whilst he gently massaged his temples and tried to dispel the dream images that still played in his mind.

The warmth of the early morning sunlight soothed the ache in his head, but at the same time, the brightness stung his eyes without remorse as he crossed the courtyard to sit with Mek on one of the many benches that ringed the courtyard. A garden of wildflowers grew around the gurgling spring-fed fountain, that ebbed and spilled forth so slowly that the pool encompassing it was nearly still and looked like a mirror as it reflected the sun's rays.

'A beautiful day, don't you think?' enquired Mek.

'As days go, it certainly rates as one of the better ones,' agreed Atiol, staring at the wildflowers.

'Baieta will be here any moment. He will introduce you to your shadow,' informed Mek.

'Ahm,' acknowledged Atiol, still gazing at the flowers.

Mek and Atiol didn't hear the stealthy approach of Baieta and were somewhat startled when he coughed politely from behind them to indicate he had arrived. 'I didn't startle you, did I?' he asked as he walked around in front of them with a sly smile.

'Just a little bit,' replied Mek.

'It was purely unintentional, of course,' said Baieta innocently.

'Of course,' agreed Mek in his most agreeable tone.

'Well, we are here this morning for a purpose, not just a little chat. There are no special ceremonies or festive banquets to mark the occasion. There will be only an introduction,' began Baieta. 'You may choose, if you wish, to never talk to the Shadow you are being assigned. You can treat him badly, make him stand out in the coldest rain, but none of these things will matter to him for he has taken an oath that all in the

Iron Shadow must take. His oath is to protect your life at all costs, even if he has to sacrifice his own to do so. It may never come to this, but if the need arises, it will be done,' assured Baieta.

Atiol gave a polite nod to indicate that he had heard and understood. 'Well, I guess there is nothing left to say. Toi-mun, come forth,' ordered Baieta.

A young man with long dark hair, wearing the studded leather armour that all the Iron Shadow wore, seemed to appear from thin air. He walked from across the courtyard with his face to the ground. Atiol realised that despite his short height, the young man coming toward him was very muscular and powerfully built, but he walked with a cat-like grace. His face remained hidden by his long dark hair as he knelt in front of Atiol.

'I am Toi-mun. I am your Shadow, sworn to protect you, and protect you I shall until I can do so no more,' said Toi-mun as he raised his head to stare into Atiol's eyes.

Atiol's face changed from a look of disinterest to one of absolute disbelief. The pain in his head flared, and he tried to rise and flee, but the stone bench caught his knee as he turned, and he went down heavily on his stomach. Toi-mun rushed to his aid, but Atiol effortlessly brushed him to the side, sending him crashing into the flowers. Flashes of last night's dreams swept before his eyes – and the scene of Galteone in ruins and of the lone man with the maimed face awaiting his fate as the figures rushed at him.

The visions slowly departed except for the lone man. Eventually, he was all that remained, but he was no longer standing. Covered in blood, he was slowly rising from the flowerbed, brushing himself off no more than ten feet away, and his face was unmarked. Toi-mun was the man in his dream.

'Atiol, are you all right?' asked Mek, pulling Atiol to his feet.

'I have seen this man before,' said Atiol in a shaky voice, gesturing toward Toi-mun with a trembling finger.

'You must be mistaken, Atiol. This is the first time he has revealed himself to any member of the Jelery besides the Council,' argued Baieta.

'No, I saw him in my dreams. He was surrounded by death and destruction,' said Atiol. The image of the old man suddenly popped into his head and he paled visibly – perhaps he was no dream either. 'I must seek him out,' he announced as he ran off towards Crawley's quarters.

'Atiol, what are you talking about?' yelled Mek as Atiol disappeared behind the closest building.

'You had better call a couple of the Blue boys to assist you.' warned Baieta. 'I don't think you will be able to control him if he cracks and goes berserk on you.' The Blue boys are those that choose to stay in the Order of the Blue second class. They act as Galteone's policing force, to maintain order in the Jelery compound.

'He has shown no sign of cracking up in the past, but I will do as you advise as a precautionary measure,' agreed Mek.

'You know what it's like; or at least, I think you remember what it is like to grow up under the pressure of expectation. Sometimes their mind can take no more of the strict rules and the learning of the vast amount of knowledge they have to retain. They lose their minds, Mek. They go crazy. You have seen it before, and you know what must be done.'

'I will take care of it myself!' snapped Mek angrily.

'Okay, Mek. I know how fond of him you are. We know you can handle it,' said Baieta.

'For both our sakes, you had better be all right,' growled Mek as he ran to fetch some help.

'Crawley, Crawley, open up the door or I will break it down,' threatened Atiol.

'Go away and come back later. I am busy,' came the reply from within. The thick door broke at the hinges as it took a huge blow. It fell slowly inward to land on the rug at Crawley's feet, causing a puff of dust to rise off the floor like a small explosion.

'I told you to open the door, and I meant it,' snarled Atiol.

'What is the meaning of all this senseless destruction?' yelled Crawley defiantly.

'I was hoping that one of you would be able to tell me,' said Atiol.

'Have you gone stark raving mad, boy? 'Tis but you and I in this room alone. There is no other, especially not that filthy–'

'–kind-hearted so and so,' said Muefrede, finishing Crawley's sentence.

'Well, Atiol, I can see that Ushwinn has made some form of contact with you, not in the way we would have wished. But, unfortunately, he is beyond even our jurisdiction,' sighed Muefrede heavily.

'Should have foreseen it,' growled Freom.

'Who is this Ushwinn and what does he want from me?' inquired Atiol.

'Ushwinn is complex–' began Muefrede.

'Ushwinn is a pain in the neck,' interrupted Freom.

'Yes, well, as I was saying before I was rudely interrupted, he is the other Anomaly, and not of our making. We think that perhaps the Earthbound Spirits found a way to inhabit a human body and entwine with the soul to become one within. What we do know is that Ushwinn was perhaps the first Raver and was extremely close to the Earthbound Spirits. Maybe, such closeness allowed them to bond – we really can't tell.'

'Like a Hiratan?' asked Atiol.

'No, boy, a Hiratan is easy to catalogue; when one of the major Spirits like a wind Spirit or a water Spirit have urges, they can impregnate human females,' explained Freom bluntly.

'Only if the females are willing, of course,' added Muefrede.

'What if they are not willing?' asked Atiol blushing at the context of the talk. 'Instead of being born in the manner of love, they are born in malice and hatred.'

'They are abominations,' explained Freom.

'What he means is they are not human-looking like normal Hiratan. They are deformed and grotesque, but are extremely powerful beings.'

'How can a Spirit, you know, do... that to a woman, when they have no form?' asked Atiol shyly.

'You ask too many questions, boy,' growled Freom.

'I will handle this, Freom. Now, Atiol, although major Spirits dislike humans, they also envy them for their bodies. They yearn to be different from one another as humans are, just enough to have some form of individuality, so they somewhat copy their form. But this is drifting from the subject at hand,' pointed out Muefrede.

'It is not Ushwinn himself we have to worry about. The Earthbound Spirits and certain major Spirits are threatening war on the humans. It is not a war in the usual way, but a war nonetheless,' said Freom.

'They grow tired of the senseless destruction of their homes, and they are threatening to withdraw themselves from the land, and you know what that will mean,' said Muefrede.

'The land will not be able to be replenished, and everything will die,' whispered Atiol in reply.

'That is correct. The land will be destroyed, and eventually there will remain only dust and memories of how beautiful the land was. Thousands of years ago they threatened the same action to teach humans a lesson, to wipe them out if you will,' said Freom.

'I will tell you the story,' offered Muefrede. 'In the beginning of the land, there was nothing – only rock and dirt. And then the great Spirit, our father, came upon the land and pitied its bareness, so using his voice, he spoke to the land and coaxed it into growing life. At first there were only the streams and the grasses, which did not satisfy the Great Spirit, so he once again used his voice to talk to the land. And slowly, the mountains rose from the land, and trees, vast and varied, sprang forth. For a while he was happy to bask in the beauty, but something was missing, and it took him eons to solve the problem of what that was.

'Once again, the Great Spirit used his voice and spoke to the earth, and huge numbers of animals emerged, as varied as the thoughts of the Great Spirit himself. Now the land was beautiful and full of life and movement, and the Great Spirit was content to watch the animals. But then something happened that the Great Spirit did not expect. The trees, the rocks, the streams began to talk to him. Perhaps his creations had been too close to his heart when he had created them, but somehow, the Earthbound Spirits came to be. The Great Spirit soon came to realise that the land was beginning to evolve on its own and the demands of the Earthbound Spirits began to take their toll. And in a bid to appease them, the Great Spirit created the Spirits for the water, the trees, the land, the rocks, and the sky. And this time, thinking one step ahead, he created another being to appease and control the Spirits, and that is how both myself and Freom came to be.'

'Then how are there two of you when he created just one?' asked Atiol.

'The two qualities he sought in this being could not be melded together, and it split into two upon its creation,' explained Freom. 'Back to the story. We came into being with the other Spirits and the land flowed smoothly, so smoothly in fact that we forgot the Great Spirit and he became lonely. He tried to reinvolve himself with the land he created, but it was too late. He had been forgotten. So, a sad, dejected figure, he roamed the land for a long while. Eventually, he sat atop a hill and wept. The giant oak tree that was beside him felt his great sorrow and, with utmost tenderness, reached out its branches and embraced the Great Spirit, and he returned the embrace. They stayed that way for decades. By the time the Great Spirit tried to release his hold, he found himself stuck. It was in this moment that the solution came to the Great Spirit, and he re-embraced the tree and became one with it, forever being worshipped by all the Spirits of the land which he had finally and eternally become a part of,' said Muefrede.

'I have never heard that before,' stated Atiol sadly.

'Wait, there is more,' advised Freom.

'It is true. There is more. Things became... how should I put this? Things became boring for us, so we created humans.'

'You created,' corrected Freom.

'Well, that is in the past. Now, anyway, as I said, humans came along, and it certainly livened up the place –but as we were to find out, not for the best.'

'That is the understatement of the millennium,' scoffed Freom.

'The humans were wild and uncaring from the beginning, and the land and the Spirits bore the brunt of it – and that sort of brings us back to the start,' finished Muefrede.

'Things were about to go pear-shaped when Ushwinn appeared, and he had with him a staff that he claimed came from an oak tree that housed the Great Spirit. He never cared to tell us how he came to be in possession of such a thing, but he claimed it contained a slice of the Great Spirit's soul, which could destroy the Spirits, and he now required a slice of our being. You see, as creators of humans, logically it could destroy them.'

'Now you see how we were in a bit of a bind because we ourselves were technically still Spirits.'

'So he blackmailed you?' said Atiol, pointing out the obvious.

'Pretty much so. We sang a slice of our being into the staff in the hope that it would never have to be used. Once that was done, the Earthen Staff of Knowledge was complete, and it was terrifyingly powerful,' said Freom.

'Armed with the Staff, Ushwinn set forth to negotiate with both the humans and the Spirits. The Spirits, being much older and wiser, agreed to the treaty straight away. They could feel the Staff's power. The humans, being much newer and less perceptive, needed more convincing. With the aid of the Staff, Crawley created a tornado that tore through the ranks of humans that were amassed at the meeting, and after that they agreed to the treaty rather quickly.'

'Then Ushwinn made a few more proclamations and conditions for the treaty, and once again blackmailed us into creating another race,' spat Freom.

'Let me explain that a little bit more eloquently,' offered Muefrede. 'The Staff could not be everywhere at once, so we created a race of people who were sensitive to the earth's needs and were able to replenish what the humans destroyed, but at the same time were able to control and keep the humans and Spirits under control, using force if necessary,' explained Muefrede.

'So Light Wielders came to be and we split into two factions – one existing within the guidelines of the law, and the other doing as they wanted, shunning the land,' summarised Atiol.

'Correct,' agreed Freom.

'A weapon with that much power should be kept secret. Who knows what could happen if it fell into the wrong hands,' muttered Atiol.

'Precisely, but it will be needed again. The Telirians are trying to win this war, and if they do, destruction will be hitching a ride on their backs. But you can stop them. The Telirians need the support of the people. You must go to Ushwinn and learn his ways. Then you must take the Staff and subdue this uprising, and restore the treaty that once stood,' instructed Muefrede.

'While you are doing that, you should look into nullifying the Telirians once and for all,' added Freom.

'Easy as that, hey? Is there anything else you would like me to do while I am at it?' asked Atiol sarcastically.

'No, that is everything,' replied Muefrede calmly.

'What if I refuse?'

'You have no choice in the matter. It is what you were born to do. Do you ever wonder why you have so much power at your disposal?' asked Muefrede.

Atiol nodded his head.

'There are very faint voices on the wind that can be mistaken for just that, but somewhere deep in your heart, you know the voices are real,' stated Freom with unaccustomed tenderness.

'You are not alone in this. The Earthbound Spirits focused a lot of their time on you. They whispered secrets into your mind that will allow you to do things that you can't possibly begin to comprehend. And all you need is the key to unlock them, and the key is Ushwinn,' explained Muefrede.

'I have heard the voices. They mostly ask for help. And I don't just hear the voices. I can also feel their pain,' said Atiol slowly.

'Do their pleas for help and their pain make you upset?' asked Muefrede softly.

A tear ran down Atiol's cheek, and he wiped his eyes to rid himself of the blurriness. 'It saddens me more than I would have thought possible,' answered Atiol with a constricted throat.

'Then you must do what we ask. You must leave Galteone and seek out Ushwinn. You must do it immediately.'

'I will need the approval of the Council before I can do such a thing,' replied Atiol.

'This is beyond the Council – and do you really think they will grant you permission to run around the countryside chasing down someone they remember nothing of?'

'If I leave without their permission, they will hunt me down as a traitor to the Jelery order. They no longer allow Light Wielders to leave Galteone without permission. Too many have been lured by the power of the Telirian ways, and the Council would prefer deserters to be put to death rather than let them return later to fight against us,' argued Atiol.

'Then they will definitely not allow this. That is why you must leave tonight,' ordered Freom.

'Mek and Baieta have a suspicion that you may be losing your grip on reality. You must act normally, for they will be here soon. They are worried about you,' cautioned Muefrede.

'I feel I have no choice in the matter. I shall leave tonight if I must.'

'You know you must, Atiol. You are right – you have no choice,' agreed Muefrede as he departed from Crawley's body.

'Atiol, it is Mek. Are you feeling all right?'

'I am fine, Mek,' he lied.

Mek appeared in the doorway followed by two of the Blue boys. 'Are you sure? You didn't look too well in the courtyard,' said Mek, scanning the room for more destruction beside the obvious lack of a door.

'I was just a little upset earlier. I got hardly any sleep last night, and I woke up with a splitting headache. I feel like such a fool. I should apologise to Toi-mun. I thought he was someone else when he clearly was not.'

'It is all right, Atiol. If you are having trouble sleeping, I can organise to get you some medicine from the healer,' offered Mek.

'Thank you, Mek. I think I will take you up on that, for sleep is what I desperately need to clear my head,' accepted Atiol.

'All right, Atiol. I will fetch something for you tonight. In the meantime, these two strapping lads will go along with you just to make sure you don't have any more of these outbursts. I hope you understand, Atiol. It is for your safety as well as everyone else's.'

'Don't feel bad, Mek. I understand that it is just a precautionary measure.'

'That is good, Atiol. You can go about your business. I will be off to find someone to reattach the door that you accidentally knocked down,' announced Mek.

'Thank you, Mek,' said Atiol as Crawley returned to himself and continued cursing Atiol's intrusion, even as he departed accompanied by his two minders.

The crow watched on and remained unmoving as a stone. It took in all that it had heard. The shrill cry of a falcon caused it to jump and scan the sky with little jerky movements of its head common to the breed. When it could not detect the falcon, it shifted slightly and resumed its watch. Then, by some freak occurrence, the crow heard the falcon just before it was able to strike, and dodged the deadly talons. Well, that was enough for the crow, whose utmost priority was self-preservation, and he flew off as fast as his wings could take him.

'Damn it, we almost had one that time,' cursed Ushwinn. 'Thank you, my fine-feathered friend. We will try for some more crows later. I will let you know when they become bold again.'

Ushwinn slowly opened his eyes after he had left the falcon's mind. 'I just hope that stupid little crow heard none of that particular conversation. Truly, those two twits can be so stupid. Delrain could get wind of my plans, then who knows what he would try. Oh, well, what's been said cannot be taken back, and we shall just have to deal with the consequences, just as long as it doesn't interfere with my afternoon cup of tea.'

Ushwinn rose painfully to his feet and shielded his eyes from the sunlight. For a moment, as he was walking along, he thought he caught a glimpse of something vaguely human in shape ducking for cover amongst the shadows of the trees. Ushwinn halted and scanned the area carefully. 'Probably just the sun in my eyes,' he thought as he continued on to his rickety little hut and his afternoon cup of tea.

The Hiratan remained perfectly still and waited for the old man to disappear inside, before it quickly launched itself into the air on its huge bat-like wings and headed for the mountains it called home.

'Here, the healer said that this medicine should make you sleep a lot better,' said Mek as he handed over a small vial.

'Thank you, Mek. I will definitely take this before I go to bed,' replied Atiol.

'Just as long as it makes you feel better.'

'Mek, would there be any chance that I could get a jug of wine to aid me in the sleeping department?' asked Atiol.

'I don't think that would pose too much of a problem. I will have the servant girl bring you some with your meal.'

'Thank you, Mek. Umm, I do not want to appear rude, but I would really like to be alone with my thoughts at the moment,' said Atiol.

'Certainly, but just remember, Atiol, I am will always be here any time you need to talk,' said Mek as he closed the door with a smile.

Atiol did not have to wait long before he heard the servant girl flirting shamelessly with the two minders who were stationed outside his door. 'Go in, sweetheart, but hurry back. It's going to be a long night, and I plan on having you included in it.' Nearly all the Jelery in the Order of the Blue Second Class were notorious fraternisers, and any female of a reasonable age was propositioned daily. It was as though they had a lot of lost time to make up for, which in most cases they usually did – a good thirty or forty years, in fact. The servant girl was no more than twenty years old, and despite her commonplace servant's garb and scruffy hair, she was extremely beautiful. Atiol had to reluctantly avert his eyes from her seductive smile and suggestive dark brown eyes.

'Just place the tray over on the small desk by the window,' he ordered, looking at his feet.

'And is there anything else you would have me do?' she asked, leaning over just enough to show the top of her well-endowed bosom as she stood before him.

Atiol went rather red in the face and coughed uncomfortably. 'As a matter of fact, there is one other thing you can do for me.'

The door to Atiol's room opened, and the servant girl slipped out. 'So, my sweet little thing, what do you think of the more powerful Light Wielders who cannot even call themselves real men?' sneered one of the men, squeezing her firm buttocks.

'I think that he is a little scared of women, but on the other hand, he is very generous,' she said as she produced a jug of wine from behind her back.

'He said to say that he is sorry you have to waste your time babysitting him when you could be doing much better things with your time.'

'Well, what are you waiting for? Hand me the wine jug, wench,' demanded one of the men as he snatched the jug and took a huge swig of wine.

'Hey, pass that jug over here. You are not the only one who has a thirst to quench.'

'Pigs,' thought Atiol as he listened to the commotion outside. Fifteen minutes passed before the noise began to subside.

'Do you know what else I like about the more powerful Light Wielders, my smelly pigs?' teased the servant girl, tugging the thick beard of one of the men. 'They pay for my services with gold,' she replied to herself, flicking the gold coin in the air and catching it with a smile as she knocked lightly on Atiol's door. 'They are sleeping like babies, very fat and hairy babies,' she giggled after Atiol had stuck his head through the slightly open door.

'Thank you. Here is another gold coin for your troubles,' said Atiol, slipping the gold coin into her palm.

'Are you sure there is not something more I can do for you?' she asked, undoing the top button of her blouse to allow a better view of her breasts.

'They are nice, but no. Now get out of here before anyone realises that you had a part in this,' ordered Atiol, dismissing the girl. She turned with a pout of disappointment and set off down the hall, swinging her hips invitingly. 'I sometimes wonder why I torture myself by even talking to them,' mumbled Atiol. He pulled his cloak tightly around his head and clasped it at the shoulders before shouldering a pack that he had prepared. He walked on tiptoes to the stairway and waited with an indrawn breath. When the only sound he could hear was drunken snoring, he crept down the stairs and into the open courtyard.

'Nice job on the Blue boys. I would have slit their throats. It's just as quiet as drugging, but twice as quick,' said Toi-mun.

'Just as quiet, twice as quick, with three times the mess,' whispered Atiol after he had recovered from his initial bout of fright.

'True, but I would not be the one cleaning it up. That is a servant's work, wouldn't you say?' asked Toi-mun.

'I do not have time for idle chit-chat, Shadow. Now be on your way and let me go about my own business,' growled Atiol, walking away.

Toi-mun shot his arm out and grabbed Atiol in a rough headlock. Atiol struggled but had to relax when he felt the cold steel of Toi-mun's blade pressed up against his neck just waiting to release some blood from his body.

'You are sworn to protect me, Shadow, and yet you have your weapon at my throat, ready to spill my blood,' said Atiol, his voice contorted with fear.

'I am protecting you, you fool. I know that you want to flee the city for some ill-begotten quest that the mad man Crawley concocted in that twisted mind of his. If you go outside these walls, you are as good as dead, so I might as well save some time by killing you now. Simple logic, don't you think?' said Toi-mun, applying more pressure to the blade.

'You won't use that sickle on me, Toi-mun. You are sworn to protect me, and if you are a man of your word, then you will release me.' Atiol assumed this was true, in the hope that the Iron Shadow lived up to its reputation.

'I know that if I release you, you will just up and leave Galteone,' replied Toi-mun.

'I will, and my mind will not be changed. There are higher powers at work here that I have no control over,' said Atiol defiantly.

'Then it would appear that you leave me no choice. I will be coming with you,' announced Toi-mun as he released his hold on Atiol and resheathed his weapon gracefully.

'You do not even know where I am going,' argued Atiol.

'That is true, and from what I can gather, you don't have a very good idea about that either.'

'I could be gone for weeks or months, and you are hardly equipped for such a long journey. You don't even have a pack,' retorted Atiol.

Toi-mun turned his back and walked a few paces, then fished a pack out of the garden and swung it onto his shoulders, and returned to stand in front of Atiol.

'Now that that little problem is solved, shall we get going?' he asked.

Seeing the futility in arguing the point further, Atiol grumbled to himself and walked on, with Toi-mun trailing a good metre behind.

'So, Atiol, something is nagging at me. Exactly how are we planning to leave the city?' asked Toi-mun as they entered the middle sector of Galteone.

'I have thought about it long and hard, and the only solution I can see is to walk directly out the front gate.'

'Walk out the front gate just like that?' said Toi-mun as he clicked his fingers.

'Just like that,' confirmed Atiol, clicking his fingers in reply.

'You will never make it out. The gate is sealed, and nobody is allowed to leave or even enter, without first obtaining permission from the Council,' pointed out Toi-mun.

'Yes, I already know this.'

'And yet I cannot help but notice that we are still walking purposefully toward the front gate,' pointed out Toi-mun.

'As you will soon find out, Toi-mun, I have some friends in very high places, higher than you think,' advised Atiol.

The pair walked on through the darkened streets to the outer sector of the city, and up to the front gate that barred their way. Toi-mun was more than a little surprised to find that the gate was slightly raised.

'You arranged this – but how?' asked a very confused Toi-mun.

A deep voice filtered down from the top of the wall, reaching their ears in a soft rhythmical chant.

'Let us just say that Crawley and I had this planned, but it is someone other than Crawley who is raising the gate. He is chanting to the earth.'

'Look at the corner of the gate,' instructed Atiol.

Toi-mun followed Atiol's pointing finger and peered in wonder as green vines as thick as a man's waist strained upward from the cobbled road, and as he watched, the gate rose higher despite its squeals of protest. 'This is not of the Jelery knowledge. How on earth is he doing this?' pondered Toi-mun in an awe-inspired whisper. The chanting became faster and more urgent as the vines began to quiver and strain under the enormous weight of the giant gate.

'Quickly, we must get under. He cannot hold it up for much longer,' said Atiol.

Toi-mun did as he was bid and rolled smoothly under the gate, and Atiol followed straight after him, a little less gracefully. The chanting changed in pitch. It became slower and thicker, almost like a child's lullaby.

Slowly, the vines retreated into the earth. The gate shut with a soft click as metal and wood touched the cobblestone. The chanting immediately ceased. Crawley poked his head over the side of the wall, and in the gloom of the night, the bright green sheen of his eyes could clearly be seen.

'Hurry, Atiol, they will be on your tail before the sun has risen,' he warned.

'Thank you both, Freom and Muefrede. Look after Crawley. He is a rare treasure and a gift to this earth,' replied Atiol.

Toi-mun stood with mouth agape, staring up at Crawley and seeing him for the first time as a being of power and knowledge.

'Look after him, Shadow, for if he dies, so will your way of life', warned Freom from within Crawley.

'I will do as you bid,' stammered Toi-mun. He turned, and had to run to catch up to Atiol, who was already moving away at a steady pace.

'You do realise that we are going to have the entire wrath of the Council to deal with if they manage to catch up with us?' he said to Atiol between breaths.

'Do you think I don't already know this, Shadow? If you have nothing better to do than point out the obvious, I recommend you save your breath,' snapped

Atiol in irritation. 'You're going to need it,' he added as he increased his pace.

'Some things are more obvious to different people,' replied Toi-mun as he sped to catch up. They ran from the towering city of Galteone, across the stone bridge that spanned the River Marset. They continued to run until they reached the outskirts of Strangle Light Woods, where they turned west and followed the river to their unknown destination.

# 11

LORD DELRAIN LOUNGED casually in his chair with one leg hanging over the armrest. He skewered a piece of sweetmeat with his dagger and chewed on it in casually. 'All right, Seker, what have you come to me with this time?' he asked, skewering another chunk of meat.

'My lord, I have done as you instructed. The men are ready and eager. All the weak of mind have been weeded out from your ranks and eliminated. The strongest have proven themselves, and at your request, I have promoted them to sergeants in your army; and those whom I noted as having special abilities are their captains,' reported Seker with downcast eyes.

'Excellent, Seker. I trust your judgement fully, so much so that I want you to lead two thousand men that are to eliminate the reinforcements from Galteone.'

'So you are going through with your initial plan, my lord?' enquired Seker.

'Of course, Seker. All I wait for is word from my delegates in Weolm. They are the last city to be under our influence. They are proving a tougher nut to crack than I first thought. But no matter. They will succumb, and when they do, the Jelery will have no allies to call upon. They will be all by themselves – ripe for the picking, so to speak,' said Delrain.

'My lord, when do you wish for me to infiltrate Monalteone?' asked Seker.

'Straightaway, Seker. You will need at least a couple of weeks to gain the confidence of the steward there. That should give the delegates in Weolm a little more time to tie up the loose ends as well. Take the men with you and have them stashed somewhere on the outskirts of Monalteone. I need the Jelery steward removed from Monalteone and destroyed without arousing suspicion – I'm sure you can think of something to achieve what I have asked.'

'Yes, my lord,' acknowledged Seker, moving off.

'Oh, one more thing, Commander Seker. If you fail in this little task that I have set, you will wish that you had never heard of me. But succeed, and the reward shall be great.'

'I will not fail you, my lord,' assured Seker, and he fought down a wave of nausea as Lord Delrain conjured a gold energy sphere that burnt the air around it.

The Blue boys outside Atiol's room woke with a groan and rubbed their eyes ferociously. 'What the hell happened?' croaked one of them.

'It feels like my eyelids been weighed down with stone blocks,' noted the other.

'Get up and check on the boy, would ya?'

One of them stood up with a slight stagger and erupted through the door of Atiol's room. A quick scan confirmed his suspicions, and he picked up the empty vial Atiol had left on the desk. He popped the stopper off and had a quick sniff. 'It's a bloody sleeping draught,' he growled, as he slipped the vial into his pocket. 'He has flown the coop, the little traitor,' he announced as he exited the room.

'Well, what are we doing? We have to get to the Council and alert them immediately. The little bastard must be caught,' ordered the other Blue boy as he ran toward the Tri Tower.

Ter-hal was smoking his first pipe of the day and perusing a pile of scrolls when the two Light Wielders burst in, breathless and reeking of wine.

'This had better be good,' said Ter-hal, puffing on his pipe and creating a thick veil of tobacco smoke around his head.

'We are sorry, high one, but our news simply cannot wait. The Jelery we were appointed to guard has managed to escape,' one of them blurted out.

'He managed to drug us with the aid of a servant girl, and left sometime during the night,' added the other, handing over the empty vial.

Ter-hal looked at the vial and cautiously sniffed its contents. 'I know this elixir. Did he leave on his own?' he asked as he re placed the stopper.

'We do not know for sure, but it would probably be safe to assume that his Shadow went with him,' replied one of the Blue boys in the hope that he was being helpful.

'Your incompetence is second to none,' snapped Ter-hal. 'You should both be dropped to the Order of the Green for a good decade or so, until you learn that even the lower-ranking Jelery still must have self-respect and discipline. If it was solely up to me, that would definitely be your fate,' yelled Ter-hal.

'Sorry, my lord. We will not let anything like this happen again.'

'Luckily for you, it is not up to me. Instead, you have the chance to make up for your mistake. Round up ten men of your choosing to aid in bringing this traitor back to me so he can face his punishment,' ordered Ter-hal.

'What if he refuses to return with us?'

'Then kill him, and if his Shadow gets in the way, dispose of him also.'

'Thank you for the chance to redeem ourselves, high one. We shall not fail.'

'It will be your heads on the chopping block if you do,' cautioned Ter-hal as he relit his pipe with a small golden sphere on the end of his finger.

Mek was walking towards Baieta's quarters when Baieta came up from behind him and gently tapped him on the shoulder. 'You were coming to see me,' he stated.

'I was,' replied Mek.

'Well, you had better cancel your little social visit. Atiol has disappeared, taking Toi-mun with him; and as we speak, a party of twelve men are preparing to leave with orders to bring him back dead or alive,' informed Baieta.

'That stupid young fool! I have to bring him back,' growled Mek as he took off in a sprint for the Council chamber.

'Thank you for letting me know, Baieta,' mouthed Baieta to himself.

Mek ran into the throng of people crowded around the twelve horsemen as they prepared to depart, and had to push his way through to reach the centre.

'This does not concern you, Mek,' said Ter-hal.

'It concerns me a great deal when I hear rumours that a pupil of mine is to be hunted down and killed with no evidence that he is a traitor,' replied Mek angrily.

'The evidence is clear, Mek, patron of the Order of the Light,' replied Ter-hal, belittling him. 'The evidence is in his disappearance. Whilst the whole of Galteone, including the Jelery, was under curfew, he decided to deliberately disobey it and slip out of the city. That in itself warrants his arrest.'

'You may outrank me, high one, but even you do not have the power to take the life of a Jelery without them first receiving a fair trial,' replied Mek.

'He will be given a fair trial if he chooses to return with the men to explain his actions. If he refuses, then he will die a traitor. That is the way it always has been, and today will be no different,' replied Ter-hal.

Mek stared defiantly into Ter-hal's eyes.

'If you continue with your actions, Mek, I will have to look into who else aided Atiol in his escape,' added Ter-hal, displaying the small empty vial that was recovered from Atiol's room. Mek turned his back on Ter-hal and walked off in a rage, swearing as he went, whilst Ter-hal watched him until he disappeared from his sight.

# 12

SEKER RAISED HIS hand and two thousand mounted men reined their horses to a halt. He strained his ears to listen past the snorts of the horses and the music of steel bits being chewed. Nothing but the sounds of the forest and its many animal inhabitants. He signalled for the men to make camp and await his further orders. He continued riding alone toward Monalteone. He rode on slowly for several hours, stopping at a large boulder with strange runes carved upon it, which read: 'Entering Monalteone, friend and allies to the Jelery Lords.'

'I would think that little rock will eventually have to be removed,' came a voice to his left.

'Or we could keep it for a laugh,' replied Seker.

'It is good to see you,' greeted the portly middle-aged man.

'It is even better to see you, Anoole.'

'We have an agreement, Seker. Why does it surprise you that I showed up?'

'It is just a thing I have when I am negotiating with a traitor. Sometimes they back out, sometimes they get caught,' said Seker casually.

'My loyalty lies with you, Seker.'

'We shall see. You still must convince Ter-hal of the impending threat to Monalteone's survival, and he is no fool,' pointed out Seker.

'He will have no reason to question me. I am in the house of nobles who serve directly under the rule of the Jelery lords. It was he who appointed me, after all,' reassured Anoole.

'Oh yes, the house of nobles. How easily they turn for the jingle of gold. Does the residing Jelery steward suspect anything?' asked Seker.

'No, not in the slightest. It took a lot of coin and a lot of influential people to put that little self-indulgent git in power,' said Anoole, holding out his hand.

'In time, Anoole, I have a few more questions first. What is his rank, for starters?' he asked.

'A modest Order of the Green,' replied Anoole.

'My, my! You have done well, haven't you? How did you pull that one off?'

'As I said, a lot of coin. But truth be told, the Jelery don't have enough Light Wielders of appropriate rank to fulfil all their needs, so it wasn't so hard to suggest the current steward. In fact, their numbers have reduced so drastically that they are expending a huge amount of manpower in rounding up any Ravers they can in a futile attempt to boost their numbers,' explained Anoole.

'They can try. We rounded up nearly all the Ravers years ago. The dungeons are overflowing with them as we speak,' stated Seker with a laugh.

'Not only that, Ter-hal has recently adopted a zero-tolerance policy on deserters, even with suspected deserters that he thinks are on their way to join the Telirian cause. If they get caught, they will be executed – no second chances,' informed Anoole.

'I am beginning to like him,' said Seker with a smile.

'He would have made a fine captain in our army if he wasn't so ambitious. He might still turn if all other options fail for him and the Jelery,' added Seker. Seker handed over a pouch of gold coins into Anoole's sweating palm. 'Now be on your way, and take this for protection. If approached by my men, just show it to them, and you will have safe passage,' advised Seker.

'Thank you, my lord. I shall not let you down,' said Anoole, accepting the bracelet of interwoven silver and gold.

'Now to go and stir up the hornets' nest,' thought Seker, riding toward Monalteone.

After abandoning his horse, Seker arrived on foot. He approached the heavy wooden gates of Monalteone, looking haggard and tired.

'Who are you and what do you want?' challenged a voice that sounded like gravel.

'I have come to talk to your steward, the powerful Jelery who resides within,' replied Seker in a soft voice.

'What is your business with our lord, stranger?' queried another.

'I have come seeking his Council as I am a lowly Light Wielder, and I have heard of your lordship's great power,' lied Seker.

He waited for a while before the gate swung outward, and two men stood in his path. One was a great ox of a man, who had his huge paw resting on the hilt of his sword, and the other man was as thin and as pale as a bleached skeleton. The skin on his face was pulled taut over his prominent cheekbones, giving his face a triangular shape; his lips were a deep blood red, which clashed horribly with his sickly pale skin. Seker had a closer look at the man and realised he was wearing lipstick. 'A vain man indeed,' he chuckled to himself.

'Yes, Light Wielder, what is it that you have come here to ask of me?' enquired the thin man.

'You must be the steward, only one radiating as much power as you could hold such a rank,' replied Seker dropping down on one knee.

The steward gloated visibly and struggled pointlessly to retain his smile as he replied. 'Come now, Light Wielder. With a little bit of training and guidance, within a few years you too could be as powerful as I. But enough of talking out here. I insist you come with me to my quarters where we can drink some wine and talk about the important matters at hand,' offered the steward, helping Seker to his feet.

'It would be a privilege, no, an honour, to talk and drink wine with one such as you on an even par,' stated Seker, bowing his head with mock respect.

'Come then, Light Wielder, we have so much to discuss, and I have vast amounts of knowledge to pass on to you.'

'I cannot wait, my liege,' replied Seker, rolling his eyes in despair. 'This is going to kill me,' he thought as he followed the steward to his quarters.

# 13

'SO, ATIOL, EXACTLY where is our destination?' enquired Toi-mun through laboured breaths.

'West, Shadow. All I know is that we go west,' replied Atiol.

So west they ran at a steady trot, Atiol drawing on the earth's energy to sustain his punishing pace whilst Toi-mun ran on his own power, which Atiol had to admire. The sun was well past its zenith when they finally stopped for a brief respite under the shade of a huge tree.

'You surprise me, Shadow. Stamina such as yours is almost unnatural. Perhaps I have underestimated you,' informed Atiol.

'Then you do not know much about the Iron Shadow or the abilities we possess. Just like you, I have trained hard to be what I am. My life, my focus, is to protect my charge, and if I fail in my purpose, then my life is forfeit,' explained Toi-mun.

'I am sorry – I did not understand the depth of your commitment to the Jelery, Toi-mun,'

'Do not apologise to me for anything, Light Wielder. You have done no wrong,' interrupted Toi-mun, tearing off a chunk of hard bread before placing it in his mouth to soften.

Atiol was leaning against the tree, chewing on some dried fruit, when his whole body began to tingle.

'What is it?' asked Toi-mun as Atiol sat forward.

'Light Wielders, two of them,' whispered Atiol.

'Are they Telirian?' asked Toi-mun, springing to his feet with his hands on his weapons.

'No. They are not that powerful. I think they are Jelery, perhaps no more than the Order of the Blue,' predicted Atiol.

'Not that powerful? Hey, I have seen someone from the Order of the Blue pick up a half-ton rock above his head and throw it several metres because he was bored,' replied Toi-mun.

'Piece of cake,' confirmed Atiol.

'Ah ha, no sweat,' replied Toi-mun sarcastically.

'The other problem is that they will not be alone. At least half a dozen or more will be with them,' guessed Atiol.

'They are for more than just moral support, I suppose,' added Toi-mun.

'Well, at least there will be none of the Iron Shadow to deal with the Order of the Blue warrants; no special protection,' pointed out Atiol.

'Yes, they themselves are protection enough.'

'We cannot outrun them. They will be on horseback. We must find some ground that will work to our advantage, and quickly,' ordered Atiol as the first echoes of pounding hooves caught his ears.

'I think I know of just the place where our backs will be protected by a sheer wall of rock. But once we are there, we will not be able to escape, for we will be boxed in, and no man can climb the walls.'

'I see no other option. Lead on, Shadow.'

They dog-legged right into the depths of Strangle Light Woods, where the air was thick and slow and filled with the smell of decaying leaf litter and moss. There was virtually not undergrowth. Only a few gnarled bushes were clinging to life amongst the towering brown-barked giants that made up the bulk of the forest, which surrounded them like the stone pillars of an ancient long-lost temple. A small speckling of sunlight fought its way through the leaves of the canopy high above and dappled the forest floor with its rays.

'We are getting closer, Light Wielder,' said Toi-mun through explosions of breath.

Atiol stole a quick glance over his shoulder and his heart pumped harder with what he saw. 'If you have any speed left in you, Shadow, now is not the time to hold it back. There are slightly more men chasing us than I first thought,' said Atiol, breathing hard.

'Exactly how many more are we talking about?'

'Just enough to make me want to run faster,' answered Atiol, pulling ahead.

Toi-mun briefly glanced over his shoulder and groaned in despair as he urged his aching legs onward. The first arrow arched overhead and landed close to his feet. 'They are not playing nicely, Atiol,' he shouted.

Before Atiol had a chance to reply, they broke into a patch of sunlight which had allowed the undergrowth to bloom like a waist-high bright green carpet that spread to the outer edges of the sunlight's limits and butted nicely up against a towering cliff-face of stone that was dotted with small shrubs and curtained by numerous vines snaking across its breadth.

'You get behind me, unless you feel as though you can dodge arrows,' advised Atiol.

As they came into the opening, the horsemen they

figured out that the fugitives had nowhere to run, and they slowed their mounts to a walk.

'Give it up, Atiol. You can see as well as I that you are trapped. I am under strict instruction to give you the chance to surrender peacefully. So come along quietly or I will have no other choice but to take you by force.'

'And if you can't take us by force?' asked Toi-mun sternly.

'Well, if that is the case, I suppose I will have to kill you both,' smirked one of the Blue boys in reply.

'I will not be intimidated by the likes of you. I warn you now – turn your steeds around and head back to Galteone. Tell Ter-hal that I have vanished as if I never was, and all will leave this place unharmed,' said Atiol.

'What an interesting proposition, Atiol! I will take it into consideration. Hmmm, let me see. How about *no*? But my offer still stands. I will give you ten seconds to think it over,' replied the larger of the two Blue boys.

Toi-mun stepped beside Atiol. He drew his razor-honed war sickles from their sheaths and dropped automatically into the stance of a seasoned warrior.

'Put down your grass cutters, little Shadow, or my men will turn you into a pincushion,' warned the slightly smaller of the two Blue boys. With a nod of his beefy head, all the bows were drawn taut and the arrow heads pointed menacingly at Toi-mun's chest.

'Lower your bows or you will die where you sit,' growled Atiol angrily, and he instantaneously conjured a golden sphere of swirling light into the palm of his upraised hand.

'You had your chance, Atiol,' yelled the larger Blue boy. 'Release!'

Atiol let fly with the sphere seconds before the arrows were released and with his arms outstretched, he conjured a bright red shield wall, with a fraction of a second to spare. Toi-mun cringed, preparing for the arrows to riddle his body. But the smell of charred wood and feathers filled the air as the arrows struck the shield wall with a fizzle and disintegrated to ash. The energy sphere Atiol threw struck one of the men as he loosed his arrow, taking him high on the chest and making a scorched fist-sized hole straight through him. He gasped in surprise and fell heavily from his saddle to the ground, where he lay unmoving. The smell of the charred flesh and the brightness of the shield wall made the horses uneasy, and they snorted and rolled their eyes in panic.

'Well, do not just sit there gawking. Get in there and cut them both to pieces,' roared the slightly smaller Blue boy.

As if a switch had been flicked in their brains, the remaining soldiers charged their mounts forward with their short swords held straight out like extensions of their arms, yelling madly. Atiol dissolved the shield wall and let fly with several energy spheres that exploded into the ground, sending a shower of dirt directly at the charging men. The horses baulked in fear and threw their riders, then followed their instincts and turned and fled for the safety of the trees.

Toi-mun seized the moment and rushed forward and slit the throats of two of the men before they could rise off the ground. The horrid sight of their comrades clutching uselessly at their throats as the blood pumped through their hands onto the ground drove the remaining men into a frenzy.

'Die, you little bastard!' screamed one of them as he came at Toi-mun and swung his sword with the ferocity of a bear. He was aiming to separate Toi-mun's head from his body; but with the grace of a ballet dancer, Toi-mun ducked beneath the sword and deftly gave it a little flick with his right sickle, helping it on its way, leaving the man's side completely exposed. With his left sickle, he sliced the gut with a sideways backhand stroke which he brought from his right shoulder. The man slumped and clutched at his ropey entrails as they threatened to spill from his stomach.

Aware of another attack from behind him, Toi-mun blocked the blow aimed at his side with his right sickle in a downward arc. Spinning with the momentum, he brought his left sickle around and cleaved the man's head from his shoulders. He watched with satisfaction as the headless body slumped sideways to the ground. The remaining soldiers looked at each other, urging anyone besides themselves to advance. They had seen the consequences of fighting with their emotions, and they all were afraid and uncertain. They had all heard of the skill of the legendary Iron Shadow, and up to this point, they had all thought it was just a myth. But now that they had seen this one's skill and ferocity, they did not want to try it out for themselves.

'Return to Galteone while you still have your lives!' ordered Toi-mun.

'Do not just sit there. Kill him! He is only one man,' screamed the larger of the two Blue boys.

'Yes, come at me. I am still only warming up,' said Toi-mun calmly, spinning his bloodied sickles in his hands.

The soldiers once again looked to each other to make a move on the smiling Iron Shadow. 'If it is as easy as you think, why don't you try to kill him?' said one of the soldiers, speaking up.

'Absolutely pathetic, and you call yourself soldiers?' With a quick flick of his wrist, the larger of the Blue boys threw a blue energy sphere at Toi-mun. The sphere made it to within a couple of feet of him before it collided with a smaller red energy sphere, knocking it off course to sail harmlessly into the cliff face. The Blue boy stared venomously at Atiol.

'There will be no more warnings,' threatened Atiol, conjuring a golden energy sphere above his head.

The two Blue boys looked on in awe at the golden light swirling within its sphere, and both shied away as they felt the immense energy it contained.

'You are nothing more than a traitor to your order, swine. I will spread the word of your deceit and treachery across the land. You, Atiol, are no longer Jelery. The Council will be informed that you are on your way, slithering like a serpent on your belly, to kiss the hand of the very people who are destroying the land, the same land you were entrusted to look after,' cursed the larger of the Blue boys.

'Say of me whatever you think fit to say. I know exactly where my allegiance lies. I just hope you live long enough to see it as well,' replied Atiol calmly.

'Naught spills from your mouth except lies. Mark my words, Atiol – you will die a traitor's death,' declared the smaller boy, and he and the others wheeled their horses around and disappeared into the forest that surrounded the clearing.

'Well, that went remarkably well, all things considering,' said Toi-mun as he wiped the blood off his blades with the tunic of one of the men he had dispatched with ruthless efficiency.

'We are alive, and that is all that matters,' replied Atiol as he watched the last of the horsemen disappear.

'Shall we continue on to where it is that we are going?' asked Toi-mun as he sheathed his war sickles.

His question fell on deaf ears, for Atiol was already twenty paces away, moving along in a hurried trot.

'I will take that as a yes,' stated Toi-mun as he fell into a jog.

# 14

SEKER PICTURED HIS hands wrapped firmly around the thin pale neck of the steward, squeezing and squeezing until the neck snapped with a satisfying crack. 'I asked, Light Wielder, what is your name and rank?' enquired the steward.

Seker regretfully dismissed the image in his head and answered with a smile. 'My name is Dorian Antecorp, and as yet, I have no rank to speak of. I have had no formal training, as it would seem the Ravers overlooked my birth. What little I do know, I have learnt from the Jelery that have been expelled from Galteone. I might add that what they taught me was definitely not worth all the gold that I paid them,' replied Seker.

'Fear not, Dorian, for I can sense power in you, and just because you are not officially recognised as a Light Wielder it does not mean that you are not one.

But, luckily for you, I have taken a liking to you, young man, and would be more than honoured to train you as my pupil,' announced the steward, patting Seker's knee with his skinny white hand.

Seker glanced at the smooth, hairless face of the steward. He was enraged with the 'young man' reference to himself. 'No, the honour would be all mine, Steward – or would you like me to refer to you with some other name or title?' he grovelled.

The steward's eyes lit up for a moment and he struggled to bring his composure back to a neutral level. 'Well now, seeing as though I am going to be training you, Dorian, do you think that it would be suitable for you to address me as Master?'

'Certainly, Master,' purred Seker, emphasising the last word.

The steward's face seemed to split in two as he smiled with self-importance at the sound of his new title. 'Yes, Master, indeed. That suits me so well,' he thought, as his already inflated ego took a giant leap toward the sky.

Seker sat looking at the steward, who was smiling like an idiot. 'Master, I am going to kill you ever so slowly and painfully, you little Jelery maggot, for subjecting me to this humiliation,' he thought as he smiled along.

# 15

THE REMAINING SOLDIERS of Galteone rode behind the two Blue boys as they plodded towards home and the wrath of Ter-hal. 'We will be extremely lucky if we don't replace Atiol on the chopping block,' moped the larger of the two.

'I don't think we shall have any luck in that department. Ter-hal is not widely regarded as being lenient,' replied the other Light Wielder.

'You could at least let me think that we will be spared a beheading,' sulked the larger one. They rode in silence with downcast eyes. Perhaps if they had been riding as normal, they would have missed the tracks that one of the Light Wielders picked up on.

'There was another horse in the area, and it was not one of ours,' announced the larger one as he dismounted from his horse. 'They are no more than a day old,' he added as he examined the hoof prints closely.

'Probably just a hunter on horseback,' dismissed the other.

The larger one ignored the comment and followed the tracks that ran along the edge of the woods, and he did not hesitate in following them as they abruptly changed direction and headed for the trees.

'Come on, let's just get back. Ter-hal does not need to find anything else to blame us for,' advised the other Light Wielder from his saddle.

Undeterred, the larger man continued to follow the tracks, and had gone no more than forty metres before they were lost amongst thousands more. He bent down and inspected them further. The hoof prints had sunk to a considerable depth into the ground. It was clear that the horses had been carrying a lot of weight. 'It was not a hunter. It was more likely a scout who had broken off from the main contingent in the forest to check on their progress before returning to them,' he pondered. Then a cold wave of dread washed over him as his brain provided him with the logical explanation.

'It is an army, a small army...' he said out loud, and he came running out of the woods and literally leapt into his saddle.

'What are you mumbling about? What has got your goat?' asked the other man.

'About two thousand men have passed this way. It is possibly a war party, and their mounts were heavily burdened,' he informed.

'Then we must make all haste to Galteone and inform Ter-hal. If it has anything to do with the Telirian, he will want to know.'

'Hold up. Not so fast. What if I am wrong, and it is actually a large village on the move, carrying all they own? If we go to Ter-hal and misinform him...'

'It would have to be a bloody large village.'

An idea was forming in the larger man's head. 'We can redeem ourselves,' he thought out loud.

'Redeem ourselves. What are you prattling on about?'

'Think about it – if we came to Ter-hal with an exact headcount and a better idea of what they are up to, he would be impressed, especially if they turned out to be our enemy. He would probably wipe the slate clean for us and that would get us out of this mess,' brainstormed the larger one.

The smaller of the two was a bit dimmer, and his meagre brain took a lot longer to process the possibilities. But slowly, a smile came to his face. 'That has got to be the best idea I ever heard. Ter-hal might be so impressed that will he not only forgive us, he may reward us with our own country estates,' he fantasised.

'Well then, what are we waiting for?' announced the larger Light Wielder as he enthusiastically took up the trail.

The remainder of the soldiers sighed heavily. They had seen enough devastation for the day and could see no glory in this new venture, only death. But like the good soldiers they were, they followed the two Light Wielders into the trees, with their hands close to their weapons.

# 16

ATIOL STOPPED ABRUPTLY and cocked his head to the side, listening intently. 'What is it?' asked Toi-mun, hearing no sound. 'Can you not hear it? Can you not hear the whispering voices?'

'He has come at last. He makes his way to the all-knowing one,' recited Atiol.

'What?' asked Toi-mun, sceptically.

'The voices – that is what they are whispering over and over.'

'Well, I cannot hear a thing, and I don't think waiting here will allow me to do so. So let's keep moving,' ordered Toi-mun, and he jolted his pack to a more comfortable position as he ran.

Atiol turned and started after Toi-mun, with the sound of faint chuckling echoing in his ears.

# 17

SEKER IGNORED THE crow that perched patiently on the roof. It looked at him with a penetrating glare that seemed to be looking directly into one's soul. He waited until nightfall before sneaking out of the steward's chamber into the courtyard, and up to the tree that poked defiantly upward through the cobblestones. The previous steward had lamely decided to nurture it, and had kept it as a symbol for the people. 'An omen,' he had said, 'to show the people that no matter what the odds are against oneself, there is always a chance to flourish.'

Seker bashed the side of his head in an effort to dispel the information. All day the steward had been in tutorial mode, and to Seker's absolute horror, he had thought it essential to brief him on the entire history of Monalteone, from its humble beginnings to its current glory. 'I will bloody well plant him in the cobblestones,' he whispered with a smirk, and he felt better for the release of anger.

The crow startled him as it landed on his shoulder and he was about to break its neck but thought better of it for the noise it would create. 'What is so important as to risk my cover?' asked Seker, scrutinising the bird.

The crow glanced around nervously as it listened attentively to Seker, then it said, 'Men from the high-walled city come. They are following tracks. They seek the men who make the tracks so they can return and tell.'

'You have done well,' praised Seker. He released the bird with a quick movement of his shoulder and it flew off into the night sky on silent wings. The news was not good, but it was something that he could check on when he went to update his troops.

The next moment, it was not a noise that alarmed him, but the sudden lack of it. A movement caught the corner of his eye and with practised ease he flung a grey energy sphere at the blur. An expulsion of air was followed by a hard thud as a body hit the ground. Several quick strides later, Seker was standing over a large guard who had been eavesdropping.

'Telirian, I knew I could smell a filthy rat,' wheezed the guard as he clutched at his stomach.

'Get used to it. You are going to be smelling a lot more of them soon. Oh, wait, what am I saying! You won't get the chance to,' growled Seker as he bent down and snapped the man's neck like a twig. Seker picked up the dead weight of the corpse as a normal man would pick up his small child, and walked with great caution to the top of the walls. Several times, despite his best efforts he had to turn tail and hide from the patrolling guards, but he never once put down his burden. He climbed the guard tower's stair to the top platform and stood looking out into the endless trees of the.

'It has been a pleasure, but now we must part,' he mocked Seker as he hurled the body with all his might. It crashed into the trees a good fifty feet away, making a louder than expected crash that made Seker cringe.

'Who goes there?' challenged one of the sentries. Seker silently cursed his error of judgement, for now he would be seen out of his room. 'It is only I, Dorian,' replied Seker.

'Nice night for a walk, eh, Dorian? But be on your guard. There is something not quite right about it. I am feeling edgy for some reason. Mark my words, those Telirians are brewing something,' predicted the sentry.

Seker bunched his fists and prepared to strike. 'Why? What would make you say something like that?' he asked.

'There has been word from traders in Taibasan that the city of Labeck no longer follows the law set by the Jelery. They are not paying their dues to them,' informed the sentry.

Seker relaxed and unclenched his fists; this did not concern him and his motives. 'Well, the cities of the north see neither hide nor hair of the Jelery. It takes them weeks to respond to requests of importance, and people have to be fed. Their fires must have something to burn, and the cities are ever expanding. All of this requires more land, more resources, and the people just cannot put their lives and businesses on hold until the Jelery show up and do a little ritual to appease the Spirits, Spirits we cannot even see, Spirits that may not exist at all.'

The guard took a step backward and put his hand on his sword. 'Blasphemy! How can you say such things? The Spirits have to be appeased. When new land is acquired, the old land is barren, and nothing will grow on it until the Spirits reoccupy and replenish it so the trees can grow on it and the Spirits can reclaim it for their use. It is the way it has always been. Equality between humans and Spirits – no more, no less.'

'Calm down, man. I am only repeating what I have heard the people from the northern regions say. I meant no offence,' said Seker, trying to calm the man before he drew more unwanted attention.

'I am sorry, Dorian. I get a little hot-headed sometimes,' apologised the guard.

'It's all right, my man. Sometimes we can't control our emotions.'

'It is just that the Jelery are getting too few in number to police the cities the way they used to. Monalteone is the last of the cities to still be governed by a steward,' replied the guard in a concerned voice.

'A true pity it is, but perhaps the Jelery will return to their former strength, and once again the land will be secure from waste and destruction.'

'We can only hope so, Dorian, we can only hope so,' agreed the guard as he moved off to resume his patrol. Seker let out a sigh of relief and made his way back to the steward's quarters unchallenged by a single sentry.

The Blue boys woke from their sleep and brushed the leaves from their clothes and hair before they stood up with a yawn.

'I tell you what, this had better be worth it,' said the smaller Light Wielder as he arched his back to alleviate the stiffness that a night of sleeping on hard ground had provided.

'There is nothing to it. All we have to do is find out who the tracks belong to, where they are going, and count how many of them there are.'

'That is going to be all, nothing else, right?'

'Relax. It is not like we are going to attack a large group of men, especially if they are armed to the teeth,' reassured the larger of the two.

The first one cocked his head and signalled to his companion to remain silent. 'Did you hear that?' he asked.

'No, I didn't hear a thing. Why? What did you hear?'

'Just for a second there I thought I heard hoof steps.'

'Bah, it was probably nothing. You are just a bit jumpy.'

'You're probably right. Well, I suppose I had better wake this lot up, then,' said the smaller Light Wielder, indicating the sleeping soldiers.

He walked over, and after a few swift kicks and some harsh words, the soldiers dragged themselves to their feet. 'There is no point in all of us going. It will just make it harder to remain concealed, so you lot can stay here and wait for us to return. Have you got that into your thick skulls?'

The soldiers nodded their acknowledgement, knowing they would be able to go back to sleep as soon as the Light Wielders left. The Blue boys mounted their steeds and continued following the tracks to their source. They had not ridden for more than fifteen minutes, when the smell of burning wood filled their nostrils.

'What do you think, cooking fires?' enquired the smaller Light Wielder.

His companion nodded his head. 'Whoever they are, they are certainly making themselves comfortable,' noted the larger man.

They dismounted and continued on foot. Moving carefully, they came upon a sleeping sentry, and the smaller Light Wielder drew a razor-sharp dagger and placed it on the sleeping sentry's neck.

'No, you fool,' whispered the other one. 'They must not know anyone was here,' he added. The dagger was withdrawn, and they crept on, moving unseen in the smoke from the cooking fires that hung like fog in the calm of the forest.

'There are more than enough men here for a small army, and they are equipped for war. I have seen enough. We must return to Galteone with all haste and inform the Council before this lot start getting serious,' decided the larger Light Wielder.

They returned to the horses uneventfully and began riding in a fast canter back to their campsite. A crow flew past their noses and settled on a branch up ahead. It carried something in its beak, which they dismissed as nothing more than carrion. The larger of the two Light Wielders felt a wave of coldness wash over him. The hair on the back of his neck stood on end, and he shuddered involuntarily. He looked at his companion, and judging by the look on his face, he had felt it as well – a Light Wielder, and an immensely powerful one at that, was close by.

They rode into camp warily and dismounted before the horses had come to a stop. The guards were asleep on the ground with their cloaks pulled completely over themselves.

'Get up, you lazy bastards. We have to get moving!' ordered the larger Light Wielder as he kicked at the closest one. The figure yielded under the blow, but remained still. With growing frustration, he bent down and ripped the cloak away. He fell to his knees, dry retching.

'What the hell?' swore the other one, and he bent down for a closer inspection.

The soldier's neck had been savaged and the bones of his spine showed clearly. Both of his eyes had been removed, and the stomach cavity had been opened and all the internal organs removed. A quick check of the other soldiers revealed the same fate had befallen them.

'They have had their organs eaten,' theorised the larger one as he scouted the camp site for the innards of the soldiers' stomachs.

'What could have done something like this?' asked the smaller one, wiping ice-cold perspiration from his brow.

'Those low-life degenerate animal Telirians must have done this.'

'It must have been their war hounds, and I would bet it was the Light Wielder we sensed that controlled them,' agreed the smaller one. 'He is still out there. I can still sense him, but it is faint.'

'We both felt how powerful he was. I'm not going to stick around and find out exactly how powerful he is. The Council will deal with this,' declared the larger Light Wielder.

'Then let's not dally here any longer. I feel as though I'm being stalked,' replied the other, agreeing readily at the idea of leaving.

At that moment, a small reverberation carried through the ground, and a large pack rat let out a squeak of alarm as it scurried between their legs undeterred by the human presence. They looked questioningly at each other before the first deer came careening toward them, its eyes rolling in fear. It was followed closely by a multitude of other animals that were fleeing desperately from some unseen foe.

'What the hell is going on around here? The animals are going mad. Quick, get behind a tree before they trample us.'

The animals rushed past with a frenzied sound, but it paled in comparison to the sound that followed. An inhuman screech that no known animal could deliver filled the air around them, causing the men to break out in goosebumps. It was answered by another deeper, throatier screech closer than the first. The larger Light Wielder looked over at his comrade, who was acting agitated and fearful. The muscles in his legs were quivering in anticipation; he was ready for flight. The first Light Wielder shook his head and mouthed the words to stay put, but he was too far gone in fright and did not take heed of the warning, or even acknowledge his companion's existence. He gritted his teeth together and took off, running in no particular direction, caring not where he went as long as it took him away from whatever had spooked the animals.

Then there was the sound of enormous wings, and the larger Light Wielder stared in transfixed horror as a monstrous creature flew overhead. Its wings that spanned at least three metres. They were formed of membranes, similar to bats' wings, and were pockmarked with small holes and rips. Apart from the size, the only difference was that the wings sprouted from the creature's back, allowing its two arms to remain dexterous. It landed lightly on the ground a short distance from the running Light Wielder. It spun around and its talon-fingered hand shot out and grabbed him by the neck. In desperation, the Light Wielder punched the creature in the chest with all he had. It was knocked backward through the air and crunched into a tree with a grunt of pain. The talons had gouged the throat of the Light Wielder, and his blood flowed freely and soaked into his clothes. His companion came running over to aid him.

'Are my wounds bad?' he asked shakily as he clutched at his throat.

'No, they are not that bad. You will need a couple of stiches, but it missed your life veins. You will survive,' was the reply.

The creature let out a screech of anger and shook its head to dispel the stars from its vision. 'You are Jelery,' it accused in a low whisper that almost came out as a growl.

'We are beast and you know what we are capable of, so you had best think about your next move wisely,' threatened the larger Light Wielder as he conjured a blue energy sphere into the palm of his hand.

'Yes, Jelery you are, but not the Jelery we seek. Where is the one called Atiol?'

'Ha, good luck to you on that one, beast. He is as slippery as an eel and has some good protection with him, possibly the best Iron Shadow in the land,' replied the smaller Light Wielder.

'You know of him, so you must know where he is,' said the creature, rising to its full impressive height of eight feet.

'We don't know where he is exactly, but we know he is heading west,' offered the larger one.

'That is all I need to know. Normally, I would have killed the likes of you, but another comes who I think will save me the effort,' warned the creature as it launched into the sky with a snap of its wings.

'They can try, foul beast,' shouted the smaller Light Wielder in defiance.

'What on this green earth were they?' asked the other Light Wielder.

'I have no idea what that creature was, or where it came from. The people of Galteone tell their children tales of Spirits twisting Ravers into ill-begotten beings to scare them to bed, but I doubt that used to be a Raver,' replied the smaller one.

'This is more news that the Council must hear.'

The tingling sensation in the smaller Light Wielder's head grew stronger. 'The Telirian is getting closer. We must flee. We cannot risk this information staying with us if we were to die – the Council must be notified.'

'Notified of what?' asked Seker as he appeared from behind a tree ten metres directly in front of them, blocking their escape.

'Seker, why do you haunt these woods with your foul presence?' asked the larger Jelery.

'Come now, man, can you not put two and two together? Oh, wait, you are only of the Order of the Blue, so I suppose you can't,' chuckled Seker. 'I am out here to inform my men that soon they will be bathing in the blood of Monalteone's steward, and also, I received a tip-off that you may be around. So I did a bit of searching and sensed you two so-called Light Wielders, and here we are,' replied Seker as he advanced upon them.

'Die, you filth,' roared the Light Wielder, and he threw the blue energy sphere he had in his hand.

Seker stopped and allowed the sphere to hit him in the chest. The blow slid him back about a foot and he smiled forebodingly. 'Thank you very much. I needed that to shake the sleep from my head. Now allow me to return the favour!'

Seker threw a red energy sphere at the Jelery, who dived deceptively fast to his right. The energy sphere struck a tree behind, and the two Jelery were showered in the leaves that were shaken from it. The Blue boys knew they had no chance of defeating Seker when it came to hurling energy back and forth, so they ran. The smaller one made a good twenty metres before a golden energy sphere struck him in the back and knocked him to the ground. The larger one watched on in pity. To help him would be folly, and the message had to be delivered. A second golden sphere struck the already fallen Jelery, causing a scream of agony to burst from his mouth. 'Sorry, my friend. Die strong, die well,' said the larger Light Wielder as he kept on running.

Seker walked up to the moaning Light Wielder, knelt down and looked upon him with disgust. 'I have always wanted to ask a Jelery – why do you care for such small things as the grass, the leaves, these pesky little insects?' he enquired as he picked up an ant. 'I mean, look at it – so small, so pathetic, so insignificant,' he said casually as he crushed it. 'It has no right to have the respect you give it. Well, man, answer me!' demanded Seker.

'All things are equal. None are better or more important than the other because all things have their purpose, and without them playing their little part, the land will fall into ruin,' he answered with a grimace.

'Oh, I agree. All things do have a purpose. Their purpose is to better our lives, you fool! And what difference does it make if the land is green in life or grey in death? It does not affect me,' sneered Seker.

'You do not see it now, but it will do, more than you know,' coughed the Jelery.

'No, I think not, but at this time I am going to show you two things that have the sole purpose of helping me to solve a little leak in my future plans. First of all, there is you lying on the ground – by the way, you smell a little charred. And then there is this.' Seker pulled from his belt a finely made silver-handled dagger with a blade that was roughly twenty centimetres long and an two centimetres wide. The edge of the blade was so honed it almost cut the air that blew upon it, and the spine was paper thin, making it incredibly light and flexible. 'Then there is this. It is known as a feather-blade dagger. Allow me to demonstrate.'

Seker grabbed a handful of the downed Light Wielder's hair and jerked his neck to the side. 'Now, when you squeal, your little friend will not be able to resist trying to help you, and I will be here waiting, thereby eliminating you both and solving my problem,' explained Seker.

The Jelery grabbed Seker by the wrist and attempted to twist it into releasing the dagger. Seker let go of the hair and grabbed his wrist in return.

'You struggle in vain, fool,' he snarled as he broke the Jelery's wrist with a quick twist. With great effort, the Jelery stifled the scream that welled up from within. 'Now, where were we? Oh, yes, I remember,' Seker reseized the Jelery by the hair and once again cranked his neck to the side, then sliced the ear away from the skull and let it slide down his neck in the flow of blood. 'You see, the blade is so sharp you do not even realise you have been cut until you see or feel the blood running. Only then does the pain realise it is not doing its job.'

The Jelery let out a little whimper, which quickly turned into a pain-filled continuous moan. 'But as you can feel, the pain does eventually do its job,' smirked Seker. 'Now, as neat as that trick was, the blade itself has several other uses. Allow me to demonstrate another one.'

Seker grabbed the injured arm of the moaning Light Wielder, then stood up and pushed his boot firmly into the Jelery's neck to subdue the struggling. He whistled to himself as he ran the bloodied blade the entire circumference of the elbow joint. He took great care to only go a certain depth. Then he ran the blade down the skin of the forearm until it reached the broken wrist, where he copied what he had done to the elbow, without the blade once being lifted.

'Does that feel good, Jelery? No? Yes? What is the matter? The cat got your tongue?' asked Seker. 'I must say, you are doing exceptionally well to stifle your pain, but let us see if you can remain that way.'

Seker slid the blade into the Jelery's chest and pushed lightly enough that it took a good twenty seconds for the blade to break free out through his back into the soft ground. 'Hold that for me, will you?' he laughed.

The Light Wielder screamed out in pain.

'Did you say something?' asked Seker with a malicious smile. He worked his fingers into the gash on the Jelery's elbow until he had a firm purchase on the skin. The Jelery cried out in pain, which seemed to encourage Seker, and he began to rip the skin away from the flesh in a series of small jerking movements. Every time he pulled at the flesh, the Jelery grunted in pain, until finally he gave in to it and began to scream and cry continuously.

Seker kept jerking on the skin the way that a dog would with a piece of rope while it played tug of war, until the last of it came away, leaving him with a handful of bloodied skin tissue which he casually dropped in front of the screaming man. 'Skinning is another use. Now, let's see. I have cut off your ear, partially skinned you, and skewered you like a pig. It leaves me with a couple of more options, and it looks like I will have to use my imagination until your friend returns, which I must say is taking him an awfully long time, don't you think?' asked Seker as he wiped the blood from his hands on the Jelery's shirt. 'But he will be along soon. If nothing else, you Jelery are rather predictable.'

The larger Light Wielder had not gone far. For a start, he was no athlete, and his conscience had urged him to stay and see if his comrade could be helped. When the screaming started, he clapped his hands over his ears. But the cries ended not long after, and he let out a sigh of relief. Perhaps Seker had left him alone, or perhaps he was dead. But when the screaming resumed and intensified, he had to make a decision. He could, and probably should, return to Galteone and report their findings. But the thought of these screams haunting his dreams for the rest of his long life urged him into doing what was right, and he took a steadying breath.

'If the filth wants to play, then so be it,' he snarled as he turned and retraced his steps to try and save the Jelery brother whom he thought of as a friend.

Seker was methodically cutting through the leather vest and cloth shirt with his knife, as his victim whimpered in pain and fear.

'You, you, d ... d ... d ... don't have to do this,' stammered the Jelery as he lay clutching his bloodied arm across his chest. 'Please, Seker,' he pleaded.

'You do know that I agree with you. I don't have to do this, but I want to. You see, I do not like your kind, and wish for all of you the same treatment you are getting, so prepare to squeal.' Seker sliced deeply from the bottom of the sternum right down to pants line with almost surgical precision. With the abdominal muscles cut, the wound gaped open and the mass of ropey blue intestines welled and threatened to spill out. 'Now let us remove your insides,' announced Seker.

But before he had the chance to plunge his hand into the victim's stomach, he was hit from the side with a hard object that sent him sprawling to the ground. 'So you have come back for your turn,' he growled as he coughed at the dust that hung about his head. Another boulder hit him squarely between the shoulder blades and exploded, forcing him back to the ground, which he was trying to rise from. Seizing the moment, the Jelery sprinted to Seker, who had struggled to his hands and knees, and kicked him in the face, crushing his nose with a splatter of blood. The kick flipped Seker on to his back, and he coughed up the blood that had sluiced down his throat. Rough hands seized him by the neck and began to throttle him. He was then unceremoniously picked up off the ground in the same hold until his feet dangled a good foot in the air, and was slammed into the trunk of a tree with such force that a shower of leaves pelted down onto the combatants.

Seker groped desperately at his attacker's face as he was slammed repeatedly into the tree. But then his thumb found the corner of an eye socket near the temple, and dug it in up to his knuckle. Bright red globs of blood burst over his hand as he ripped the eyeball from its socket. The Jelery screamed in pain. He released his hold on Seker and applied pressure to his vacant eye socket.

Seker slumped forward and gasped for air, but he had only taken a few deep breaths when the Jelery came at him again, the pain in his eye socket forgotten. He had slipped into a berserker's rage and would not stop until death befell him or he had dealt it out. A mighty punch was aimed at Seker's mangled nose, and all he could do was lower his head and let the blow take him in the forehead. A bright burst of stars filled his vision as he stumbled sideways. The stars cleared just in time to allow him to counter another charge from the Jelery. He dropped to the ground and tripped his attacker, sending him to the ground with a thud.

Seker scrambled to his feet and conjured a large red energy sphere, which sucked the life from everything within a two-metre radius. The undergrowth browned and wilted, as did the leaves, and an unfortunate bird that flew too close dropped dead from the sky.

By this time, the Jelery had struggled to his feet and he spat blood from a split lip. Seker threw the energy sphere with a yell, and it hit the Jelery in the chest, sending him skidding through the leaf litter for three metres, leaving deep gouge marks in the soil. But he had held his footing. His clothes smouldered and smoked, but the flesh underneath remained untouched.

'You exceed your rank, Jelery. You should not have the knowledge or the strength to absorb a sphere of that magnitude. Your flesh should be burnt, yet you remain standing and whole. Impressive!' acknowledged Seker. 'Of course, you could throw one of your blue energy spheres at me, but we both know that it does not possess the strength to even mar my clothes. It wouldn't even burn paper, but you knew that all along, so you used your strength and threw those stones at me. Smart move on your behalf. I should have expected it. And that kick, well, you can see what it did to my face. I am going to enjoy your demise, Jelery. You have been a worthy foe.'

Seker raised his hands above his head, and a golden energy sphere began to grow above them. Its power was immense. Even an untrained eye could see the tiny particles of energy glittering and sparkling as they were drawn from all the living things around him into the ever-growing sphere. The Jelery was nearly spent and could only stare on in wonder. When the energy sphere was a metre in width, Seker threw it. It came as fast as a bolt of lightning, and the Jelery could do nothing except take it like a man. As it struck it seemed to envelop him before exploding with a brilliant flash. All the trees within a ten-metre radius were reduced to pillars of grey charcoal that toppled in a cloud of soot. Flames licked at the trees outside the radius, and the blackened figure of the Jelery lay smoking on the ground in a twisted heap. Seker studied his throbbing hands and frowned at the blisters that had formed on them. He looked at the destruction they had caused and smiled.

'A small price to pay for the power,' he stated.

Seker strolled back over to where his blade had fallen and picked it up, then advanced on the surprisingly unburnt smaller Jelery.

'Thank you for your help,' he said as he slit his throat and wiped the blood from the blade on the pants of the dying man. 'This is going to make my story a lot more convincing when I return to Monalteone,' said Seker as he gently prodded his bloodied and broken nose.

# 18

ATIOL STARED INTO the flickering flames that danced around the wood that sustained them, lost in deep thought.

'Do you have a clear idea of where we are supposed to be going?' inquired Toi-mun.

'No, not really. I only know that I am being drawn to the south like a moth to the light,' he answered.

'There is naught to the south except the cliffs of the sea, and they are void of human life,' Toi-mun informed him.

'I know this, Shadow, but I do not trouble my mind with it. He is there and that is all that matters.'

'Then to the south it is. You should sleep, Atiol. Save your strength. Something or someone is stalking us. The night is too silent,' warned Toi-mun. 'I do not sense anything with power that might concern me, but nonetheless, there may be more than Light Wielders with malevolence on the agenda.'

A strong wind swept in, snuffing out the fire completely. Toi-mun drew out his weapons and dropped into the fighter's stance ready for action. A golden sphere grew from Atiol's hand, illuminating them both in its golden glow.

'I have no ill will toward you, Atiol. I have come to warn you,' echoed a voice, soft and feminine.

'Who are you? I will speak with no one who will not show themselves,' replied Atiol.

The wind intensified and began to howl through the trees, stirring up a great cloud of dust and leaves, causing Atiol and Toi-mun to throw the hands up to protect their eyes. Then as suddenly as the wind had begun, it ceased. Atiol felt a warm hand upon his own as it was pulled from his eyes. A young woman, if that was what she was, stood in front of Atiol. She came only up to his chin in height, and was finely featured with large almond-shaped eyes that seemed to fill her face. The eyes were gentle and deep, yet stern, and Atiol could only gape as her long black hair blew about her like a silk sheet, whipping at her body, which was young and supple with the outward signs of womanhood.

Atiol had no real experience in dealing with women, especially one as achingly beautiful as this. With an embarrassing realisation, he tore his hand from her grasp and apologised sheepishly. In response, she gazed down at her bare feet as she smoothed the dress that clung to her like a second skin.

'Who are you?' asked Atiol once he had regained his composure.

'She is one of the Hiratan,' whispered Toi-mun.

'You are a Hiratan? I have never seen your kind before. What is it that you want from me?'

'Firstly, yes, I am a Hiratan. My father was human, and my mother was a wind Spirit, who was able to somewhat take on the form of a human female.'

'Much like yourself,' pointed out Atiol.

'Well, sort of, but I had a huge head start. Seeing that my father was human, I had to learn to take on the Spirit form.'

'Would not that have been difficult?' asked Toi-mun.

'Somewhat so, yes, but now it is as natural as, well, the wind itself,' she replied with a smile.

'Wait a moment – I thought only male Spirits did... that sort of thing with humans,' said Atiol awkwardly.

'What a silly notion. Wherever did you get it from?' The Hiratan giggled.

'So what is it that you have come to warn us about?' interrupted Toi-mun, trying to get the conversation back on track.

'I have come to warn you both that there are other Hiratan about, Hiratan born of the more malevolent Spirits from beneath the mountains; and they mean to do you harm,' she informed them.

'How are we to recognise them for Hiratan, as you pass rather well for a human?' implored Atiol.

'They have not the ability to take on the human form or, in fact, the Spirit form. They are stuck looking like creatures from your nightmares.'

'Why can they not take on such forms as you do?' asked Toi-mun.

'The malevolent Spirits that made them are primitive, and are only male. Though they can take the fleshly form, it has never been wholly human; and the humans that they have had relations with were never willing participants. They were raped. So the Hiratan that the human females bore were created in hate, spite, and pain, and were twisted from birth, and born into a rage that clouds their thoughts and renders most of their abilities useless. Do not get me wrong – they are powerful in their own way, and right now they are hunting you down. They intend to stop you from reaching Ushwinn. They want chaos. They want Spirits to rule the land. They despise the human race.'

'Well, they should go and confer with the Telirians. Their goals are nearly the same. They would be perfect bed partners,' said Toi-mun hatefully as he sheathed his weapons.

'They want the Jelery to disappear as much as the Telirians do, and although the Telirians do not know it, they are helping them when they can,' advised the female Hiratan.

'It would seem as though everyone would strive to see us fail in this task,' said Atiol despairingly.

'No, not everyone, Atiol, not everyone,' soothed the Hiratan as she ran the back of her hand gently down his cheek.

'You have not told us your name, Hiratan. I mean, if you have one,' said Toi-mun.

'My name is Shi-liarne,' she replied.

'We thank you for the warning, Shi-liarne,' said Atiol humbly.

'You are more than welcome, Atiol. I only hope that the next time we meet, it will be under better and friendlier circumstances. Farewell. Guard him well, Shadow,' she added as she disappeared in a swirl of leaves and dust.

'I wonder what she meant by friendlier circumstances,' pondered Atiol.

Toi-mun smiled and gently patted him on the back. 'I think she means to rob you of your purity, Atiol,' he said with a big smile.

Atiol blushed furiously. He walked over to the dormant fire and brought it back to life with a small golden sphere.

'Well, I cannot say that we were expecting anything like that,' announced Toi-mun.

'No, definitely not. Let us hope that nothing else unexpected happens tonight. I do not like the sound of a Hiratan hunting us,' confessed Atiol.

'If the Hiratan are made of flesh, then they can bleed, and if they bleed, they can die. Rest, Atiol. I will let no harm befall you,' promised Toi-mun.

Atiol took comfort in Toi-mun's reasoning and quickly fell asleep by the fire.

# 19

SEKER STUMBLED INTO the steward's quarters, trying to look as pathetic as possible. He had dry blood caked on the front of his shirt where it had flowed freely from his crushed nose. 'Master,' he blubbered as he sank to his knees.

The steward emerged from behind a large drape, clutching a quill that dripped red ink to the floor. 'Dorian, what happened to you? I mean, my gosh, look at you!' exclaimed the steward, discarding the quill.

'Master, I was set upon by a large group of bandits, who were going to rob me, slit my throat, and leave my corpse for the animals to feast upon,' explained Seker.

'What did you do, man?' asked the steward as he placed his hands on Seker's shoulders.

'My lord, I remembered all that you have taught me in such a short time, and with those skills, I fought them off as best as I could. But as you can see, I came off the worse for wear. Unfortunately, I am not on the same level as you, master.'

'Well, come now, Dorian. You cannot be expected to run before you have learned to walk,' gushed the steward.

'I know that you would have survived unscathed, and killed them for having the audacity to attack you in the first place. As it still stands, my master, I believe they are still lingering in the woods, waiting to prey upon the next unlucky citizen of your great city that stumbles upon them,' warned Seker.

'This atrocity will not go unpunished, though it is a blessing you survived this brutal attack, Dorian. A lesser man would have perished at their hands. I will send fifty of the city's finest guards to dispense with this rabble of thieves,' consoled the steward, squeezing Seker's shoulders with his thin pale fingers.

'My lord, can you spare so many men in such times? The city of Monalteone should keep all the men it can within its walls, especially with the disappearance of one of its guards under somewhat suspicious circumstances.'

'Come now, Dorian, fifty men will make no great impact on my city's overall defences. You must remember that there are people outside these walls who deserve my protection as well, and they shall receive it.'

'If that is your will, my master, then who am I to argue?' conceded Seker, smiling inwardly.

'Though I would ask one more thing of you, Dorian – it would please me greatly if you were to lead my men into battle,' stated the steward.

'My lord, you do me a great honour, and I will accept on the condition that you will accompany myself and your men. The people need to see your greatness, to have confidence in their patron,' began Seker as the steward listened intently. 'They need to feel safe in the knowledge that their steward is a man of action who will go into battle to defend his city and his people. If you do these things, the people will be saying your name for years to come. You will be remembered as the greatest steward in Monalteone's history, but you have to start doing things for yourself,' said Seker passionately, embracing his role.

'Dorian, your words send shivers through my body. You are a man of great foresight, and you are right – I will show the people my greatness, and my name shall become legend, the greatest Light Wielder of all. Yes, I can see it now. My name will strike fear into the hearts of my enemies,' fantasised the steward, whose face had become flushed with the thoughts of grandeur.

'Then you will lead your men?' asked Seker.

'We leave in the morning for battle and glory, Dorian.'

'For battle and glory, my master,' echoed Seker as the steward disappeared behind the curtain with his long green robe trailing after him on the polished floor.

# 20

ATIOL WOKE TO the smell of breakfast being served and Toi-mun's cursing.

'I did not think that the cooking of breakfast warranted such strong language,' Atiol said, yawning.

'It does when you don't exactly know how to cook it,' replied Toi-mun.

'Toi-mun, I am so hungry I could eat a lump of charcoal and enjoy it,' stated Atiol.

'Then that is a good thing.' Toi-mun handed Atiol a plate with several lumps of blackened food. Atiol raised an eyebrow and took a sample bite from one of the lumps. It crunched alarmingly.

'Charcoal for breakfast, it is,' said Atiol, smiling.

'My apologies. Cooking was not one of the skills that I felt I had to excel at.'

'Well, at least I can taste a faint trace of sausage, but the main thing is that it will fill my empty stomach,' consoled Atiol.

They sat in silence and chewed their food as they stared into the slowly dying flames. After their breakfast, they continued on. As they gradually made their way south, the voices in Atiol's head became more frequent and urgent to the point that he feared he might become as mad as a Raver. But when they came upon the vast expanse of the River Marset, the voices vanished as if they had been.

'The voices have finally quelled in my head,' said Atiol with great relief.

'I wondered why you were starting to act weird. Perhaps they stopped telling you all their troubles so that you could deal with your own,' answered Toi-mun, sweeping his arm at the fast-flowing water.

'I did not factor this into my plans,' admitted Atiol.

'Well, it is too deep and wide to cross. If we tried, the fast-flowing current would have us at its mercy, so what are we to do, Atiol?'

'We think our way around the obstacle. There has to be a way. There always is,' said Atiol matter-of-factly.

Ushwinn looked intently into his cup of tea, whispering in a strange tongue. The liquid rippled before solidifying with an image of Atiol and Toi-mun standing on the banks of the river. His tea rippled again and the landscape flew by with a bird's eye view, before descending rapidly into Strangle Light Woods in the exact vicinity of the two-winged Hiratan that were walking slowly, sniffing at the air and tasting it for traces of their prey. Ushwinn broke off his contact and drained his cup of tea in a single gulp.

'The Earth Spirits and their offspring could not resist an opportunity like this to interfere,' he said to himself, and he got to his feet with a sigh.

He shuffled over to a small cupboard and unlocked it with a small key he produced from his pocket. He reached in and retrieved a small silver case, roughly four inches in length, five inches wide, and two in depth. He placed it on his rough wooden table and opened it carefully to reveal four beautiful crystals lying in individual compartments that were lined with soft green felt. They were each as long as the little finger of a man and just as thick. The four crystals were individually coloured. There was green, blue, grey, and clear. They represented different elements of the land: the blue was for the water, green was for the trees and growing things, the grey was for the weather and lightning, and the clear crystal represented the wind.

Ushwinn carefully picked up the blue crystal. As he touched it, it sprang to life with a soft blue glow. He peered into the depths of the crystal and watched with a smile as the water contained within began to flow around in its confined space. Ushwinn picked up his staff from the table and placed the glowing crystal into a hole at the top of it which had been specifically designed to accommodate the crystals. He opened the door to his humble hut and went outside to a patch of bare ground. The sea breeze assaulted his sense of smell, and he breathed in deeply, filling his lungs with the cleansing salt air. He closed his eyes and firmly planted the staff onto the ground, with both his hands remaining on the polished wood. There he stood for a good thirty seconds before he began to chant in a low tone that seemed to resonate from the depths of the earth. And the crystal responded by glowing brighter until the faint sound of rushing water could be heard from it.

Atiol was startled from his thoughts by a large splash. An animal driven by a deep-seated primal fear had hurled itself into the river and was quickly caught by the swift current. Atiol and Toi-mun watched on as its head disappeared from view. Before they had a chance to comment on the strange event, a large boar ran past them and hurled itself into the river; it covered a good metre and a half across the surface before the river remembered it was a fluid and dragged the boar down to squeals of fright.

'What on earth is going on around here?' asked Toi-mun, springing to his feet.

'I think that whatever has been hunting us of late has decided to show itself at last,' answered Atiol.

With his hands on his weapons, Toi-mun looked around, carefully scanning for danger. Atiol firmly grabbed him by the shoulders and spun him around to look at the river. A hand made of water had emerged and was beckoning them to the river.

'Now, what do you make of that?' inquired Toi-mun.

'If I am not mistaken, I believe it is a water Spirit.'

'I know that, but what does it damn well want?' snapped Toi-mun.

'I think it is pretty clear,' replied Atiol, moving to the edge of the water.

'I would probably think through what you are considering,' warned Toi-mun, but he followed.

At first sight the hand resembled a clear glove filled with water. It disappeared under the water as they drew closer.

'Well, here goes nothing,' announced Atiol as he took a step out into the river. He almost thought himself a fool as his foot went below the waterline, but a strong hand caught it just below the surface and held it there, waiting. Atiol stepped off the bank with his other foot, and it was caught in the same fashion. He peered down into the water, and the strong handsome face of a male water Spirit, glowing a faint blue, looked back at him and winked mischievously. Atiol was almost thrown off balance as the water Spirit bore him across the river at great speed, leaving a trail of whitewash. As he neared the opposite side of the river, Atiol was launched out of the water. He landed momentarily on his feet before the momentum caused him to pitch forward into a tumble. The water Spirit popped its head above the surface and chuckled.

After seeing this display, Toi-mun was eager for his turn, and as the water Spirit caught his feet, he could not help but smile. The only difference between the two trips was that after being launched into the air, he landed gracefully on his feet.

'Now, that definitely gets the adrenaline pumping!' he exclaimed.

'That could come in rather useful. What do you make of those two?' asked Atiol as he gestured back across the river. On the other side of the river, the two Hiratan emerged from the trees, sniffing the air like a pair of hunting dogs. Toi-mun drew his weapons with shaking hands. The sound carried across the water, and the Hiratan's heads pivoted toward its source. They let out a screech of anticipation and want, then they both jumped into the air. Their wings snapped out to their full length, sounding like a slack sail suddenly hit by a strong breeze. They came across the water with tremendous speed, and bore down on Atiol and Toi-mun with malicious intent. When they were about three-quarters of the way across, a wall of water sprang up, and the two Hiratan smashed into it at full speed. The wall collapsed onto them like a giant fist closing, and dragged them down the river. They broke free of the water's grasp a little further down the river. They rose into the air again in an attempt to gain the riverbank, but another wave of water welled up to engulf them – but this time, it bore them back to where they'd started and slammed them viciously on to the rocks lining the river.

'I think we should leave while we still have the chance to do so,' advised Atiol, jogging away from the river.

'I think that would be advisable,' agreed Toi-mun as he followed Atiol.

The water Spirit grabbed the ankles of the two Hiratan and dragged them down under the rushing water. The Hiratan were dazed after the initial onslaught but they were thinking with more clarity as they sank deeper into the river's depths. They allowed the water Spirit to take them to the rocky bottom of the river before they sprang into action. They grabbed the water Spirit by his wrists with their taloned fingers, and pushed off from the riverbed with their enormous muscular legs. The water Spirit tried to free itself, but the Hiratan held firm. They broke free of the water with their struggling captive and ascended into the air. The water sprang up, tailing them high into the sky, then formed into a hand and clutched desperately at the panicking water Spirit, catching him around the midriff. The Hiratan's momentum slowed, but their height was too great for the water's hand, and it lost its grip. The hand crashed back down into the river like a huge boulder, displacing vast amounts of water onto the riverbanks and into the forest, drenching all that was in the vicinity. The

Hiratan chuckled to themselves. The chase had been momentarily forgotten. They had a gift to deliver to their father Spirits, deep within the mountains.

Ushwinn collapsed to the ground. His failed rescue attempt had left him spent and breathing heavily. The breaths soon turned into sobs of grief for his lost friend.

The two Hiratan flew with their captive high into the sky. On several occasions, they dropped the water Spirit and waited until the last possible moment to catch him before he hit the ground, just for their amusement. It took several hours to reach the mountain range they called home, and they entered via a cave halfway up the northern slope. They had to stoop as they navigated through the maze of tunnels to reach a large central cavern lit by the faint green glow of fungus that hung from the roof. The two Hiratan held their captive tight, digging their talons into him and drawing pale blue liquid from the wounds as they dragged him to the centre of the cavern.

'A gift for you, my fathers,' said one of the Hiratan as the water Spirit was thrown roughly to the ground.

A segment of rock broke away from the wall with a groan and an earth Spirit formed of solid rock walked toward the Hiratan. 'What happened with the Light Wielder?' it asked.

'We were closing in on him, but the Keeper of the Staff interfered,' replied the Hiratan with a bowed head.

'And what of this one?' it asked again, grabbing the water Spirit's jaw with one of its huge stone hands.

'He got in the way and tried to stop us from eliminating the Light Wielder,' informed the other Hiratan.

'Do you not see that by helping the Keeper of the Staff, we will all remain bound by it to share the land with the users and destroyers called humans?' asked the earth Spirit, squeezing more tightly on the water Spirit's jaw. The water Spirit remained silent and looked upon the earth Spirit with contempt.

'We will deal with you soon,' stated the earth Spirit as he released his hold.

Another segment peeled itself away from the wall. 'The Keeper of the Staff is aware of our intentions. We should not have expected anything less,' stated the other earth Spirit.

'We shall have to be a little less subtle,' said the first earth Spirit.

'What would you have us do?' asked the Hiratan.

'There is not much that we can do now that the staff keeper is alert to us. We must remain vigilant and wait for an opportunity to present itself,' replied the first earth Spirit.

'Yes, we could do that, or we could try to take the Staff from the Keeper,' supplied one of the Hiratan.

'And would you wield it, my son?' asked the other earth Spirit.

'No, I suppose not. I forgot in my haste that we cannot touch it lest it destroy us,' replied the Hiratan ashamedly.

'Be not so harsh on yourself. You had a good idea; it just wasn't thought out properly. If only humans could touch the Staff, how easy it would be to corrupt one to do our bidding,' said the first earth Spirit.

'Another Light Wielder would be able to touch the staff, just as long as he did not try to use it,' replied the other earth Spirit.

'Forgive my ignorance, father, but why can they not use it?' asked one of the Hiratan.

'Oh, they can use it if they want, but the Staff is... how would you say it?... enthusiastic. It has vast power within, and if they did not have the power to control the staff's enthusiasm, it would destroy them by trying to be helpful and filling them with its power to do the task they were attempting, or until they become overloaded with energy and exploded,' explained the earth Spirit. 'Go and find such a Light Wielder of the Telirian order. They are always greedy for power and will jump at the chance to have such a trophy,' it added.

'Take this and explain its use when you find the Light Wielder,' said the other earth Spirit, handing over an Iron Shadow's dagger. 'It may give him an edge when it comes to dealing with the Staff Keeper.'

'It will be done, father,' replied the Hiratan, and he exited the chamber followed by the other Hiratan.

'If the Light Wielder succeeds, what do you think he will do with the Staff?' asked the first.

'I could not care less, just as long as it is taken far away and forgotten; or better still, he destroys himself by trying to use it and the staff lies abandoned in the middle of a forest for all eternity. But enough talking, for I have a hunger that needs to be satisfied,' replied the other earth Spirit.

The earth Spirits converged on the cowering water Spirit, and its screams could be heard resonating throughout the mountain as they feasted.

# 21

THE FLAGS AND banners on the walls of Galteone stirred a little. Their white and green colours broke up the starkness of the ancient stone city. The members of the Council watched from a small balcony high in the Tri Tower as half of the city's armed guards marched in unison out of the city toward Monalteone.

'Do you believe we have acted wisely in our decision?' asked Yolstane.

'Of course, we have, you fool. Monalteone calls for our aid. Are we to ignore the pleas for help from the last city that holds true to our rule?' retorted Ter-hal harshly.

'No, of course not,' conceded Yolstane.

'I believe what Yolstane was trying to ask is, can we fully trust the character of this Anoole?' added Xaryn.

'What do you mean – the same way that you and Mek trusted that Raver Crawley in his selection of a Light Wielder?' enquired Ter-hal testily.

'There was more than one Raver heralding Atiol's coming, and it was agreed by the Council – all the Council – that it would be in our best interests to retrieve the child,' added Alourin calmly.

'It was only agreed to by the Council for the sole purpose of denying the Telirian another number, and in the end, it did us no good,' replied Ter-hal.

'Then who are we to believe the word of Anoole, if we do not believe the Ravers?' challenged Yolstane.

'Enough! Enough of this petty squabbling. Anoole is no crazy unstable Raver. He is a member of the house of nobles and was appointed to the position with my blessing, so if you are indirectly asking me whether I trust my own judgement, of course I do, and my decision is final!' screamed Ter-hal.

'Yet all this time, I thought the Council as a whole made the decisions,' stated Alourin quietly.

'I grow weary of this useless conversation. I am returning to my quarters, and I will not be disturbed,' growled Ter-hal, and he stormed off in a swirl of white cloth.

'Make sure the walls are manned with twice as many guards. We can at least make it look like we have a fair-sized army,' ordered Alourin to a guard standing near him.

'If the Telirians catch wind of this, they are sure to pounce. I just hope we are ready,' thought Alourin as he watched the departing guard.

# 22

SEKER RODE BESIDE the steward, who fidgeted around uncomfortably in his saddle. It had been a while since he had felt the need to ride, and his backside was suffering for it now. A quick glance at the steward showed he was white-knuckling his reins, which indicated to Seker that his nerves were beginning to fray.

'So, Dorian, are you entirely sure of their numbers?' asked the steward nervously.

'My lord, I am confident that with half a dozen men by your side, you would be able to subdue twice the number they have.'

'Yes, yes, of course I could, Dorian. It is just that I do not wish to see you get hurt again. I brought along the extra men for your protection. I mean, what sort of teacher would I be, if I allowed my star pupil to get killed hunting bandits?' stammered the steward nervously.

'My lord, you continue to astound me with your thoughtfulness, and I must confess I am fearing for my safety. It is as if you read my mind,' brown-nosed Seker.

'Come now, Dorian, you sing my praises too soon. I have not yet shown you what I can do,' gloated the steward.

'I wait in anticipation, Master.' A wave of power washed over Seker as he sensed his men, and he welcomed the upcoming slaughter with a deep breath as he closed his eyes.

'What is it, Dorian?' asked the steward.

'Oh, it is nothing, my lord. I am just enjoying the beautiful smells of the forest,' lied Seker smoothly.

The steward breathed deeply through his nose, trying to catch the same scent. 'It just smells like a dirty old forest to me. Give me the smell of fresh incense burning in my quarters any time,' he announced.

The group rode further into the forest under Seker's guidance, when the steward stopped abruptly. 'Do you sense it, Dorian?' asked the steward as he scanned the area worriedly.

'Sense what, my lord?' replied Seker with feigned ignorance. The steward had not the time to answer before the forest around him erupted with yelling armed men that swarmed toward his group. Fortunately, most of his men were not as cowardly as he and they reacted instantly, answering the charge with a volley of arrows that felled several of the closest attackers. But they came on undeterred and another volley did little to their momentum.

'Form to me, form to me!' ordered one of the steward's men in a voice that could be heard over all others. The men obeyed fluidly, and within seconds, the steward was surrounded. The attackers now faced a wall of horse flesh and sharpened steel.

'My lord, we have to get you out of here. You will travel in the centre of the wedge where it is safer. It will be nothing fancy – just a hack-and-run retreat. Are you ready?' asked the soldier.

The steward looked about feverishly. His face had turned ashen in colour. 'I said, are you ready, my lord?' asked the soldier more firmly.

The steward looked at the man with wide fright-filled eyes and nodded quickly.

'Charge the swine!' hollered the soldier, swinging his sword overhead.

The horses advanced and ploughed into the wave of attackers. Steel clashed against steel and what steel did not, cleaved flesh. Slowly, the wedge moved forward lubricated by blood. Seker could see that the wedge was working all too well and had almost broken free. For the sake of his mission, he had to act. He conjured up a golden energy sphere and in quick succession took down the horse of the self-appointed leader and the horses either side of him. With the tip of the wedge blunted, his men were able to cut into the horses from within the wedge, and they men poured into the gap like water into a bottle, cutting the steward's men's mounts out from underneath them with brutal efficiency, forcing them to the ground. But still they fought on.

'To me, men, to me!' came a screaming command above the din of battle.

Seker recognised the voice and cursed aloud. That man was a born leader. The men rallied to him, and again they formed the wedge. But without the horses to support them, the wedge failed, and soon only half a dozen men remained.

'Lay down your arms, you fools,' boomed a voice from amongst the attackers.

Seker's men halted their attack and allowed the steward's men to consider their options. They were all breathing heavily, and blood flowed freely from several wounds. Their self-imposed leader threw down his weapon, and the men followed suit.

'A very wise move,' said a man as he emerged from the packed ranks of Seker's men to stand in front of them.

'You are now all prisoners of Lord Delrain, and will remain so until further notice,' he announced coldly.

The steward was still on his horse and a strange look came into his eyes. 'Die, you Telirian scum! Prepare to feel the wrath of my power,' he screamed in an uncustomary burst of gusto.

'Stay behind me, Dorian. I will protect you,' he added.

The steward conjured a green energy sphere but never got to release it, as he slumped forward onto his saddle with a groan. 'Dorian?' he implored as he looked back at Seker in confusion.

Seker let out a snarl and hit him again with his elbow, knocking him out cold.

'Dorian, your protector seems to have had a little accident,' mocked one of his men with a chuckle.

Seker rolled his eyes in disgust and kicked the steward out of his saddle; he landed with a thump on the leaf litter of the forest floor. 'I leave you to disperse of this ragtag bunch of men calling themselves soldiers. You damn well nearly let them escape back to Monalteone,' he scolded. 'Learman, you are a halfwit. You knew very well that we would be coming on horseback, and yet you decided to attack on foot. That could have been forgiven if the horses were amongst the trees, and yet you let us come into a clearing,' he added angrily.

'They have all been accounted for, be it dead or alive,' replied Learman defensively.

'Shut up, you fool. Not only did you let them come into a clearing, you then mindlessly unleashed my men to fall upon the sword. This little endeavour of yours has cost far too many lives. You make an error of judgment like this again, and it will be you lying on the ground bleeding your life away into the dirt,' threatened Seker.

'Yes, my lord,' spat Learman as he stared venomously at Seker.

'Oh, and Learman, if you wish to test yourself against my authority, you have only to ask.'

'No, my lord, I do not wish that,' conceded Learman, lowering his eyes.

'Then, in future, do not look at me as you just did, or I will act before asking your mind. Now assemble the men, for I wish to speak to them,' ordered Seker, riding off.

# 23

'ATIOL, IS YOUR entire life going to be as eventful as the last couple of days? If so, I wish to resign immediately,' stated Toi-mun.

Atiol laughed out loud and shook his head, but he kept on walking.

Another night and day went by uneventfully, and slowly the grasslands became sparser, only to be replaced by outcrops of rock and boulders. Few trees were growing amongst the boulders, and when they crested a large hill, it became apparent why. They were immediately assaulted by a strong wind that whipped their clothes into a jig, and they were forced to seek shelter behind a large outcrop of rock as the gusts became fierce.

'If you can ignore the ferocity of the sea wind, you will find it to be rather informative.'

Atiol and Toi-mun flicked their attention toward the voice.

'Do not be startled, Shadow. I mean your Jelery no harm.'

'That is a little hard to swallow when you stand in the midst of a strong gale and yet neither your hair nor your robe moves at all,' replied Toi-mun, resting his hands on the handles of his weapons.

'Oh, I am sorry. Does it make you feel uncomfortable? There, is this better?' asked the man, and his clothes and hair came alive.

'No – my hair is so long it whips me in the face. You shall just have to put up with it,' stated the figure, stopping the flow of wind upon himself. As he approached them, Toi-mun drew his weapons. 'Are we really going to have to do it this way?' enquired the man.

'That is entirely up to you,' replied Toi-mun.

The stranger let out a long sigh. 'I really do not like weapons,' said the figure, gesturing gracefully with his hands. Two snake-like vines shot out of the ground and tangled themselves around Toi-mun's wrists and held him tight. With another little flick of his hands, Toi-mun was blown off his feet, sending him skyward. Still bound to the ground by the vines, he flapped around in the breeze like a human banner.

'A rather feisty fellow, that Shadow of yours! Now, am I to introduce myself?'

'No, I do not think that will be necessary, Ushwinn. After all, it is you whom I seek,' replied Atiol.

'Is it really me you seek, or is it the knowledge I possess? You do not have to answer that,' said Ushwinn, chuckling.

'That is a relief. I was not about to answer a question where the answer may offend the person who asked it.'

'I can see that the attitude of Ter-hal has influenced the teaching of Galteone's pupils. I imagine you could probably recite the one thousand and one rules and regulations of the "how to" and "when to" of conjuring an energy sphere,' scoffed Ushwinn.

'No, I never cared much for the so-called etiquette of the lordly Light Wielders. As for what I said before, my teacher Mek told me to "never knowingly insult someone that you are not sure you can defeat in battle",' replied Atiol smoothly.

Ushwinn chuckled to himself. 'Wise man, that Mek. If all that he taught you is as intelligent as that last statement, then you and I shall get along just fine. Well, I suppose we had better get out of this wind and get ourselves a nice cup of tea.'

Ushwinn placed his hand on Atiol's shoulder and steered him in the direction of his hut. 'Umm, do you think it would be at all possible to let my Shadow down?' asked Atiol.

'What? Oh yes, I suppose I could do that for you,' agreed Ushwinn. Behind them Toi-mun fell to the ground with a solid thud as the wind and the vines retreated into obscurity. 'You are invited as well, Shadow, as long as you can play nicely,' said Ushwinn.

Toi-mun replaced his weapons angrily and dusted himself off, muttering curses under his breath as he hurried to catch up.

# 24

THE STEWARD OF Monalteone awoke with a groan and a dull ache in his wrists that flared dramatically when he tried to move them.

'Your wrists and ankles are bound in iron, steward,' a voice informed him.

'I am not a steward anymore. Do not call me by that title. My name is Manar,' he replied sulkily.

'Well, Manar, are you going to sit up and hold a decent conversation with me?'

Manar struggled upright into a sitting position that was relatively comfortable. 'Oh, it is you. It is good to see you are still alive... I am sorry, I do not know your name,' said Manar.

'It is Thaloss.'

'Well, Thaloss, we almost made it out back there,

but it is apparent that I was being led by the nose, so to speak, by that sneak Dorian.'

'His name is Seker. I have heard the men of the camp whispering his name. He is Delrain's second in command, his general,' supplied Thaloss.

'Well, I suppose I should be flattered that one so high up in the Telirian ranks was sent to deceive me,' muttered Manar, consoling himself.

'That was just the first part of his scheme. While you have been snoozing this last day and a half, a force, some two thousand strong, is drawing near. They were sent from Galteone to their deaths. There is a traitor named Anoole on the house of nobles. He has somehow convinced the old cronies on the Council that Monalteone is in danger and needs immediate reinforcements.'

'How do you know of these things?' asked Manar.

'Seker gave his men what he believed to be a stirring little speech about the imminent demise of the Jelery, and how they will rise to their rightful place, and a lot of other such nonsense he thought was important.'

'When are the troops from Galteone set to arrive to the slaughter?' asked Manar.

'They would be almost at the site of the ambush as we speak.'

'I am such a fool. Why did I not see the deceptiveness of Seker? If I had been paying closer attention, I would have alerted Galteone to be on the lookout for Telirian mischief; but now, because of my ignorance, a lot of good men are going to die,' moaned Manar in self-pity.

'Stop. You're snivelling. We may not be able to save those men, but there is a whole city full of people under your protection. Where do you think this murdering horde of bastards will be going to go next? They will sack Galteone, kill all within, and then they will come to Monalteone and do the same, unless we can warn everyone to get out before it happens.'

'What did you have in mind for getting us free? I am bound in chains,' despaired Manar.

'Have some faith in yourself, man. Are you not Jelery? Do you not possess great strength?' scolded Thaloss. 'If I could slap you, I would, you fool. Now break those damned chains.'

Anger flashed across Manar's face, and he began to pull against the chains that bound him. His muscles trembled and began to ache, but finally he felt the power surge into him. His hands felt as if they were being drawn apart by unseen helpers and slowly the chains came apart as if the links were made of soft clay. With the power still surging through him, he snapped the chains on his ankles. Then the power left him abruptly. It left him with pain in his hands that felt like molten fire.

'You did it, Manar,' said Thaloss excitedly. 'Now untie the knots and free my hands – hurry!' urged Thaloss.

'I thought a lot more of us were taken captive,' speculated Manar.

'There were. They have been taken one by one for the amusement of the soldiers, who had to stay behind. I think they're still occupied with their latest victim,' replied Thaloss, clenching and unclenching his fists to stimulate a bit of blood flow into his hands. He helped Manar get to his feet, then carefully lifted a corner of the tent flap up and cautiously peered out. 'Finally, a little bit of luck. The guards have abandoned their post. Hurry up, and stay behind me,' he ordered.

The two of them slipped quietly into the back alleys of the tented city that had popped up like mushrooms between the trees of the forest. The sounds of boasting and laughing interspersed with muffled cries of pain caught Manar's ears and he strayed toward the sound.

A tree branch served as the torture rack, and the man – if that was what he had been – was strung from it by his hands. His face was a pulped mass of meat, and several of his teeth were stuck to his chest in the blood that sluiced from his wounds. His arms were bent at odd angles, and the white of a bone stuck through the skin on one of them. The blood welled freshly where the ears once were and splattered on the victim's shoulders. One of the captors broke away from his comrades and lifted the victim's head up by the hair and spat into his face. Manar was flushed with rage, but a hand clamped around his mouth and silenced him.

'Shh, it is only I,' announced Thaloss. 'Let us go while we still can.'

They slipped out of the camp unimpeded, and were soon in the forest heading toward Monalteone.

They arrived at the gates just as the cool of the evening was upon them.

'There is much to be done. There is no telling when the bunch of murderous bastards are going to come knocking at the gates,' advised Thaloss.

'You are right. These walls were not designed for a siege and we must evacuate the city. It will take several days to prepare, and we have but two hundred men at the city's disposal. We must make our way to Galteone,' agreed Manar.

'That would be for the best, but if Galteone itself is under siege, head to Weolm. Skirt through the forest out of sight and you will come upon Weolm Pass. That road should be unguarded, and you will have freedom of movement whichever way you go. And you must do this alone,' advised Thaloss.

'And what of you?' asked Manar.

'I will make my way to Galteone. The Council must be informed of this treason. Good luck, Manar, until the next time we meet,' replied Thaloss as he slapped Manar on the shoulder and set off to commandeer a horse.

# 25

ATIOL AND TOI-MUN followed the old man into his shabby little hut and sat themselves down on the only chairs available to them.

'Unfortunately, I do not have a vast range of tea available, but I think this brew will suffice,' said Ushwinn as he passed them two steaming wooden cups brimming with liquid. Atiol took a sip, and a calming warmth spread throughout his body and left a spicy, orange-flavoured residue in his mouth. 'Tea is like an outfit that you only wear at certain events or times of the season. You're drinking what I like to call autumn rays. It is perfect for chilly evenings such as this one,' explained Ushwinn.

'Well, whatever you call it, the taste is delicious,' agreed Toi-mun as he drained his cup.

'Of course, tea has other uses than just warming the body. Look into yours, Atiol, and tell me what you see.'

'I do not see a thing besides the tea,' confessed Atiol.

'You have to open yourself up to the Spirits that are all around you. They have a great deal to show you. Now look again,' encouraged Ushwinn.

Atiol gazed deeply into his cup, and its inky blackness slowly morphed into blurry shapes: a forest, armed men that he somehow knew were not good in heart or mind, marching single-mindedly toward something. The cup exploded unexpectedly and showered his hands with its scalding liquid.

'If you let the Earthbound Spirits into your being, then you also let in their power,' advised Ushwinn.

'What was I looking at?' enquired Atiol as he wiped his hands on his pants.

'Simple. You were seeing something that the Earthbound Spirits wanted you to see. In time, and with practice, you will be able to control the scrying to see what you need to see,' replied Ushwinn.

'I saw many, many armed men...'

'I know what you saw for I have also seen it myself,' interrupted Ushwinn.

'Who are they and where are they marching to?' asked Atiol.

'Come now, Atiol. With everything that is happening in the land, I think you know the answer to that.'

'The Telirian war machine is on the move, and they are heading toward Galteone. They plan to finally strike at the heart of Jelery power. For them, the war has started in earnest,' theorised Toi-mun.

Ushwinn raised a snowy white eyebrow at Toi-mun in surprise. 'Your Shadow seems to have some brains to go along with his brawn, but he has only guessed the half of it. Lord Delrain's right-hand man Seker has led a sizeable force into the outskirts of Monalteone and has sprung a cunning trap against some two thousand soldiers from Galteone. They believed that they were on their way to bolster Monalteone's forces, who were supposedly under siege by the Telirians.'

'What of the soldiers, Ushwinn? How have they fared?' asked Atiol with worry in his voice.

'I am afraid they have suffered the same fate as your teacup, Atiol.'

'Two thousand soldiers – all of them dead,' despaired Atiol.

'That is one-third of Galteone's armed forces. Word must be spread to the other major cities. They will send many men to our aid. They must,' said Toi-mun.

'In the past, such a course of action would have proven to be fruitful, but the cities have been poisoned by the Telirians. For many years, they have been planting their agents throughout them. Their numbers have grown extremely well and they now hold much sway within the political circles of each city,' said Ushwinn.

'Then what size force will Delrain send against Galteone, Ushwinn?' asked Atiol.

'Some ten thousand or so,' he replied.

'That many soldiers will wipe Galteone off its foundations and kill all the people who dwelt within. We must return and warn the Council of this impending doom,' declared Atiol rising to his feet.

'It cannot be you. That is not your part in all of this,' rebuked Ushwinn, placing a steadying hand on Atiol's forearm.

'Then what is my purpose, old man, if it is not to save my closest friends?' asked Atiol, roughly shrugging away the hand.

'Your task is to learn what you need to save the land and all its inhabitants,' said Ushwinn with neutrality.

'No easy task in any case,' added Toi-mun.

'Your Shadow speaks the truth, Atiol. What you need to do will be no easy task.'

'I care not for what he has to say. I am going back to Galteone right away!' shouted Atiol as he made his way to the door.

The door locked with a soft click, and Atiol glanced angrily at Ushwinn. 'I would advise you not to try and stop me, old man,' he threatened. He grabbed the door and tried to wrench it back, but the door did not budge an inch. Atiol tried again, assisted by the energy from the land, and the whole cabin shook as he pulled on it with all his might. But still the door stood fast.

'Now you leave me with no choice,' he growled. He threw a golden energy sphere at the door. But about an inch before it made contact, it sizzled and sparked as it hit a shield wall that flushed purple as it absorbed the energy.

'Just a little shield wall I had ready in case you became a little foolish,' supplied Ushwinn. 'Your energy spheres will have little to no effect on it. Are you ready to learn yet, Atiol?' asked Ushwinn.

Atiol stood fast and snarled his reply. 'It would seem as though one has no choice in the matter.'

'I knew you would come to your senses. Now sit down, please,' asked Ushwinn, patting the chair. Atiol sat down stiffly. 'You must understand, Atiol, that things have been set in motion that cannot be stopped, and the sooner you grasp the concept, the more at ease your mind will become.'

'You knew this was to happen a long time ago, and you did nothing to stop it,' accused Atiol.

'Yes, I know a lot of things that are going to happen, but I do not know the events leading up to them nor the time frame in which they are to happen. The Spirits have no concept of time. It is one of their shortfalls. I suppose that would happen if you lived as long as they have,' explained Ushwinn. Atiol and Toi-mun stared silently at the old man. 'But the one thing I do know for certain is that these current events have brought you to me, and I know that this is a good thing. I can feel it in my heart, as I know you do. Otherwise why would you have travelled all this way? It certainly was not for the cup of tea, even though it is quite good.'

Toi-mun smiled to himself. 'He is right, Atiol. The tea is rather good.'

Atiol chuckled deeply despite his mood. 'Yes, I suppose he is right.'

'What, about the tea?' asked Toi-mun.

'Yes, about the tea, and about everything else, you fool,' answered Atiol half-heartedly.

'Then you still wish to learn, Atiol?'

'Yes, Ushwinn, as I said earlier, it would seem as though I have no choice in the matter. But promise me this, Ushwinn – you will send word to give Galteone some warning.'

'Fear not, Atiol. There will be warning, but not from me, for what good will it do?' replied Ushwinn with softening eyes.

'Well, then where do we begin?' asked Atiol.

# 26

THALOSS RODE HARDER than he ever had in his life. His mount was wavering, and he had to alternate between riding and running along beside the horse. He slept little and ate even less, stopping only occasionally to drink, and to water the horse. One foot in front of the other was the only thought in his mind as the sweat dripped into his eyes and blurred his vision, so he did not immediately pick up on the fact that the packed dirt and leaf litter had given way to dirty cobblestones. The sweet sound of the River Marset had begun to fill his ears, and he looked up to see the giant Tri Tower looming over the city of Galteone.

The guard pounded on the door of Ter-hal's more opulent quarters.

'Why are you bothering me?' snapped Ter-hal.

'I am sorry to bother you, my lord. A soldier from Monalteone needs to speak to you, and it looks as though he rode hard to get here.'

'Then you had better show him in,' ordered Ter-hal.

'Straightaway, my lord,' replied the guard.

Still breathing and sweating heavily, Thaloss stepped into Ter-hal's chambers.

'You asked to speak with me,' accused Ter-hal as he cringed from the strong odour that Thaloss emitted.

'My lord, a small army has infiltrated your lands, and they bear the mark of the Telirians–'

'And they are laying siege to your city as we speak,' finished Ter-hal. 'This is old news to me. I have sent some two thousand troops to the aid of Monalteone.'

'My lord, we were never under any siege,' stated Thaloss.

'No siege! Then why call for aid?' muttered Ter-hal as he sat heavily in his armchair.

'My lord, are you all right?' asked Thaloss as he saw Ter-hal's face whiten in shock.

Ter-hal waved him away. 'I am fine, I am fine. You must tell me everything, and leave no detail out no matter how trivial it may seem to you.'

Ter-hal's face grew visibly paler as Thaloss recounted all he knew, from the day that Seker first appeared at Monalteone's gates, to his own feverishly fast journey to Galteone and his arrival at Ter-hal's quarters.

'I have been openly deceived.'

'As have we all, my lord,' consoled Thaloss.

'Guards!' bellowed Ter-hal angrily.

'Yes, my lord,' replied the guard as he entered the quarters.

'Take a few of the city watch and go round up the traitor Anoole. I dearly wish to speak to him,' ordered Ter-hal.

'My lord, what you command is impossible. The noblemen Anoole departed the city some two days ago.'

'What? To where?'

'To his estate, I assume, my lord.'

'My lord, this is just confirmation of Anoole's treason. What sane man would willingly venture into the countryside knowing full well that the enemy was beyond the gate?' interjected Thaloss.

'A man who has nothing to fear from our enemies because he too is our enemy,' replied Ter-hal.

'My lord, while it is too late to stop Anoole, there are going to be some four hundred men, women, and children and the remaining soldiers of Monalteone, heading to Galteone via the Weolm Pass. As we speak, it is most likely that they are deep in the forest and may need further protection,' advised Thaloss.

'Your words ring true. I will send two hundred men to wait on the Weolm Pass, to assist them in whatever way they can. Let us just hope that the Telirians are not to be enticed by the entrée, but hunger for the main course – Galteone.'

'I thank you for your assistance, my lord,' replied Thaloss, dropping his head in submission.

'It is I who should be thanking you, good man. Now, it looks as though you could certainly use some food and a good bath. I will call one of my personal servants to attend to you.'

'My lord is too kind, but I wish to travel with the soldiers. After all, they are my friends out there,' thanked Thaloss.

'As you wish. I will not detain you if that is your will. Good luck. I hope you find them all and bring them to safety.'

Thaloss bowed deeply and left Ter-hal's quarters.

Later that day, the promised troops, accompanied by Thaloss, rode out of the gates of Galteone, over the River Marset and on to the Weolm Pass in the hope that Monalteone's people had not fallen into enemy hands.

Bodies littered the forest floor. Those that twitched or still showed signs of life had their throats cut or their skulls caved in with a mace to make sure they were deceased.

'It was a complete rout, Seker. All are dead, and there will be no prisoners just as you requested. We only lost about one hundred men,' reported Learman.

'An acceptable loss. Tell the men to collect all the reusable arrows from the fallen, for they shall need them later,' replied Seker, wiping the blood from his dagger. 'When they are finished, tell them to prepare for departure. We make our way to Galteone. Lord Delrain meets with us in less than two days' time. Pick thirty or so men to stay behind and wait in ambush. There may be others to catch in this trap,' he commanded.

'So we are not to proceed to Monalteone?'

'No, it would be a pointless endeavour, for when the news of Galteone's demise reaches their ears, they will swear allegiance to Lord Delrain. They will have no other option.'

'And if they refuse to do so?' asked Learman.

'Well, then you get to kill them, Learman, my blood thirsty friend. Perhaps you may get your fill of blood when we sack Galteone.'

'It is possible but highly unlikely,' replied Learman as he thumped Seker on the shoulder.

# 27

THE DAY WAS warm and bright, and a gentle breeze caressed their clothes as Toi-mun followed Atiol and Ushwinn to the edge of a towering cliff that overlooked the ocean.

'Toi-mun, this is as far as you can go,' informed Ushwinn.

Toi-mun looked over the edge of the cliff at the waves crashing onto the rocks far below, and pulled back. 'It would seem the same for you as well,' replied Toi-mun.

'Do you trust me, Atiol?' asked Ushwinn.

'So far, yes,' he replied.

'Good. Because that is our destination,' informed Ushwinn, pointing to a small island.

'Now follow me,' he ordered. Ushwinn took a step out over the edge of the cliff between two inconspicuously placed boulders, and disappeared into thin air as he fell.

'Well, off you go. Follow him,' said Toi-mun, smiling.

Atiol looked hatefully at Toi-mun, who was still smiling. He took a deep breath as he stepped off the cliff, half expecting it to be his last. He fell freely and began to yell, then landed solidly on his feet and pitched forward on the wooden planks of a rope bridge.

'Graceful, so good of you to join me,' uttered Ushwinn.

'This certainly was not here before,' noted Atiol as he stared at the great length of the bridge that swayed alarmingly in the breeze.

'Well, you have not been here before, but the bridge has been in this place all along.'

Atiol spun around and checked to see if the ropes of the bridge were firmly anchored into the stone of the cliff face. He gingerly placed his hand on the rock and was reassured to find it solid enough.

'Toi-mun!' he yelled.

'Do not bother with that. He is unable to hear you,' informed Ushwinn.

'Nonsense. He is only just above us on the edge of the cliff,' retorted Atiol.

'That is true, but he is not in the same time as us. We are in a time rift, Atiol, for we are going to be here for a long while. At the same time, it will seem like a short while for him,' explained Ushwinn.

'Then why did we not see the rope bridge from above, and yet we can see the island in both here and back there?' asked Atiol, gesturing over his shoulder to where he thought Toi-mun to be.

'The island has always been in the same spot, but like I said, it is just in another time. And as for the bridge, it has not yet been built in the other time, and by the time it has been, it would have well and truly rotted or been replaced with a new one.'

'So in years to come, if I came across this place and saw the bridge and deemed it safe to cross, I could very well find myself dead on the rocks below, having stepped off thinking that there was a bridge, when all the while it could have rotted away an age ago?' said Atiol full of confusion.

'Yes, precisely. Now you are getting it. Start to understand these simple things, and the rest will be easy,' confirmed Ushwinn enthusiastically.

'What if other people come onto the island when we are there? Will not they see us?' asked Atiol, trying to understand.

'Yes and no. They will see us but only as – how do the humans put it? – as ghosts, because we will both be there but at different times, and it is unavoidable to detect someone else in the same space even though it is technically not the same space, if you know what I mean,' said Ushwinn with a wink.

'No, I'm afraid not. So Toi-mun can't hear us because we are not here?' replied Atiol, rabbit-earing his fingers on both hands.

'Nor can he try to follow us. If he tried, he would fall to his death, for only Light Wielders can enter a time rift.'

'What! So even if in the future he could see the bridge, he would still not be able to walk on it even though it is in his time, so to speak?'

'Yes,' replied Ushwinn.

'Is that not a little dangerous for anyone who happens to walk by in the future?'

'Most likely. You could erect a sign if you like, when we return,' offered Ushwinn. 'But it would be a bit confusing for most to understand. *Here, in the future, which would now be the present, if you see a bridge, do not try to cross it, and if you are reading this in the past and cannot see a bridge, do not try to cross what appears to be thin air, for both cases will result in death on the rocks below.*'

'Yes, I suppose you are right,' replied Atiol sheepishly. 'So why has no other Light Wielder known about this time rift?'

'Because both of the Light Wielder factions have become ignorant and are too wrapped up in their self-importance to remember the old teachings.'

'So there are more than one?'

'Many more. Now come along. You have a lot to learn and, I dare say, a lot to clean. I have not been here myself for over three months,' ordered Ushwinn.

'When you say three months, what time frame are we talking about – the here and now, or back there?' asked Atiol cautiously.

'You can decide that for yourself when we get there,' replied Ushwinn.

'That never means anything good,' muttered Atiol as he followed behind the old man.

Toi-mun shook his head in disbelief and walked away from the cliff. 'They can keep that sort of thing for themselves,' he said to the breeze – the breeze that had picked up considerably. Then a prickle of recognition washed over him and he chanced on an idea. 'Shi-liarne, is that you?' he asked, feeling instantly foolish for talking to the wind.

A soft feminine chuckle echoed around him. 'Oh, well done,' she congratulated. him 'Most never even have the inkling that I am around,' she added as she materialised before Toi-mun's eyes.

'Do you spy on people often?' asked Toi-mun with a raised brow.

'Only those who have the same agenda as mine, and in whom I have a certain other interest,' she replied with a raised brow on her own. Toi-mun coughed uncomfortably under the seductive stare and turned away quickly to avoid the arousing thoughts that had begun to sink into his brain. 'But fear not, Toi-mun. My interest with you at this time is simply to warn you. Keep an eye on Atiol. The Spirits are stirring into action, and they will soon set their plans in motion if he fails at reinforcing the age-old treaty.'

Toi-mun went to respond, but Shi-liarne had already drifted off into the breeze and disappeared into clear air. He shook his head and kept walking to Ushwinn's hut, which was to be his home for a while.

# 28

TER-HAL WAS STANDING beside the open window of his quarters, watching the birds circle slowly over the city, when a loud knock interrupted his birdwatching. 'Enter,' he ordered.

The guard entered and said, 'My lord, Crawley wishes to speak to you.'

'Send him away. Tell him I do not have the time.'

'My lord, even though it looks like Crawley, I have the distinct impression that is not he who has brought himself to you. He will not be turned away,' said the guard.

'Indeed he will not,' said Crawley as he pushed past the guard and came into Ter-hal's quarters. 'I can clearly see that you are run off your feet,' he added sharply as he looked around the room.

'Leave us,' ordered Ter-hal, waving the guard out of the room. 'And who am I speaking with?' he asked with a slight sneer.

'It matters not, but what does matter is what you decide to do with the thousands of lives in your care. The time has come to evacuate the city!' demanded Crawley.

'I must be talking to Freom, judging from the irrational content. Well, Freom, on what basis do you make this call?'

'It is imminent, Ter-hal. You cannot win this battle. Do not condemn all in the city to death. You must leave for Weolm. It is neutral in this war. It still has not chosen either path, and will welcome you, at least for now.'

'If my people cannot be defended here in Galteone, then there is nowhere that they can be. No, my friend, there will be no evacuation,' announced Ter-hal calmly.

'You fool, the Earthbound Spirits hear the sound of many feet coming, and they head for Galteone. They toll like a drum. They toll your demise, and grow louder with each passing minute!' yelled Crawley.

'I have made my final decision on the matter. Now if you would not mind, you can show yourself out,' replied Ter-hal, and he turned his back to Crawley.

A green sheen passed over Crawley's eyes, and he stared blankly around the room, attempting to gain his bearings. 'Oh, I am sorry, Ter-hal. I must have been daydreaming and accidentally wandered into your quarters.'

Ter-hal spun around and eyed Crawley with suspicion. 'That is quite all right, Crawley,' he replied as he relaxed his face into a smile. 'Sometimes we just forget ourselves,' he added, guiding Crawley out through the door with his hand on his back.

# 29

THE CAVE BLOCKED out the chilly sea breeze, and a damp musty smell took over from the tang of the salt air.

'Well, it is not much, but it is to be home for a little while,' announced Ushwinn.

Atiol scanned the cave, and as his eyes slowly adjusted to the gloom, they saw a rudimentary fireplace with the usual cooking utensils (and judging by the amount of dust, it had been a long while since it had seen use); a worn but well-built table housed a couple of chairs; and several large screens of ageing thatch which blocked the rear of the cave that housed the sleeping quarters.

'As I said, I have not been here for a while,' confessed Ushwinn. He ran his finger along the length of the table, gouging a grove in the dust. 'You will find a spring-fed well at the back of the cave. Fetch a pail of water, and

I will get the fire going whilst you clean up. And then I will see what I can rustle up for supper.'

Atiol soon returned with the pail of water, but unfortunately, the pail's best days were well behind it, and only a few cupfuls of water remained in it.

'Well, you will not get a lot of cleaning done in a great hurry if that is all the water you could collect,' remarked Ushwinn.

'Do you have another bucket, then? This one is full of holes and leaking rather badly at the seams,' retorted Atiol testily.

'Umm, no, I do not. You will just have to pick it up,' replied Ushwinn.

'Hence the bucket.'

I told you I do not have another.'

'Well, it seems as though we have a problem,' stated Atiol.

'No,' chuckled Ushwinn, 'not we – you. And I already told you to pick it up.'

Ushwinn looked with intent at the leaking pail, and much to Atiol's dismay, the small amount of water rose like an energy sphere made of water, then dropped back down into the pail with a splash. 'You have a lot to learn, but on the positive side, your previous training has given you a good start. You can already conjure the energy around you and shape it into a ball of visible energy,' explained Ushwinn. 'That task that is a lot harder than shaping a pre-existing and readily available substance into a ball, wouldn't you say? So go fetch me some water.'

Atiol walked back to the well, muttering curses all the way. He sat down heavily. He knew the water was down there as he could smell it. So he sat in silence and concentrated on the water. He had lost track of all time when a single drop of water rose above the top of the well. He smiled triumphantly, but in doing so relaxed his concentration, and the drop fell back down. Atiol smashed his fist into the floor in frustration, skinning his knuckles in the process. 'Damn it!' he growled as he sucked the welling blood from his knuckles.

'Frustration will only impede your progress,' said Ushwinn, as he walked over to where Atiol sat.

'I know. It is just so damn–'

'–frustrating,' finished Ushwinn.

'Exactly. I have had no trouble in the past with my learning abilities. In fact, I excelled in all the aspects of Jelery learning, but this is perplexing me,' conceded Atiol as he dropped his head.

'Perhaps you are going about it the wrong way. Sometimes you cannot force things. Have you tried working with the water?'

'I do not understand,' said Atiol.

'Stand up, boy,' commanded Ushwinn. 'Now get me to move to the wall, if you can,' he goaded.

'I don't see the point in this,' argued Atiol.

'Just do it!' yelled Ushwinn. Atiol shoved the old man, but Ushwinn did not budge.

'Put some effort into it.'

Atiol placed his hands on Ushwinn's chest and pushed with his whole body, but Ushwinn, stood like a rock, unmoved. 'Keep going. Try harder, harder, Atiol.'

He struggled with Ushwinn for a good five minutes and had not achieved any backward motion when Atiol dropped to his hands and the sound of his heavy breathing filled the cave.

'Well, that got you nowhere fast, did it?' Atiol shook his head. 'Why did not you just ask me to move to the wall? Well, are you going to ask me?'

'Ushwinn, can you please move to the wall?' asked Atiol.

'Certainly. It would be my pleasure,' replied Ushwinn as he moved to the wall. 'Much easier than pushing, don't you think?' asked Ushwinn with a smile.

'You didn't tell me that I could just ask you to move,' replied Atiol, feeling a touch embarrassed.

'Nor did I tell you to start pushing me. You came up with that bright idea on your own, and on your own the rest of this exercise must continue. I will have dinner ready for you when you feel the need.'

Atiol watched Ushwinn walk out of sight and felt an even greater sense of awe and confusion about the old man. He immersed himself in the task and lost track of time, until a while later he emerged with his hands cupped together and came over to where Ushwinn was seated. He carefully opened his hands, and a three-inch sphere of water hovered a moment, then slowly rose up to his face where it distorted his smile of triumph. It rose above his head and slowly began to orbit his head like a personal moon before it came back to rest lightly on the palm of his hand.

'Well done, Atiol, and to think it only took you two and a half days to learn that. Now you must be hungry,' congratulated Ushwinn.

At the mention of food, Atiol's stomach ached with its emptiness, and he dropped the sphere to the floor with a splash. 'Well, now that you mention it,' said Atiol.

Ushwinn served a thick fish stew that was lightly seasoned, and a good solid chunk of freshly baked brown bread. Both disappeared very quickly, and Atiol was on to his second bowl of stew before Ushwinn's comment had sunk in.

'Two and a half days to learn, hmm, not bad,' he thought as he inhaled another spoonful.

# 30

TOI-MUN COLLECTED THE snare, and tied the rabbit to the others. It had been over a week since Atiol and Ushwinn had departed, and the food in Ushwinn's hut had all but disappeared. In his search for fresh game he had travelled northwest, and back over the River Marset at a ford close to the mountains of Telirian-held land; and he'd travelled northeast for several more days until the forest once again supported life and was not poisoned by its proximity to Arama. He picked up his collection of rabbits and set off in search of a farmhouse that would be willing to trade some of their food staples for his freshly caught bunnies.

Delsain crouched low behind the snagging thorn bush and watched as the unknown man slung the rabbits over his back. Seeing them had caused an explosion of saliva in his mouth, and his stomach rumbled along in sympathy.

He had eaten very little since he had hauled himself out of the brackish water, coughing and vomiting.

For two days he had drifted in and out of pain-filed consciousness until he was discovered by an old woman who was in the process of collecting plants and fungus. She was too old and frail to move him any considerable distance, so she had constructed a crude shelter over him where he lay. She had fed him, and luckily for Delsain, had a good knowledge of the healing arts, and had taken care of the burns that covered his body. He had shown his gratitude by throttling her, which almost proved to be a big mistake. She had fought like an animal, and he was almost throttled himself. He had lost his great strength and the ability to conjure energy, an infliction he believed was only temporary.

He collected anything of use that he could find. But the old lady's meagre supplies had not lasted long, and he was in the process of finding a new victim to donate their belongings to him. He clenched his hands into fists then unclenched them, testing for the strength which, as he predicted, had slowly started to return. He was by no means outrageously strong, and although the stranger was short and muscular, he had no doubt that with a little bit of surprise on his side, he would take him down easily enough.

Delsain picked up a large rock and threw it as hard as he could into the undergrowth. The stranger turned his head and his attention to the sound, and Delsain ran toward him. Delsain dove through the air, planning to ram his shoulder into the spine of the stranger. The worst-case scenario would be that he only knocked the stranger to the ground, and the best case would be if he were to hit him flush enough that he would break the stranger's back and paralyse him. The stranger, however, stepped elegantly to the side, moving impossibly quickly for someone his size. He allowed Delsain to crash to the forest floor, where he landed with a short bark as the wind was knocked out of him. Within the blink of an eye, Toi-mun had his knees on his attacker's back and one of his sickles pressed up against his throat.

'Now do you wish to try that again, or have you had enough?' asked Toi-mun as he applied more pressure to the blade.

'Please, I was... I am starving and need something to eat. Please,' begged Delsain.

'If you are hungry, the polite thing would have been to ask,' replied Toi-mun, and he hesitantly withdrew his blade and got to his feet. Delsain rolled over and Toi-mun gawked at the sight of the man's burnt flesh and turned to hide his revulsion.

He turned back and offered his hand to the fallen stranger. 'Let us start again, shall we?' Delsain looked at the hand that was being offered to him and took it, knowing it was his only option. Toi-mun pulled him to his feet, noting, but not showing, the repulsion that filled him when he touched the man's scarred and scaly hand.

'I am Toi-mun, and you are?' he enquired as he sheathed his sickle.

'Delsain. I am Delsain,' he replied, taking back his hand.

Toi-mun studied Delsain's burnt face and neck. It was obvious that he had sustained massive burns that were still freshly healing, all of which raised questions. But the questions could be answered later. 'Well, Delsain, I was going to trade a few of these when I found a farmhouse, but since you and I are here, I say that we have some lunch.' Delsain nodded his agreement. 'Well, as the guest, I must insist that you gut and skin, and I will get a fire going,' added Toi-mun.

Toi-mun drew out his dagger and cut two rabbits from the string. Delsain saw the oily sheen of the black dagger and had to stifle a gasp. This at least explained his quick reflexes and confidence. This man was one of the Iron Shadow. But where was his ward?

'Do you have a knife to perform the job?' asked Toi-mun, interrupting Delsain's train of thought.

'Yes, of course,' he replied, pulling out a small knife with a curved blade.

'A herb gatherer's blade,' thought Toi-mun, 'yet he is definitely not one.' Toi-mun got the fire going, and soon the rabbits were roasting over the flames. Their juices sizzled as they dripped onto the coals. 'So, Delsain, tell me about yourself.'

'There is not all that much to tell,' replied Delsain as he ripped a back leg off one of the rabbits.

'Well, it will not take too long to tell,' stated Toi-mun.

Delsain looked over his rabbit leg and swallowed a mouthful of meat. 'No, I think I will keep my past to myself, for as you can see, it has not been kind to me,' said Delsain, pointing to his face.

'Then what are your plans for the future?' Toi-mun asked with growing anger.

'Ah, an easy one. I am travelling to Taibasan. It is where my family resides. Well, not my immediate family, but I have an uncle, a spice trader, and I am hoping to join the business.'

Toi-mun could not detect a lie on Delsain's face, for it was the truth. Delsain had just failed to mention the numerous murders it was going to take to get him there.

'A man can get rich trading in spices. I wish you luck with that.'

'Thank you, and what of yourself, Toi-mun? Where is your ward?' he asked before he bit another chunk of meat from the bone.

'You are more observant than I first thought, Delsain,' complimented Toi-mun, throwing a twig on the dancing flames. 'He is being taught by another in a place where I cannot go even if I wanted to, so here I sit, waiting, not knowing when, or even if, he shall return.'

'A hard thing it is to wait. An even harder thing it is, not knowing for how long,' said Delsain. They ate the rest of their lunch in silence.

'Well, I still have to find a farmer to trade for some supplies, so I will bid you farewell, Delsain.'

Toi-mun got to his feet and gathered his remaining quarry. 'I hope our next meeting will be a bit less eventful than this one was,' replied Delsain, also getting to his feet.

The two men went their separate ways. As Toi-mun walked, he had a bad feeling that he had done the wrong thing in allowing Delsain to live.

The Hiratan had watched Delsain intently. From the moment he killed the old woman, it had perked the Hiratan's interest. 'Perhaps this is the one I seek,' it thought as it followed high in the sky. The only thing now was to verify if the man was indeed a Light Wielder. That was something that only time could tell him, so he watched, and waited for time to tell him what he needed to know.

# 31

GALTEONE'S BANNERS SNAPPED in the breeze as thousands of pairs of eyes focused on the surrounding countryside. They searched and waited for the imminent arrival of the Telirian army that had been spotted by the scouts of the Iron Shadow less than an hour before, scarcely three miles from the city. All the Council members were gathered on the walls, along with the troops.

'They should be here by now,' grumbled one of the soldiers.

'And are you complaining that they are not here trying to kill you?' retorted another with a smile.

The little bit of banter broke the tension that had been building, and a ripple of nervous laughter spread to all who were within earshot.

'The men are in good Spirits at least. How is the Council leader holding up?' asked Mek.

'He is fine under the circumstances,' replied Ter-hal sharply. He stared at Mek.

'They come at last. I can hear their footsteps,' announced one of the soldiers.

With strained ears, Galteone's defenders picked up the sound of thousands of feet pounding the ground in unison. The banner of Arama, blood red with a black fist at its centre, materialised over a slight rise in the plains.

'So they forded the river, leaving the way clear to Monalteone via the Marset Bridge. But to what purpose?' thought Mek.

Baieta must have been having the same thoughts, for he whispered in Mek's ear, 'A trap perhaps.'

'It very well could be, but who can tell?' replied Mek.

'There are still two hundred of our troops out there with who knows how many of Monalteone's soldiers and citizens,' said Baieta.

'If they had any sense, they would not try to return here. They would be better off heading to Weolm, where it is safe,' said Mek.

'For now at least,' pointed out Baieta.

'Yes, for now,' agreed Mek.

Delrain's army halted just out of range of Galteone's bowmen. They stood passively and in silence, except for the constant barking and howling of the Telirian war hounds that were held somewhere toward the rear with the siege engines.

'Something is happening,' yelled one of the soldiers as he gestured to the mass of men below him. The army parted slowly, and a tall figure clothed in fine black leather strode into the growing gap. The sun shone brightly on the studs in his armour.

Mek clutched onto Baieta's shoulder as he nearly doubled over with a wave of nausea.

'Are you all right, Mek?' asked Baieta, concern etched on his brow.

Mek straightened up, and a cold bead of sweat snaked over his face from his hairline. 'It is his power. I have never felt anything like it,' he confessed.

A quick glance at all the Jelery present informed him they had felt it too. The only one standing firm was Ter-hal, who starred venomously at Delrain, trying to kill him with his gaze. 'Good people of Galteone, for all of you who do not know it, my name is Delrain, and I, like your beloved Jelery lords, am a Light Wielder. But that is where the similarities end,' announced Delrain.

He paced back and forth as he spoke. 'Your leader, Lord Ter-hal – your nanny, your father, your dictator, your prison warden – has you locked up behind these.' He gestured at Galteone's vast walls. 'It is supposed to be for you own protection, or so he would have you believe.'

'Blow it out your arse, you Telirian scumbag,' yelled one of the soldiers.

Delrain looked up from under his brow. 'You are a brave man – stupid, but nonetheless brave,' he commented. 'As I was saying, the walls for your protection? Or a prison where your lords can keep an eye on you all? I would not have you penned in like cattle for the convenience of the farmer. I would not force you to live under a ridiculously outdated set of laws that have no bearing on how we should live our lives.' He paused for effect. 'We have our own minds to make the choices that we deem fit to better our lot in this world. That is what I offer. That is the Telirian way. That is the way of the future!' yelled Delrain, shaking with conviction. His troops let out a roar of approval, and he silenced them all with a gesture from his hand. 'I am a man of mercy, and I offer you a way out of your current predicament, your imminent destruction; a way out of your prison. I will leave the way open across the River Marset for all who wish to take it. You have only to swear your loyalty to me. However, I cannot offer the same option to the members of the Council, for they have only one option left to them, and that is death. I will give you all some time to decide what you wish to do with my generous offer. You have two hours.'

Delrain turned around and disappeared amongst his men.

Ter-hal massaged his temples and expelled a breath, then he opened his eyes and looked at the Council, that were gathered in the Tri Tower. He lowered his hands and crossed them on the table, and sat up straight before he said, 'It would seem as though we have an opportunity to save the good people of this city.'

'We had that opportunity before we were set upon, Ter-hal,' replied Xaryn with annoyance.

'Indeed we did, but that was before the enormity of the situation decided to set up camp at our walls. I never imagined they would be so many in number.'

'Your stubbornness knows no bounds, Ter-hal,' added Solatt, smashing his fist on the table.

The other Council members murmured their agreement with Solatt. 'My stubbornness has served its purpose in the past and has kept the citizens and the Jelery in order. Without it, there would be no Jelery!' replied Ter-hal, raising his voice.

That comment set off several arguments amongst the Council members.

'Enough, enough of this!' yelled Alourin. 'Here I sit with the all-powerful and all-knowing Council of the Jelery and they are squabbling, yelling, pointing fingers, having apparently reverted to children. Shame on you all, that I have lived so long to see the Jelery consume themselves with petty argument. We all have our strengths. We all have our weaknesses, and we all have made mistakes, but now is not the time for division. It is the time for unity. Our fate, it would seem, is sealed, and if this is to be our end, then let us meet it proudly and defiantly. Let us be remembered for our mercy as much as our power. We shall give all the choice to stay and fight or flee and live, and we shall not hinder them in their decision.'

'Once again, old friend, you have shown that your wisdom knows no bounds,' said Xaryn.

Ter-hal got to his feet and an unspoken agreement passed through the Council. 'United until the end, my brothers,' he said proudly.

'As it always shall be,' replied the Council as one.

At the Council's request, the citizens had gathered beneath the balcony of the Tri Tower. The ultimatum had been given: stay and fight or flee and live, while there was still a window of opportunity to do so. A low murmur broke out over the crowd, and from their vantage point, the Council members could see arguments flaring up, mostly between family units.

'My lords, how are we to know that we are not going to be walking into a trap?' asked one in the crowd.

'There is no way of knowing that, my good man,' replied Ter-hal. His answer produced a new wave of conversation and argument amongst the crowd.

'You have not led us astray so far, and this is our home. I would rather die defending my home than amongst the trees with a Telirian blade sticking out of my back.'

Most of the crowd agreed with the speaker and his logic. Although they were no soldiers, they would fight to the bitter end nonetheless.

'Good people of Galteone, none shall be frowned upon if they choose to leave, and all who stay shall be welcome to. And none shall pass judgement on either.

But the time draws near and a decision must be made, so if you wish to leave, then please do so now,' advised Ter-hal.

The people in the crowd eyeballed each other questioningly, but all stood firm.

'We shall be by your side, my lord, to whatever end,' declared a voice from the people gathered. The crowd cheered their support.

'To whatever end,' thought Ter-hal as pride caused tears to well in his eyes.

The cheering of the crowd resonated to the Telirian army, and a look of confusion crossed many of their faces. When Delrain heard the commotion, he walked to the head of his army and turned to address them.

'Perhaps they want to die,' he joked to the men, who laughed in reply.

'My lord, the gate is opening,' noted one of the soldiers.

Delrain squinted to allow himself a better view. A stream of horsemen, roughly fifty in number, galloped through the gates with Crawley at the head, and disappeared over the Marset Bridge into the cover of the forest beyond, away from the city and the impending battle. 'Strange indeed,' he thought.

'Delrain!' boomed Ter-hal as he came into view at the top of the walls.

'Is that all who would take advantage of my generosity?' sniggered Delrain as he stepped closer.

'It matters not that a Raver and a few horsemen wish to flee, but apart from them, the city holds firm,' declared Ter-hal.

'Is that to be your reply, then?' Delrain asked smiling.

'No, not in its entirety.' Ter-hal raised his arm and dropped it. 'Loose!' he cried, and the sky darkened with arrows as the men complied. Most of Delrain's men were beyond the reach of the arrows, but a few of the archers with strong arms found their mark and a couple of his men slumped to the ground, clutching at the arrows that protruded from their bodies. Delrain himself, who had approached the walls when Ter-hal appeared, was amid the deadly rain but calmly surrounded himself with a large energy shield that glowed red and sparked as the arrows touched it. He slowly turned and walked back to a safer distance where the arrows held no threat.

'If that is what he wishes, then so be it,' thought Delrain. 'Bring down the walls!' he yelled to his men. Those in the front row moved aside as the catapults were moved into place, and soon the air was filled with huge boulders that smashed into the walls of Galteone in an attempt to reduce them to rubble.

# 32

DELSAIN HAD HAD a fruitful few days as his power returned to him. Each murder had become easier and easier, and he had acquired all the possessions and equipment he would ever need to continue his journey to Taibasan. He stopped at about midday and set about fixing himself a meal. He started a small fire with an energy sphere, and gazed deeply into the flames. He had to shake his head to clear away the fogginess that had been settling into his conscience. This was not the first time that he had been a little distracted; a few nights past he had woken up to a whispering in his ear, but when a speaker could not be found he dismissed it as a dream. He ate his meal and kicked dirt onto the fire to douse it, then he shouldered his heavy pack and headed in the general direction of his destination.

As the day wore on, he found it harder and harder to remember what he had done a moment before, and it was not too long before his lucidity evaporated altogether and his mind drifted into the fog.

*So cold, so cold*, were the first coherent thoughts his brain had been able to process in a while, and he opened his eyes slowly with confusion. He soon realised that he was flat on his back, as he noted a couple of swollen grey clouds drifting by. He had been hearing a sound for a little while without realising what it was and sat up like a rocket when it became clear. A cold wind hit his face, and the salty tang of the ocean filled his senses. Delsain was at the top a cliff overlooking the ocean, listening to the waves pounding on its base below.

'You may be a bit disorientated, but that will soon clear.'

Delsain spun around and recoiled in fear at the Hiratan's grotesque and frightening appearance. It leered at him in response and uncoiled its wings to their impressive fullness, then folded them into a leathery bunch behind its muscular back. 'You are in no danger,' it reassured.

'All right, you have my attention, Hiratan,' replied Delsain, reaching for the sword on his belt.

'Good, Light Wielder, good. You are a Light Wielder, are you not?' the Hiratan asked as it threateningly leaned closer.

'I am, or at least I was part—'

'I care not for what you once were or what you did, or what you had to eat for lunch,' interrupted the Hiratan abruptly.

'Yes, I am a Light Wielder,' replied Delsain warily.

'And you are not Jelery?'

'No, definitely not.'

'Good. Then you will do something for me that I am unable to do myself,' demanded the Hiratan.

'What makes you think that I can do this something?' asked Delsain.

'Let me just say that you have certain abilities that I do not.'

'That of a Light Wielder,' provided Delsain.

'Precisely. Plus you have other qualities I admire. I have been watching you, and you are a survivor. You have – and will do – what it takes to ensure that you succeed.'

'What is it that you would have me do and, more importantly, to what gain?' asked Delsain, rising to his feet.

'You will steal the Earthen Staff of Knowledge and kill all in the vicinity, then the Staff shall be yours.'

'Bah! That is but a story. Such a thing does not exist,' dismissed Delsain.

'It exists, as you will see, and Ushwinn has it.'

'Ushwinn, you say? I have heard many stories about him. Apparently, he can control the elements, the wind, the water–'

'Yes, yes, yes, and all of the others,' interrupted the Hiratan with growing impatience.

'Well, if that is all true, then how am I supposed to be able to kill him?' implored Delsain.

'With this,' replied the Hiratan, throwing a dagger into the ground at Delsain's feet.

Delsain studied the dagger, and its black oily sheen screamed its origin. 'An Iron Shadow's dagger,' he said dismissively.

'I can hear from the tone in your voice that you are no wiser than those who carry them, for even they have forgotten the dagger's true purpose other than that as a symbolic item of prestige. Allow me to demonstrate its proper use.'

The Hiratan reached down and plucked the dagger from out of the earth. 'Give me your hand, Light Wielder,' ordered the Hiratan. Hesitantly, Delsain extended his hand. The Hiratan clasped Delsain's wrist with his taloned fingers and forced the palm upward.

'Ahh,' winced Delsain as the blade was drawn across his palm. He tried to pull it back, but the talons of the Hiratan bit deep. The blood flowed and formed a pool in the cup of his palm and the Hiratan smeared the blood upon the blade and released Delsain's hand, which closed instinctively on itself to stem the flow of blood. The Hiratan held up the dagger coated with thick blood. A drop had begun its bid for freedom when suddenly, it was drawn back to the blade. Delsain watched on in disbelief as his blood began to drain into the oily depths of the blade until none remained upon its surface. Delsain extended his wounded hand and experimentally squeezed a drop of blood onto the blade. For a few moments it sat there like a heavy drop of scarlet dew and then it disappeared into the dagger. He ran his finger over the surface of the blade and inspected it for traces of blood.

'You will find no evidence of blood upon it, for as you have seen, an Iron Shadow's dagger feeds upon the blood of a Light Wielder,' explained the Hiratan.

'To what end?' asked Delsain.

'Plunge this blade into a Light Wielder's exposed flesh, and the Light Wielder's abilities turn off, leaving them as weak and pathetic as a human. Leave it in there long enough, and it will drain their life completely; or once it is in there, you could easily snap his neck like a twig.'

'Or I could just slit his throat,' offered Delsain.

The Hiratan let out a deep, throaty chuckle. 'Perhaps, there are many ways to end someone's life; but getting close to another Light Wielder can prove rather difficult, for as you know, a Light Wielder can detect another of its kind within a certain distance.'

The Hiratan closed his eyes and concentrated. The dagger shimmered and enveloped itself in a black haze which grew in length before it solidified into a spear. The spear was seven feet long and had the same oily black finish as the dagger. 'A bit better for long range, wouldn't you say?' Delsain picked his jaw up off the ground and clamped his mouth shut. 'It is impressive, yes?' asked the Hiratan.

'Thoroughly,' replied Delsain with his gaze fixed upon the spear.

'The blade still has its limits. It can be formed into any sort of stabbing, cutting, or clubbing instrument, but it requires to drink after each transformation in order to do so again,' explained the Hiratan as it willed the spear back to its original form. 'The dagger will be yours, along with the Earthen Staff of Knowledge and the focus crystals that go with them.'

'What are the focus crystals?' asked Delsain.

'Four crystals were presented to Ushwinn as a gift when the treaty between the humans and Spirits was formed. They came from the major Spirits of each element – water, wind, earth, and weather,' explained the Hiratan. 'They were intended to extend Ushwinn's reach of power far beyond his and the Staff's normal capabilities, making him a threat almost anywhere within the land,'

'And they all will be mine to use,' gloated Delsain.

'Only if you do what I have asked. But be warned: while the focus crystals on their own can be used in relative safety, the Staff is dangerous. Use it if you will, but be warned – if the staff finds you wanting in power, it will destroy you,' warned the Hiratan.

'Well, what am I supposed to do with it, then?'

The Hiratan shrugged his shoulders. 'Keep it as a family heirloom, or you could gift it to someone you think has the power to wield it. I am sure you would be greatly rewarded for it. Just do not give it to any in the Jelery order, or I will seek you out and all my brothers will see to it that you have a long and unbelievably painful death,' threatened the Hiratan.

'Another thing, Hiratan. Where is the Earthen Staff of Knowledge and its Keeper?'

'On a small island off the coast of the south sea, in a time rift. That is why I need you. Only Light Wielders can enter time rifts.'

'It will take me at least two weeks to get there from here!' exclaimed Delsain.

'It took you nine days, Light Wielder,' corrected the Hiratan.

'What do you mean "took"?'

'Look around you, Light Wielder, and get your bearings.'

Delsain looked around and studied the surrounding countryside and the direction of the sun. 'I am already at the south sea. But how?'

'Not all the Earthbound Spirits wish the humans goodwill. They took over your body whilst your mind floated in the fog, and they brought you here at my bidding. It's amazing how much ground you can cover when you don't have to stop and eat, but only drink,' explained the Hiratan.

'Well, that was very convenient for you,' stated Delsain with a hint of annoyance.

'Light Wielder, the island is accessed by an unseen bridge that will require a leap of faith on your behalf. It is marked by two boulders that line up with the width of the island at that distance.'

'I do not understand how the island is visible if it is in a time rift,' pondered Delsain.

'It matters not, and I do not care to waste my time in the telling,' snapped the Hiratan.

'One last thing, Hiratan. It appears I have everything to gain from doing this, and yet you are getting nothing. So tell me, what are you getting out of this?' asked Delsain with genuine curiosity.

'Chaos,' replied the Hiratan.

'Chaos! Is that it?'

The Hiratan peered at Delsain and gave him an evil grin. 'Chaos is everything, Light Wielder, everything.'

# 33

FOR OVER TWO weeks, the walls of Galteone had been pounded relentlessly. Numerous manned assaults had been repelled, with heavy loss of lives on both sides. Ter-hal had been resting in his quarters ever since it had begun. A guard knocked on his door and was granted entry. 'My lord, the enemy are concentrating their barrage to the right side of the wall,' informed the guard.

'And how is the wall withstanding the punishment?' asked Ter-hal as he swung his legs over the side of his bed.

'Not so well, my lord. Cracks are beginning to appear at its base.'

'Summon all the Council members and inform them that the walls are under duress, and the time has come,' commanded Ter-hal.

The Council members were roused from their chambers. All had been sleeping more or less continuously since the attack had begun, in an effort to conserve their strength. The walls of Galteone ran deep into the earth, and that is where the Council made their way via the Tri Towers' ancient dungeon. Several passageways lit by smoking torches in the walls led to strategically placed chambers. The passageways were old and had been rarely used. Cobwebs choked up all available space, and had to be brushed aside for them to pass. The damp earthy smell of being underground infiltrated their senses and the chambers themselves were barely large enough to stand up in. The stones of the wall were uniform in appearance, except for the two that bore the perfect imprint of someone's outstretched hands. In separate chambers, the Council members placed their hands into the depressions and began to chant in a low monotone voice. The guttural words they spoke had been unheard by human ears for an age.

The sun began to set on a city under siege. Its outer walls glowed with a deep purple hue that radiated out into the growing darkness. Delrain emerged from his tent and smiled at the glowing walls of Galteone.

'Playing your last hand are we, Ter-hal?' he said to himself. 'And what will you do when this fails?'

Delrain raised his hands above his head, and a golden energy sphere appeared and grew in size until it had reached a metre in circumference. The light of the orb swirled within itself, bathing Delrain's face in its yellow glow. He threw it with all his might at Galteone's radiant walls. The sphere hit the walls and a shower of sparks erupted, filling the air with a metallic odor. The wall rippled like the disturbed surface of a pond, and deep below the walls, the Council members' faces twitched slightly with the impact.

'Increase the barrage from the siege engines, and tell the Telirian Light Wielders to bombard the walls with everything they have.'

# 34

DELSAIN STOOD AT the top of a cliff overlooking the island out to sea. He eyeballed the rocks to his left and right with mistrust.

'To trust the word of a Hiratan...' he thought. He had traversed the length of the cliff that overlooked the island several times, and whilst he had found singular rocks, these were the only two that came close to the description that the Hiratan had given. He stepped to the edge of the cliff and threw a precautionary glance at the jagged rocks that would greet him if he happened to be in the wrong spot. He went to step off and baulked, falling backward with panic.

'Leap of faith, my arse,' he growled, getting back to his feet.

He unsheathed his sword, using his great strength, he drove it into the ground up to its hilt. He retrieved a recently acquired rope from his pack and tied it to the protruding hilt. He tested his knot a few times and found it pliable enough. 'Let's try again, shall we?'

He threw the rope over the edge, and saw it disappear roughly eight feet below. 'Well now, there is something that you do not see every day,' he said to himself out loud. He descended into the nothingness, following the rope, and breathed a heavy sigh of relief when his feet touched the planks of the bridge. He released the rope and made his way toward the island.

Two-thirds of the way across, he stopped to formulate his plan of attack. He knew he would not go undetected on the island, and the prospect of an all-out brawl with the might of Ushwinn did not tickle his fancy. But how could he sneak up on him without being detected, when his very being would give him away? So he waited silently while his brain fed him alternate solutions to his dilemma. All were dismissed almost as quickly as they were formulated. Subconsciously, his fingers had been tapping on the hilt of his newly inherited dagger, and he stopped when he realised what he was doing. He drew the dagger from his belt, held it out in front of himself, and studied the oily blackness of its make. The Hiratan's words came flooding back to him.

'Plunge the dagger into a Light Wielder's exposed flesh, and that Light Wielder's strength and abilities instantly shut off.'

He knew now what he had to do, and he knew that he had to be quick about it as the warning of death rang in his ears. He stepped off the bridge onto the island and hid behind a tall tussock of grass. The island was not overly large, but he knew nothing of its landscape, except for the large rocky outcrop that dominated its core. So he decided to study what he could see. He looked around. Rocks, rocks, rocks covered in bird guano, smoke. Smoke. His eyes darted back, and yes, there it was, a thin column of smoke spiralling into the sky to disappear with the breeze. Where there was smoke, there was fire, and he was willing to wager it came from a cooking hearth. His plan was crude and violent: get as close as he could, transform the dagger into a spear, throw it into Ushwinn's chest, then rush forward and break the old man's neck.

Easy, simple, foolproof, he thought, but not this part. He placed the dagger's point on the underside of his forearm as it lay on the ground palm upward, which caused the flesh of the forearm to flatten, exposing nothing besides the skin and muscle. He was not going to risk a permanent injury if he didn't have to. Delsain drew a deep breath and pushed the blade through the flesh of his arm so it would stay in unaided. He stifled a scream as the pain began to build, and he had to fight the instinct to pull the blade free. He opened his eyes and rose to his feet.

He had to wait until the dizziness passed before he moved forward with haste. Time was now against him. He sprinted from cover to cover and swiftly advanced toward the stone outcrop. He sprang up from his hiding place and nearly ran into the back of Atiol, who was perched cross-legged on a large flat boulder.

Delsain pulled up a mere foot away from Atiol and thought that he would be discovered for sure. Atiol, however, had his eyes closed. His attention was tuned to the wind, listening to it, studying it, and was oblivious to all else.

The dagger in Delsain's flesh had become a white-hot fire, and he felt the blade drawing on his life energy. The young Light Wielder in front of him was a saving grace. This was not Ushwinn before him, so he figured that there were two on the island, and they would be expecting to feel each other's constant presence but not a third. So he would keep it that way, but he had to be quick. The relief was immediate when Delsain pulled the dagger from his arm. Atiol's eyes flicked open in recognition of another Light Wielder, but before he could act the dagger was driven deeply into his shoulder, up to the hilt. He let out a cry of pain that was cut off when two strong arms wrapped around his neck and stemmed the flow of blood to his brain.

Atiol thrashed and fought with his attacker, who was slowly taking the vision from the corner of his eyes. He hadn't the strength to fight any longer, and he slipped into blackness without a whimper. Delsain held on to Atiol's the neck for thirty seconds after the body went limp, to ensure he was truly dead. The body fell heavily to the ground when he released it. Delsain was breathing heavily, and sucked in deep lungfuls of sea air to calm himself. Luck, it seemed, was on his side.

Delsain crept to the entrance of the cave. He had been sensing Ushwinn for a good forty seconds and was positive that the feeling was reciprocated. A strong smell of baking bread reached his nostrils, and the homely comforting smell caused his stomach to rumble. Delsain held the dagger in front of himself and willed it into a spear. He studied the spear and noted that it was not entirely the same as when the Hiratan had transformed the dagger. 'I suppose we all have different visions of what the perfect weapon should look like,' he thought. He rounded a small bend in the cave's entrance hall and spotted a white-haired old man tending the fireplace, poking at its coals, stirring the flame back to life. He strode purposely toward him.

'Now, Atiol, there is no way you could have possibly finished the exercise I had set for you,' scolded Ushwinn.

'No, I am afraid he did not get the chance to do so, for he is the only thing that has been finished.'

Ushwinn turned with incredible speed, swinging the fire poker at the intruder's head. It connected with Delsain's temple just as he thrust forward with the spear. Delsain was knocked backward off his feet, and he lost his grip on the spear as he fell to the ground. He got to his feet with his vision swirling and he prepared to fight as best as he could, but he need not have bothered. Ushwinn's hands groped at the spear shaft protruding from his chest and tried to pull it free, but it was slick and wet with his own blood, and they kept slipping up the shaft.

'So here stands the mighty Ushwinn. I thought you were but a myth, a childhood story to scare little children to sleep. I must confess I am rather disappointed,' confided Delsain.

Ushwinn raised one of his blood-covered hands and a small golden, almost white, energy sphere began to grow. It grew to the size of an apple before it petered out to nothing. He tried again, but this time only raised a few small sparks from the palm of his hand.

'How?' he mouthed as his hand slumped to his side.

'You have been stabbed by a Shadow's blade,' explained Delsain.

'Ah, that would explain my situation. But I thought that information had been lost,' replied Ushwinn faintly before he staggered backwards, 'So you know all about the dagger's abilities?'

Ushwinn nodded.

'Well, then I would expect you know what is to come now.'

Ushwinn tried to draw air into his lungs and took only rasping breaths, barely drawing any. 'It matters not... You cannot wield the Staff.' He gasped as the pain flared in his chest.

'No, perhaps not, but I think I may know someone who might be able to.'

Anger flared in Ushwinn's dying eyes, and he let out a groan as the dagger began the painful process of drawing his life force from him.

'It would be a shame to waste all this food you have so lovingly prepared,' said Delsain with a chuckle.' I haven't had a thing to eat for days.'

Ushwinn toppled to the ground, knocking over a cupboard full of cooking utensils that clattered across the stone floor. 'Be still, old man. I am trying to eat over here,' said Delsain, stuffing a chunk of hot bread into his mouth.

The pain flared with each heartbeat that reverberated in Ushwinn's ears – thump, thump... thump, thump – and as they drew further apart, he shed a tear for mankind, and for all the Spirits and all that was good in the land. But mostly, he shed a tear for Atiol. Thump... silence.

Delsain watched on passively as he ate. After the meal he ransacked the cave for anything of use or value, but found the pickings to be rather slim. The Staff was not very hard to find as it was leaning against the wall in a casual manner. His heartbeat intensified as he extended his hand toward it. The wood pulsed with a life of its own and was warm to the touch. Delsain had felt power like this before, when he had been in close proximity to Lord Delrain, but never in an inert item such as this. The small silver case that housed the focus crystals were unearthed as he rummaged in Ushwinn's pockets, and he deftly slipped it into one of his own. The spear still protruded from Ushwinn's chest, and

Delsain grabbed it close to the wound and tried to withdraw it, but found it stuck fast.

'Plan B,' thought Delsain, grabbing the shaft of the spear once more. This time, he willed the spear back to its original form, and he watched as it shimmered and reverted to its former shape. His hand began to burn, and the smell of scorched flesh filled his nostrils; he released his hold on the searing dagger. He experimentally touched the glowing white handle with his index finger. 'Damn it!' He withdrew his finger and popped it into his mouth. 'That hurt,' he said as he examined the blister growing upon it. He gathered all that he could put in his pack, and shouldered it and tightened the straps until it sat comfortably. He grabbed the staff and made for the exit of the cave. He stole a final glance at the still glowing dagger and sighed at his loss.

'I will have to acquire myself another as soon as possible,' he promised himself. 'They are rather useful.' He stepped out of the cave, into the bright sunshine.

Thoughts of power and control had begun to seep into Delsain's thoughts. The staff was actively tempting him and in the few days since he had left the time rift behind, he had found himself on the verge of taking the leap many a time. He shifted the Staff to his other hand and rested it against his shoulder, then halted to consider his options. One, keep the Staff and hide it away in an undisclosed location known only to himself. He could steal away and look upon it, caress its smooth polished surface, and listen to it whispering, tempting him to raise it up and smite all who opposed him.

'Bloody hell! It was doing it again. You have one little thought, and it jumps all over you with plans of grandeur and fills your head with images,' he said to himself angrily. He realised that option was definitely out of the question, for sooner or later, he would be tempted to wield it and would inevitably destroy himself in the process.

The other option was to wield it.

'Perhaps I am powerful enough to wield it,' he thought. 'Ahh!' he screamed in horror and he threw the Staff to the ground. He looked at it and realised that every conceivable possibility where he still possessed the Staff would end up with him a pile of smoking ash and charred bone.

It was evident that he had to get rid of it. That meant giving it away to someone, and at this stage, he didn't care who that was. His brain ticked over at a frenetic rate, and a thought popped into his head, causing him to smile. He could re-enter the Telirian order if he offered the staff to Delrain as a gift. It would be more than a humble allowance of re-entry. He would be greatly rewarded, even revered. He would be second only to Lord Delrain, and rewarded with wealth and power beyond his imagining.

'Yes,' he said out loud. 'I will make my way to Lord Delrain and present him with the Staff.' He knew – as did most of the land, since it was the hottest topic of conversation amongst scullery maids and masters alike – that the Telirian army were laying siege to the Jelery stronghold of Galteone. He changed his direction toward Galteone, and the glory and praise and wealth that awaited him there. His head was filled with images of gold filling his pockets, spilling to the floor in their abundance. Smiling, he picked up his pace.

# 35

A SHARP PAIN in his eye brought Atiol out of the blackness. Again it flared, and he struggled to move. He opened his eyes a little, and saw a blurry beak attached to the white face of a seagull. He swiped weakly at it, forcing it to retreat into the air with a squawk of surprise. When he sat up slowly, the movement produced a burst of pain in his shoulder, and a warmth flowed down his chest. Blood, he realised as he fought the wave of nausea that followed.

Atiol had no recollection of the time that had passed from the moment he was first attacked, but the heat of the sun indicated that it had been longer than he cared to fathom. He was sunburnt, his throat was parched, and the desperate need for water overrode all his body's other signals of pain and discomfort. He rolled onto his knees, using his good arm to prop himself up. A nearby boulder provided the much-needed leverage and he pulled himself to his feet, where he swayed groggily. The short walk to the cave took an eternity, and several times he fought back the blackness that formed at the corner of his vision. The coolness of the cave welcomed him as he entered, and he slumped to the floor, soaking up the cooler temperature of the stone underneath.

'Get up, Atiol. Get Up!' his mind screamed at him. He rose on shaky legs and stumbled further into the cave's entrance, and almost cried in relief when he saw the large stone jar they used for storing drinking water. The stone lid shattered as he threw it to the floor, and he plunged his head into the cool liquid, taking huge gulps of water. He surfaced, coughing and spluttering, and immediately repeated his actions. When he surfaced, the fresh water washed the sweat from his scalp into his eyes, causing him to squint, and he wiped it from his stinging eyes with his sleeve. The water had revitalised him somewhat, and his thoughts began their return to rationality. The smell of blood, copious amounts of it, invaded his nostrils, and then the sickly-sweet smell of decay.

'Ushwinn, are you in here? Ushwinn,' he called.

Atiol entered the chaos of the kitchen, and his heart immediately sank.

'Oh, Ushwinn!' he wailed as he knelt beside the old man, who was lying amongst the clutter. He stroked his cool brow. 'You did not deserve an ending like this.'

As he looked around, it was evident that the Earthen Staff of Knowledge and the focus crystals had been stolen. The dagger still protruded rudely from Ushwinn's chest. Atiol noticed it for the first time, and it took a couple of minutes of rifling through his catalogued mind before he found the answer.

'It is the dagger of an Iron Shadow.' But instead of the oily black colour he was used to, this one was a brilliant pearly white, and the oily sheen caused a rainbow of colour to run up and down its length. 'Such a thing of rare beauty, and it was misused for evil,' thought Atiol angrily.

He took hold of the handle and pulled it from Ushwinn's chest. It slid out with ease, and to Atiol's surprise, it was completely free of blood. The blade filled the air with a high-pitched honing noise. He looked at Ushwinn and, for the first time, noted that there was hardly any blood surrounding the old man's body.

'Strange,' he thought, and then he realised that the smell of blood was coming from himself. He slipped the dagger into his belt. With the staff gone, his priority now was Galteone. At least he knew he would be of help there. He could fight the Telirians. The staff had been taken and could be anywhere by now and he did not have the patience to scour the land from end to end. Moreover, he had the niggling thought that, like himself, the staff would be heading to Galteone.

Atiol stood facing the cave's entrance. He had wanted to bury Ushwinn but found that when he tried to move him, his shoulder exploded with pain and hundreds of tiny stars clouded his vision. He could not bury him, nor could he leave him, so here he stood. He concentrated and concentrated. As the minutes ticked by, sweat beaded his brow, but slowly the earth responded and began to tremble. The trembling increased drastically until soon the whole little island was heaving violently. Rocks began to fall in the cave's entrance, and it was not long before the whole cave collapsed in on itself, sealing his mentor within.

Atiol ceased his effort, and the island once again became stable. He said his final farewell and walked away from the mound of broken rock that had become the burial tomb of Ushwinn. He didn't look back.

# 36

THE RELENTLESS ATTACK on Galteone's walls had continued, and yet, they stood unwavering. Delrain had begun to lose his patience, for he had greatly underestimated the Jelery resolve.

'My lord, may I come in?' asked Seker.

Delrain beckoned him to enter with a wave of his hand.

'My lord, the Telirians grow weary. They have been exerting themselves continuously for two days, and they need to rest,' he informed Delirian.

'Seker, my general, what of your little army? Are they too tired? Have they exerted themselves?'

'My lord, such a notion offends me. My men could carry on for several more days at this pace, but the other...'

Delrain silenced Seker with a dismissive wave. 'Perhaps you are right. You usually are, Seker, and if you think the Telirian Light Wielders need to recuperate, then let them do so. They will rest, and the siege engines will increase their rate of fire. I want you to gather all available men. The last thing we need to do is give the Jelery a rest,' ordered Delrain.

'We must break them. It is the only way,' he added.

'Yes, my lord, your bidding shall be done,' replied Seker as he turned sharply and departed the tent.

So the energy spheres ceased, and were replaced with a thicker aerial assault from the siege engines.

In the bowels of Galteone, the Council members endured all. By now, a small army of servants attended each member of the Council as well as they could. They hand-fed them and held cups of water to their lips so they could drink. The sweat was mopped from their brows, and they even helped them to relieve their bladders and void their bowels when required. Every six hours on the hour, they were administered thimble-sized cup of a potent brown elixir that was heavily spiced to make it palatable; it burned as it was swallowed. The elixir chased away any traces of exhaustion from the old men, and with this constant intake of fluids, food, and the elixir, the Council members could continue to protect the city for a long time.

Thaloss watched from the cover of the woods when the city first came under siege. And he watched on as a band of horsemen emerged from the city and rode past where he and the other refugees were hiding in the forest. Galteone was no longer a city at peace.

'We cannot enter the city,' said Manar as the first stones cast by the catapults smashed into Galteone's walls. Thaloss turned to him and thought to rebuke him for the comment, but realised the pointlessness of it and remained silent. 'Where do we turn to now for protection?' asked Manar with despair.

'Weolm will take us in, or at least I hope they will,' replied Thaloss.

The entire remnants of Monalteone's people and the two hundred soldiers from Galteone turned from the stricken city and began their march to Weolm. They arrived at the Weolm plains a good week later, and stood silently staring at the huge white walls of Weolm and the immaculately manicured gardens that stretched out all around it. For all those who had not seen the spectacle before, it took their breath away. A column of mounted men approached them on the cobblestone road as they came near the gates.

'Halt. State your business,' demanded a finely dressed man, prickling Manar's senses.

'I did not realise that the Telirians spoke for Weolm,' said Manar calmly.

The other man stared with contempt at Manar. 'They do not, my friend. Here is a diplomat from Arama,' said another, who came forward bearing the pips of a captain on the shoulders of his uniform.

'I am sorry. Allow me to introduce myself. I am Gelarne, the captain of the city watch.'

'Hail, Gelarne. I am Manar.'

'That man is Jelery,' hissed the diplomat from Arama into Gelarne's ear.

'Is that true, Manar? Are you Jelery?' asked the captain.

'I am,' replied Manar. 'And I seek refuge for all that travel with me,' he added.

'Impossible. Weolm is in deep negotiations with Arama, and it has been stipulated that no refugees from Galteone are allowed entry to the city whilst they still resist against the Telirian rule,' declared the diplomat triumphantly.

'I am afraid that what he says is true, Manar. I cannot allow your entry,' confirmed the captain.

'None from Galteone, you say? Then we are in luck, as we hail from Monalteone,' said Thaloss.

The diplomat's face turned red with rage. 'If that is correct, then I see no just cause in denying you entry,' said Gelarne thoughtfully.

'This is not allowed. They are Jelery and are not permitted to enter!' screamed the diplomat.

'No, Ramos. I have read the proclamation myself, and it only stipulates that those Jelery who are from Galteone shall not be given access to the city. These Jelery hail from Monalteone,' replied Gelarne with steel in his voice.

'I shall have this rectified at once,' the diplomat declared as he steered his mount back toward Weolm. 'Do not get comfortable, Manar. You will be wandering the roads before the day is out,' he threatened as he kicked the horse's flanks and took off toward the city.

'I would not worry too much about him and his threats. It took him a good three months to have his current proclamation sighted and agreed to,' assured Gelarne. 'But I do have a slight issue: you travel with a fair-sized force of armed men bearing the mark and dress of Galteone,' he added.

'Perhaps I can persuade them to discard all items declaring their origin,' offered Thaloss hopefully.

'I can see no issue with that,' agreed Gelarne with a smile.

It took far less time to persuade the soldiers of Galteone to discard all things bearing the mark of Galteone than Thaloss feared, but only with the promise that they could stash their armour and other identifiers in the forest for safekeeping, in case they required it at a later time. So it came to be that a fair-sized group of Jelery refugees entered the city of Weolm, seeking sanctuary.

# 37

THE WIND BLASTED the door off its hinges. Toi-mun sprang out of his bed and rushed to the doorway. 'You must make haste. He is badly hurt.'

Toi-mun turned around and faced Shi-liarne. Her eyes were red and swollen from weeping. 'Who, who is hurt?' demanded Toi-mun.

'It is Atiol. He has returned from the time rift. I felt him emerge, but when I went to greet him, I found him lying in the grass, unmoving, and I could not rouse him.'

Toi-mun had been pulling his boots on as she spoke and was strapping his weapons on as she concluded. 'Show me where. Take me to him.'

Shi-liarne disappeared in a gust of breeze and reappeared fifty metres away. Toi-mun sprinted after her, and when he got close, she disappeared again, popping up further away. Their unconventional travelling technique continued until Toi-mun's throat burned with every breath. Shi-liarne had Atiol's head cradled in her lap by the time he caught up to her.

'Move,' he commanded as he pushed her out of the way. He quickly examined Atiol and grimaced when he came upon the wound in his shoulder, which he bound as tightly as he could with strips of his own shirt. 'He is at least breathing deeply, but he has a serious shoulder wound and has been burned severely by the sun,' pronounced Toi-mun.

'Why does he not wake then? Why is he so still?' sobbed Shi-liarne.

'Most likely he has not had enough to drink or to eat. And who knows what he had to endure in the time rift? We have to get him to the cabin as quickly as we can,' replied Toi-mun.

He picked up Atiol and carried him over his shoulder. On the way back to the cabin, Atiol opened his eyes briefly and lifted his head and looked directly at Shi-liarne, who gave him an encouraging smile before his head slumped back down.

# 38

THE ENTIRE CONTENTS of the tent had been smashed into pieces, but despite this, Delrain scanned around for something else to take his frustration out on. His impatience had turned into outright rage because for three more days Galteone had been attacked alternately by the projectiles of the siege engines and the energy spheres from the Telirian Light Wielders, and occasionally both at the same time. He had reluctantly agreed to give the entire attacking force a break, knowing full well that in doing so he was also giving the Council members a chance for reprieve. Infuriatingly, as he predicted, the purple shield wall receded back into the ground half an hour after his attack had quelled.

The Jelery Council members had been administered a sweet, fruity elixir that had dropped them almost instantly into a deep slumber. They were covered in blankets where they fell in the personal chambers underground, because they had to be close at hand when the next onslaught began. Mek checked in on each member of the Council, and spoke in depth with all that were charged with their care, and their concern became his.

'They cannot keep up this pace. They are extremely powerful but they are also old men, and it is inevitable that their hearts will give in,' stated Baieta.

'To be completely honest, I am surprised that they have lasted this long. We must do something. We cannot just sit here waiting for our enemy to resume their attack and kill the Council. We must strike back,' replied Mek.

'Well, since the Council is unavailable at the moment, as a senior member of the Jelery Light Wielders and the only available member of the Order of the Light, is it not your duty to take up the reins?' advised Baieta with a wry smile.

Mek mulled this over briefly, and a small smile played across his face as he slapped Baieta on the back. 'Gather all the Jelery Light Wielders you can,' he ordered. 'It is time we gave them something to worry about.'

All the Light Wielders had gathered along the top of the city walls, from the lowest Order of the Grey to Mek in the Order of the Light.

'All have come as you requested,' Baieta informed Mek.

Mek looked around at the twenty or so faces of his fellow Jelery Light Wielders, and nodded to each in recognition when their eyes meet. 'Brothers, let us show that the Jelery are still a force to be reckoned with and not some dying animal waiting for the peace of death. We have to make this as short and as devastating as possible. Those with the ability of the Order of the Red, I want you to concentrate your attack on their tents. I want them to burn. Those of a lower order, I want you to aim at the men and any visible fires or braziers that are out in the open. Even though your energy spheres can't cause flames, they can certainly encourage existing fires to spread,' he ordered. The men nodded in understanding. 'I want the Telirians to lie awake in their cots, each wondering will he be next. I want them to taste fear.'

Mek raised his arm and let it fall. A small barrage of energy spheres descended into the mass of Telirian tents. After the third wave of the attack, most of the tents were now well ablaze and those who had not been injured or killed spilled out of them, only to be randomly picked off by the lesser energy spheres. A particularly well-aimed green energy sphere scored a direct hit on a large fire and sent flaming pieces of wood and ash into the fabric of the surrounding tents; several men emerged from the thick smoke, coughing and choking. As the tents were densely packed, the fire spread at an alarming rate, and the men who had been on the front line keeping watch were forced to retreat to assist those who were trying valiantly to douse the flames. All around, confusion reigned.

Mek nodded his head at a burly, barrel-chested soldier, who raised a small flag and waved it vigorously as if his life depended on it. A horn resounded in reply and the gates of Galteone opened. Two hundred mounted men spilled out of the city. Their armour glowed orange in the late afternoon sun. They charged headlong, straight into the Telirians' confused front line. Their swords cleaved limbs and heads from enemy torsos and blood flowed freely. With the fires burning through the encampment and a small savage contingent of the enemy ploughing a path through the front lines, most of the Telirian army began a confused retreat from the front line. With nothing but their unprotected backs on offer, the mounted men cut them down with ease.

A Telirian sergeant could be heard bellowing from somewhere amongst the confusion, and finally the retreat halted and they regrouped under the sergeant's orders and began to counter the mounted men. Overwhelmed by the far greater number of soldiers who were now organized, the men of Galteone sounded the retreat. Several men were pulled from their horses and stabbed to death; those who remained in the saddle were viciously stabbed and hacked at, and a number of them died where they sat, unable to move in the crush of humanity and horse flesh.

Mek gestured to his Light Wielders and a supporting volley of energy spheres cut into the enemy, gaining precious seconds for the horsemen. They eventually broke free of the Telirian front line and spurred their mounts into a full gallop, riding low in the saddle to minimise the target for the enemy. Surely enough, the first wave of arrows fell amongst them. But the arrows caught a couple of the men, who tumbled from their horses and hit the ground with a clang from their armour, but the riderless horses kept pace with the others. They returned to the gate and had to duck as the gates were hastily lowered to prevent access to the enemy on their heels. As the gate shut with a boom, Mek signalled a halt to the Light Wielders' attack. It had gone a lot better than he could have hoped.

'How many men did we lose?' asked Mek later, as he sat in his quarters holding a half-full cup of wine.

'Fifty did not return to the city, and a further eleven have serious injuries and will most likely not survive the night. All the rest bear some minor injury or bruise. The healers will have their hands full, in any case,' informed Baieta.

'Sixty-four brave souls lost. And what of the enemy?' he asked, taking a long swallow of the wine.

'Initial estimates put their losses at around three hundred, but it may be more. We have no way of knowing the number of casualties caused by the Light Wielders' attack and the fires that followed,' answered Baieta.

'Now we only have to repeat the feat thirty more times, and we will have this thing won,' joked Mek half-heartedly.

'How many?' screamed Delrain.

'We have the count at roughly four hundred, my lord,' repeated the soldier warily. Delrain sat heavily in his chair and scratched irritably at his stubble. 'Do you require anything further, my lord?'

'No, be gone with you, and tell everyone that I shall not be available this evening to anyone or for any reason,' commanded Delrain.

The captain departed from the tent in a flash, and Delrain sat staring into the burning brazier. He went over his entire campaign from the very beginning and for the first time, a small fear of failure arose and he began to doubt himself.

'Ahh, my lord,' called a wary voice from behind the tent walls.

'Are you entirely stupid? I said no one was to disturb me,' he threatened.

'My lord, I know what you said, but I must insist. This particular visitor has something that I think you would want to see,' answered the voice, shaking with fear.

Delrain muttered angrily to himself and spat on the expensive rugs that covered the floor of his tent. 'For your sake, I hope you are correct in your assumption.' he snarled.

A cloaked figure slid between the flaps of the tent opening and bowed deeply. Delrain could sense that the robed figure was a Light Wielder and smiled smugly to himself as the man trembled in fear. 'My lord Delrain, I have travelled hard and fast to come before you.'

'For what purpose? I assume that this is more than a social visit,' asked Delrain.

The man reached under his cloak and produced a staff. Delrain leant forward on the edge of his chair. 'Is that what I think it is?' he asked eagerly.

'Yes, my lord. It is the Earthen Staff of Knowledge, stolen from Ushwinn himself,' replied the visitor. He held the Staff out horizontally in his outstretched hands, offering it to Delrain.

Delrain exhaled sharply at the enormity of what the man was offering him.

'My lord, please take it from me, I beg you. I cannot stand to possess it any longer for I fear I shall be tempted to use it,' pleaded Delsain as he fell to his knees.

Delrain reached out tentatively and plucked the staff from Delsain's trembling hands. His mind was instantly filled with thousands of images supplied by the staff. Mountains collapsed and the earth tore itself apart. Lightning struck thickly wooded forests which burst apart trees with a crescendo of flying wood chips, and all the while, the wind howled hauntingly and obliterated everything in its path. And he was at the centre of all, holding the staff, wielding the destruction like the deranged conductor of an apocalyptic symphony.

Delrain wrestled his mind back to awareness and was surprised to see the sweat dripping from him in copiously. 'I know you are a Light Wielder,' he said, 'and I must insist that you remove your hood so I can look upon the man who has brought before me such a mighty gift'.

Delsain slowly pulled back his hood, and raised himself off the floor to look Delrain in the eyes. 'My name is Delsain. I am, or used to be, a Telirian Light Wielder until I was deemed unsuited for such a role, and I was cast out with a little token for the time I served you faithfully,' he said, indicating his burnt and scarred face.

'A great misjudgement, Delsain. Of that I am sure, my brother,' said Delrain, stepping forward. 'You are still a Telirian, but instead of following orders from the other Telirians, you will answer to no one but myself,' declared Delrain.

'I thank you, my lord,' replied Delsain humbly.

'Furthermore, Delsain, as a show of thanks for this timely gift, you will have the choice of whichever city you want to reign over as a mark of your prestige and high rank amongst our fellow Light Wielders.'

Delsain dropped to his knees and kissed Delrain's soft leather boots in gratitude.

'Delsain. There is no need for that, and besides, what would someone think if they were to see the second most important Telirian Light Wielder on his knees? Now, stand up, man.'

Delsain rose to his feet, and Delrain placed his free hand on his shoulder and squeezed it lightly. 'I have family in Taibasan, my lord. I wish to rule there,' said Delsain.

Delrain laughed and shook him gently. 'You are not wasting any time. All right, Taibasan is yours, as soon as we clean out this little nest of Jelery which, thanks to you, should be a hell of a lot easier,' agreed Delrain, offering his hand.

Delsain took the hand offered to him and shook it heartily. With his free hand he produced the small silver case that contained the focus crystals. 'A little something extra, my lord,' he said as he handed Delrain the case. 'They were a gift from the Spirits to Ushwinn. They can be used on their own to control the elements they represent, or they can be used with the staff to greatly increase its range,' he explained.

'Now that is an interesting concept,' said Delrain as he pocketed the case. 'Now tell me, Delsain, how did you come to be in possession of the staff? I want to hear it all. Leave nothing out,' ordered Delrain, indicating a chair for Delsain to sit on.

Delrain rose early and washed his face, and realised he needed a good shave as his hands scraped over the rough stubble. Sleep had been somewhat hard to obtain. The Staff had been very close to him, and he had discovered that it kept popping random images of grandeur and destruction into his head. During the night it finally occurred to him that the Staff wanted to be used; needed to unleash its power and was doing everything in its power to do so. 'It need not have tried so hard,' he thought with a smile. 'It shall see plenty of use with me.'

He dressed and ate the leftover meat and cheese from the previous night's meal, then strolled outside, brandishing the Staff in his right hand and saluting his troops with the other as he passed. He was in a good mood and began whistling a tune which roused strange looks from the men that were huddled around small cooking fires preparing their breakfast.

Seker emerged from his tent and stood enquiringly in the path of Delrain.

'Seker, a beautiful morning, is it not?' asked Delrain, halting in front of him.

'Yes, I guess so, my lord,' he replied perplexed.

Seker moved aside and allowed Delrain to pass then turned and followed at his heels. 'My lord, that staff you have – is it the Staff that I think it is?' he asked.

'Why, yes, Seker, it is,' replied Delrain.

'How did you acquire such a thing?' he demanded abruptly.

Delrain stopped and turned to face Seker, who immediately apologised for his curtness when he noted the look of anger in Delrain's eyes. 'Apology accepted. It is an interesting story, and I will tell you about it later, but right now, I have far more important things to attend to. Now come along,' demanded Delrain.

Delrain made his way to the highest vantage point, and the men parted and formed a curious ring around Seker and their lord. The morning sun was warm, and the sky was brilliantly clear. Delrain planted the tip of the Staff into the ground and took a deep, steadying breath. He felt a little fear as he began to concentrate, but realised he was aboard a wagon without brakes that had begun its descent down a treacherous ravine.

The Staff's power had been unleashed. The sky began to darken with thick storm clouds, and thunder rumbled ominously. The first lightning strike landed amongst his own troops, and he opened his eyes in an attempt to control it.

He focused on the looming Tri Tower that dominated the skyline. A massive bolt of lightning struck it halfway up, sending a shower of rocks on to the city streets below it. The power surged through Delrain's body, and the lightning began to strike randomly and indiscriminately. Numerous strikes rained down into the city, but just as many struck amongst his own men. Delrain's eyes glowed white hot, and he began to laugh wickedly as his clothes began to smoke. Seker rushed forward and tackled him when his concern became too great, and they landed heavily on the ground. The lightning continued for a few more minutes, and then the storm clouds dissipated almost as fast as they had emerged. Delrain sat up with his clothes still smoking and chuckled in triumph. He pulled Seker into a sitting position beside himself and thumped him on the back excitedly.

'Ha, it is a thing of beauty, a thing of beauty!' he declared.

A few rocks still fell from the damaged Tri Tower and then without warning, it teetered and began to collapse.

Delrain's men cheered as they watched it fall to the ground, crushing numerous buildings in the act.

'My lord!' exclaimed Seker as he got to his feet. 'Your power is absolute,' he added, pulling Delrain upright.

The soldiers around him dropped to their knees and bowed their heads in submission and reverence to their leader and lord.

# 39

ATIOL SAT BOLT upright, screaming and clutching at his ears, as if they were on fire. 'They will not stop,' he moaned.

'Who will not stop?' asked Toi-mun, rushing to his side.

'The Spirits are screaming in fear and pain. Something terrible has occurred,' he replied between clenched teeth. 'Oh no, it cannot be,' he added despairingly. 'He has the Staff and the Tri Tower has fallen,' he wailed as he rose to his feet and swayed dangerously, threatening to topple.

'Here, lean on me,' offered Shi-liarne, coming up under his good shoulder and taking his weight.

He looked at her with surprise and Toi-mun answered his questioning eyes. 'She has been with you since you emerged out of the time rift,' he explained.

The time rift, Ushwinn, the Earthen Staff of Knowledge, all of it came flooding back to him. He was overwhelmed with emotion and began to sob. Toi-mun turned away uncomfortably from the open display of emotion, but Shi-liarne stayed with Atiol and gently stroked his head as he cried himself out on her shoulder. It took a while for the weeping to subside, and Atiol found it hard to pull away from the warmth and intoxicating aroma of the little dark-haired Hiratan.

'I must go at once,' he declared, gently disengaging from Shi-liarne.

'Atiol, you are in no condition to travel anywhere,' advised Toi-mun.

'Do not tell me what I should and should not be doing,' snapped Atiol.

'I was not telling you to do anything,' replied Toi-mun calmly.

'I'm sorry, Toi-mun. I have to get to Galteone. I have to try and save it,' Atiol apologised.

'It is not a good idea, but I am always at your disposal – even if it means walking into the back of a huge armed force.'

'Thank you, Toi-mun.'

'Now, shall I gather everything for the trip?' asked Toi-mun.

Atiol nodded in agreement, and in a mere matter of minutes, all had been gathered, and they were ready to set out for Galteone.

'Shi-liarne, what exactly do you think you are doing?' asked Toi-mun.

'What does it look like?' she replied sweetly.

'We are most likely walking into the middle of a war zone, and that is no place for a female to be,' he advised strongly.

She laughed lightly and placed a hand on Toi-mun's shoulder. 'You seem to be forgetting that I am not an ordinary female,' she said lightly.

Toi-mun opened his mouth to speak, but a raised eyebrow from Shi-liarne closed it. 'Wise beyond your years,' she noted. 'And besides, someone has to look after Atiol,' she added as she moved off.

Toi-mun looked at Atiol, who looked back blankly in response. 'Perhaps she can cook better than you,' he said as he fell in behind her. Toi-mun muttered to himself and kicked at a some tall grass before he too fell in behind Shi-liarne.

# 40

ANOTHER ATTACK WAS unleashed on Galteone whilst its citizens were busy clearing away the rubble and shattered bodies that had been crushed by the Tower when it fell. It did not take long for the Council members far below to redeploy the shield wall.

'My lord, the attack proceeds as you directed,' reported Seker.

'Ah, Seker, do sit. I want to reacquaint you with someone.'

Seker did as he was told and took the seat that Delrain indicated. 'Delsain, you can come in now,' called Delrain.

Delsain appeared in the entrance of the tent and came to Delrain's side and sat down on a slightly lower but no less ornate chair. Seker felt a little put off as he looked at the plain chair upon which he was perched. Delsain removed his hood, and Seker visibly recoiled at the sight of his face. 'Hello, Seker,' he greeted venomously.

'Delsain, I would be lying if I did not tell you that I am surprised to see you,' replied Seker, staring coldly.

'Yes, well, I can imagine that it is not every day that you get to hold a conversation with a man you killed,' he sneered in response.

'You are obviously not as soft as I first thought,' smiled Seker.

'That is quite enough. We are all on the same side!' yelled Delrain, silencing them both.

'As you can see, Seker, Delsain sits at my side. That is because he brought me a great gift. He answers to none but myself, and any attempt to belittle or harm him will result in a rather unpleasant reprisal,' said Delrain.

'And Delsain, Seker is my general and the same applies for him. He answers only to me. Anyone with half a thought rattling around in his head can see that you two do not like each other. I am not asking you to become friends. I am only asking that you tolerate each other when you come in proximity of each other. Do I make myself clear?' he asked with steel in his voice.

'Yes, my lord,' they answered in unison.

'Excellent. Now I have something for each of you as a token of my respect,' announced Delrain.

He got up from his chair and went to a small table and picked up two small brown leather pouches. 'I had these made for you by the smith, who happens to be rather deft in jewellery making.' Delrain picked up a pouch and threw it to Seker, then threw the other pouch to Delsain. 'I do not know which of the two you shall receive. I left that to chance, or fate if you like,' he added.

Seker opened his pouch and a soft green glow emitted from within. He tipped the contents into the palm of his hand. He picked up a thick silver chain and gazed in wonder at the focus crystal as it continued to radiate. Delsain let out a gasp as he produced his own focus crystal, that glowed blue in his hand.

'Here, allow me,' offered Delrain as he took the chain and fastened it around Seker's neck. 'I personally selected these two focus crystals as a gift for you both to use as you deem fit,' he said.

'My lord, I do not know how to thank you enough,' said Seker, dropping to his knee.

'There is no need. You have served me well, and I reward those who serve me well,' replied Delrain, guiding Seker to his feet.

'Ah, earth and water! I cannot live without either. Enjoy getting to learn the power they possess, just as I am enjoying the power of the Staff. Now, whilst we wait for the men to soften up the Jelery, let us eat.'

Delrain clapped his hands and the servants floated in, placing onto a large serving table platters of meat, cheese, breads, and several varieties of exotic fruit that Delsain had never seen in his life. Delrain got to his feet, grabbed a jug of wine, and filled three silver goblets to the brim.

'A toast to the fall of the Jelery and to the glorious rise of the Telirian Empire.'

The three men raised their goblets to their lips and drained them in one gulp.

Mek walked through the fallen debris and watched in silence as the city's inhabitants cleared away the manageable pieces of stone from the top of the Tri Tower, all the while searching in the hope that the people who were still missing may yet be found alive.

'My lord.'

Mek turned around and looked directly into the eyes of a middle-aged woman with a weary face. She was covered in the fine dust that coated all in the immediate area.

'It was lightning, my lord. He brought the lightning down upon us,' she stated simply before walking away.

Mek looked upon the empty patch of sky where the Tower had stood, and his brow creased in concern. He had been on the walls when Delrain unleashed the fury of the staff, and when the Tri Tower came down he had felt the same helplessness and dread as the rest of the men. 'It is only a matter of time before he reduces the walls to rubble,' he thought. 'I need to get as many people out as I can when the time comes.'

He sprinted off to find Baieta, and prepare for the inevitable.

This time Delrain was prepared for the raw rush of power that flowed through the Staff and he channelled it more effectively. In hindsight, he considered himself lucky that he had not been overwhelmed by his first encounter with the Staff. The ground trembled slightly as he directed the combined power of the Staff's knowledge and power into it. The tremors grew steadily in intensity and built into a violent shaking that knocked down the men around him. The earth creaked and groaned as it dipped and rose like the surface of a turbulent sea. He bent the Staff's force to his will. The walls of Galteone lurched alarmingly, and terrified screams came from within the city. The shield wall stretched like elastic, trying to accommodate the weakened walls, and it became increasingly obvious to all within its vicinity that it was the only thing holding the wall in place.

Beside Delrain, Seker watched with interest, and he had been alarmed when the crystal began to vibrate from within his shirt. The walls of Galteone threatened to tumble. It seemed as if they needed a further push. He and drew the crystal free of his shirt and released the crystal's power at the walls. The earth near the walls heaved up and grew like a small hill, pushing the walls out to an unnatural angle. Below the walls, the Council members strained. The shield wall flared a brilliant hue of dark purple, and the wall halted its fall. But then, as predicted by Mek, the sustained effort asked too much of the old men, and one by one, their hearts burst in their chests and they dropped like stones to the floor until only Ter-hal remained; later he too fainted and slumped to the floor. The shield wall snuffed out like a blown candle. With nothing holding them up, the walls of Galteone fell heavily, sending great clouds of choking dust into the air.

Delrain ceased his efforts and turned to Seker. 'I see the focus crystal works well,' he noted with a smile.

'It seemed like the right thing to do at the time,' Seker replied, returning the smile. He let out a bellowed command, and the entire army rushed toward the city, screaming madly.

The wall had been breached in several places throughout the city, and the inner walls had almost collapsed entirely; but on the whole the outer walls had stood up fairly well, with only a few places large enough to breach. Galteone's archers flocked to them and fired indiscriminately at the mass of screaming men as they rushed at them.

Baieta stood before a collapsed part of the wall. 'Ready yourself, men,' he commanded. 'Wait until you see the whites of their eyes,' he added, unsheathing his sword.

They came through the swirling dust, searching for blood. For Baieta, time slowed. He calmly looked behind him at the nervous faces of the soldiers of Galteone, and smiled encouragingly before he let out a roar that drowned that of the attackers. He then launched himself toward them, and the soldiers of Galteone responded and charged into the fray, roaring defiantly.

They came together and the clash of steel on steel rang through the air. Screams from the fallen added to the chaos in the air, and the cobblestones around them soon became slick with blood and was treacherous underfoot. The soldiers of Galteone fought with courage beyond the grasp of ordinary men, and they died the same way. No one surrendered, and all around, Baieta could see isolated pockets where his men were totally outnumbered and cut down.

A scream of absolute defiance rose above the general chaos, and Ter-hal emerged from the stub of the Tri Tower with his eyes glowing white, hurling foot-wide white energy spheres at the attackers, who fled in fear of the old man as his tattered cloak whipped about him. He was no longer Ter-hal. He was a Light Wielder of the old legends, a god to be feared by humans and Spirits alike. The raw power of the earth flowed through his body unimpeded and burned the very air about him.

A score of Telirian Light Wielders came to the fray and charged at Ter-hal, throwing energy spheres of their own at the old man. The bodies were piling up around him, and the golden energy spheres of the other Light Wielders seemed to be absorbed into him. But his clothes were not made for such punishment and burned on his body; slowly, a blinding light began to surround Ter-hal. As it grew in intensity, everyone near to him had to shield their eyes from it. Captivated, they stopped, the battle forgotten as they gazed upon the spectacle. Then from within the light there arose a defiant scream that prickled the hairs on the back of their necks. The light exploded with a deafening boom, sending shock waves outward and knocking all to the ground. They had been the lucky ones, as dozens and dozens of charred smoking bodies surrounded a large circle of melted and scorched stone that still glowed red with intense heat.

Baieta heard the huge explosion and felt the outer shock wave go by him. He knew they could not hold much longer. There were no other men in reserve, and retreating would be pointless as all the inner walls of Galteone were not defendable. He rallied the remaining men to him, and they fought on for what seemed an age. As he ran his sword through another of the enemy, he just hoped that he had bought Mek enough time.

# 41

ATIOL'S CONDITION HAD deteriorated drastically as the day wore on, and they were forced to stop well before nightfall. Atiol lay on his bedroll, and Shi-liarne examined his shoulder. She unwound the crude bandage, and the smell of corrupted flesh wafted from it. She applied a small amount of pressure, and a drip of pus leaked from the swollen red wound.

'His wound is putrefying. It must be cleaned,' said Shi-liarne.

'How are we going to do that? We do not have the proper medicine for that type of wound. We do not even have anything to stitch it closed,' replied Toi-mun.

'Do you have any salt, Toi-mun?' she asked.

Toi-mun scrounged through his pack and pulled out a small pouch of rock salt and handed it to her. 'You do realise how expensive that stuff is, don't you?' he asked.

She smiled sweetly and dumped the entire contents into a cooking pot. 'I need you to fill this with water and bring it to the boil. I have to go and find something that may help keep the wound clean,' she said, disappearing with a gust of wind. Toi-mun filled the pot with water, and set it on the fire and watched restlessly for the water to boil.

Shi-liarne returned as the water began to boil and placed a small bark-wrapped package beside Atiol, who was sweating profusely. She rummaged through Toi-mun's pack and pulled out a relatively clean shirt and began ripping it into strips. Toi-mun removed the pot from the fire and set it aside to cool.

'Atiol, Atiol,' called Shi-liarne, gently rousing him from his sleep. 'I have to clean your wound, and I am not going to lie to you – this is going to hurt,' she advised.

Atiol nodded in consent and closed his eyes. She dipped a piece of the torn shirt into the salt water, removed it, and while the steam still rose from it, cleaned around the wound. She threw the cloth to the side and gathered the edges of the wound between her hands, and squeezed. Atiol grunted in pain as th thick yellow pus was forced from the wound.

'Toi-mun, can you wipe it away for me?' she asked. Toi-mun complied, and he wiped away what seemed to be an endless supply of the thick, putrid excretion. She eventually stopped squeezing and picked up the pot of boiled salt water, and tested its temperature.

'Can you pull the wound apart for me, please?'

Toi-mun manoeuvred into position and did as was bid. She tipped the salt water into the wound in an attempt to flush it free of infection. Atiol groaned and clenched his teeth as the hot water hit, but could not suppress a cry of pain as the salt stung his raw flesh.

'I am sorry, Atiol,' Shi-liarne repeated over and over until the pot was empty. She placed the pot to one side and picked up the bark-wrapped package and carefully opened it. She removed a piece of honeycomb dripping with its sweet filling. She tried to get as much of the amber liquid into the open wound as possible, then heated the wax in the pot and poured it onto the wound to seal it. 'I know it is crude, but it is all we can do for now,' she said to Toi-mun as she bound the wound tightly with the remaining strips of the shirt.

'Will it stop the corruption in the wound?' asked Toi-mun.

'I do not know. Only time will tell,' she replied.

# 42

AS THE SOUNDS of battle grew close, Mek herded as many people as he could to the front gate of Galteone.

'We will only have one shot at this before they spot us and try to stop what we are doing. So at my command, the gate will be opened, and you will all head straight for the trees beyond the river,' he ordered.

'It is too late, my lord,' shrieked one of the women, gesturing to an oncoming group of men, waving their weapons above their heads menacingly.

Mek swore colourfully and ordered the gates to be opened. 'Quickly, get out now!' he yelled, casting energy spheres at the charging enemy.

The gate ground to a halt with a screech a half metre from the ground, and refused to budge further. They were effectively bottled in, with only a few able to roll under the prostrate gate at a time. Their enemy was too great in number, and Mek alone could not stop them. The women and children around him began to cry and scream with fear.

And then Baieta emerged from a side alley and charged straight at the oncoming men. At the last moment, he dropped low and swung at the knees, cutting them down like wheat.

'Get the gate, Mek!' he yelled as he parried a blow and cleaved the head off his attacker.

Mek pushed his way to the gate and bent down and grabbed underneath it. He took the full weight of the gate and strained as he lifted. The wall had buckled, and the track was bent from the earthquake. It screeched in protest but it began to rise. Mek kept up his effort, and inch by inch, he forced it past the kink, straightening it out enough to allow the gate to rise under its own power. Mek fell to the ground as the citizens of Galteone made their escape toward the cover of the trees.

A and familiar hand pulled him to his feet. 'The city is lost,' said Baieta.

'It was lost the moment they arrived, Baieta. We can only hope that more have managed to escape. By the way, you look terrible,' replied Mek as he watched the city burn from several deliberately lit fires.

'It has been a somewhat terrible day,' said Baieta solemnly.

'The order has failed, my friend. After thousands of years, it has failed,' stated Mek as he dropped his head.

'No, it can never fail as long as there are people who believe in our way – and if there is at least one who can show them the way,' replied Baieta, pulling Mek into a rough embrace.

An arrow clinked against a stone wall and fell at their feet. Mek looked around, and saw around fifty men advancing on them position swiftly.

'Can you bring the gate down, Mek?' asked Baieta as another badly aimed arrow clinked against the wall.

'If I can get through the chains, then yes,' he replied.

'Then do it, Mek. We need to give them as much time as we can to escape,' ordered Baieta.

Mek looked at his old friend and smiled, knowing what it would mean when the gates slammed shut. 'Yes, we owe them that much,' he agreed. He threw a golden energy sphere at the chains that held the gate open. Sparks flew on contact, the chains glowed white hot, and soon they began to stretch like soft clay.

'Good-bye, old friend,' said Baieta, and he shoved Mek with all his might. Mek landed heavily on the ground and turned in time to see the chain give way completely. The gate came crashing down.

'Baieta, Baieta!' he screamed.

'Go, you fool, you also need time to escape, and I can give that to you. I cannot let you die. I swore an oath,' replied Baieta, yelling his response.

Before Mek could reply, the first sounds of ringing steel on steel rang out on the other side of the gate. 'Give them hell, old friend,' he said quietly as he ran off towards the forest in pursuit of the other refugees.

Thaloss was sitting with a few of the soldiers from Galteone when Manar burst into the small house they had been occupying for the last few weeks in the slums of Weolm. 'Slums' was just a name, as the city of Weolm was wealthy, and the area would have been regarded as a regular suburb in another city.

'Galteone has fallen to the Telirian forces,' he announced.

The soldiers murmured amongst themselves before one of them spoke up. 'Did any survivors escape?' he asked with concern.

"Tis hard to say. There have been a few reports confirming that there were, but it is still unclear,' replied Manar.

'If there are any survivors, they will be heading here,' said Thaloss.

'A fat lot of good that will do them. They will not be granted refuge while that diplomat from Arama slinks around in the palace, poisoning the minds of the officials,' replied the soldier, who had spoken earlier.

'That is unfortunately true, but nothing is stopping us from going out to meet them and offering whatever supplies we can muster,' said Thaloss.

'You are right once again, Thaloss. If we ever go back to Monalteone, I believe I will require an advisor,' replied Manar. 'Well, what are we doing, sitting here on our backsides?' he demanded as he leapt to his feet.

'Steady up there, my good man. We have yet to procure the supplies we will need. Give me until the end of the day, and we will head out at first light,' said Thaloss. Manar reluctantly agreed and sat back down.

The sun rose early, but the several hundred horsemen rose earlier and departed Weolm, carrying as much as they could muster in the way of supplies. On the way, the two hundred Guards of Galteone retrieved their stashed equipment, dressed proudly in the colours of Galteone, and set off at a steady pace along the Weolm Pass in the hope of encountering any survivors.

Mek and the small group of refugees had had a rough couple of days as they had been pursued doggedly by a group of Telirian soldiers. On several occasions, they had to flee for their lives into the thick undergrowth to remain unmolested. At around midday, they were walking on the side of the road when he felt a prickle of recognition.

'Everyone off the road into the trees!' he ordered. It took a couple of minutes for everyone to be safely hidden amongst the trees, and they remained deathly still as the first sounds of hoofbeats reached their ears.

'They cannot have been this delayed, if they escaped at all,' said a voice.

The mounted men came into view, and one of the horsemen in the lead turned and peered into the forest where Mek lay. 'There is a Light Wielder in there,' he announced.

Mek's heart sank, and he sighed heavily. '

You had best come out of there,' commanded a voice.

Mek weighed up the options and decided to do

as they said. He rose to his feet, and with a gesture behind his back signalled the others to remain where they were. He stumbled out onto the road and was instantly surrounded by the men. 'Perhaps, if I comply, they will not realise there are others,' he thought as he studied his feet.

'Mek, is that you?' asked a soldier. Mek raised his head and stared into the smiling face of Manar. 'It is you,' Manar confirmed.

Mek looked around at the mounted men and saw that they bore the marks and garb of Galteone and Monalteone, and he sighed gratefully. 'You have no idea how good it is to see the likes of you,' he announced.

The refugees slowly emerged from the trees, and the soldiers dismounted and offered them food and water, which they took readily with many thanks.

'We travel to Weolm, seeking refuge,' said Mek, after a long swig of water.

'It will do you no good. While Weolm remains neutral, there is a Telirian diplomat residing within its walls, and he has convinced those in power to deny refuge to all from Galteone,' informed Manar.

'How did you fare when you attempted to gain entry?' asked Mek curiously.

'A small loophole that the diplomat forgot to close.

I am from Monalteone, not Galteone, and they could not deny us refuge.'

Mek smiled in reply. 'Yes, that sounds like the governing body of Weolm. They are sticklers for protocol and documentation,' he agreed.

'So we decided that since you cannot gain refuge within, we would bring the refuge to you,' said Thaloss, joining the conversation.

Mek looked at the heavily burdened animals and smiled at Thaloss with genuine warmth. 'So we will be denied refuge in all the cities of the land and shall be forced to live like nomads,' he sighed.

'It will not be as grim as that, Mek. We have brought more than enough supplies to keep you going for months, and I am sure you can find a good place to reside in the woods. There are building supplies as well. You will not go unhoused,' replied Thaloss.

'Nor unprotected, my lord,' added another of the soldiers. 'The soldiers of Galteone will protect our people and stay with you,' he added.

'I thank you all,' said Mek.

'Mek, my soldiers and I must return to Weolm. We will keep you well supplied until we too are banished, or when your numbers have grown enough for us to join you permanently,' announced Manar.

'It sounds as if you have it all worked out. I will look forward to your visits. At least I still have one other Jelery Light Wielder to impart my wisdom to,' said Mek with a broad grin.

'I would be honoured to receive the teachings of one in the Order of the Light, but for now, I bid thee farewell,' he replied, and prepared to leave.

'Farewell and thank you,' said Mek as his growing band of people gathered the supplies and headed into the forest, protected from behind by the remaining troops of Galteone.

# 43

'My lord, the city has been taken,' informed Seker.

'Excellent. Tell the men to kill anyone they find. Give them a day to loot all they can,' ordered Delrain.

'And after that?'

'After that we regroup and make for Monalteone. I want it reduced to ashes as if it never existed,' he replied.

'It will be as my lord requests.'

When Seker had departed, Delrain picked up the earthen Staff of Knowledge and caressed it lightly. Its raw power sent tingles up his arm.

'Ahh, my beauty,' praised Delrain as he gazed into the deep red colour of the staff. 'Today Galteone. Tomorrow the entire land.' He burst into maniacal laughter.

# 44

AS HE TRUDGED on toward Galteone, Atiol's condition did not appear to be getting any worse, nor did it appear to be improving.

'How are you feeling, Atiol?' asked Shi-liarne.

'I have been in better shape, but I think I will live,' he replied.

'Do you still think it is a good idea to return to Galteone?' asked Toi-mun.

'No, probably not, but what else is there for us to do? The city is under siege, and we may be able to help.'

The talk dried up after that exchange. And no one commented when they detected a hint of smoke on the breeze. The day was growing dark as they stopped to set up camp for the night. Toi-mun started a small fire, and Shi-liarne cooked them all a simple hot meal.

'I must apologise to you, Atiol,' said Toi-mun.

'For what?' asked Atiol.

'It would seem as though you were right in your assumption. She can cook a hell of a lot better than me,' answered Toi-mun, taking another mouthful of food.

Atiol struggled to suppress a laugh. 'Idiot,' he said, throwing a small rock in Toi-mun's general direction. That simple act relieved a lot of tension that had built up within the trio since they'd left the cabin, and they all went to sleep in a better mood.

They woke up early and with their more improved mood, they covered a lot of ground. By late afternoon, the smoke that had been just a hint the evening before hung thickly in the air, casting them all in an eerie yellow glow as it covered the setting sun.

'How far do you reckon we have left to travel, Toi-mun?' pondered Atiol as he poked at the small fire.

'A day, day and a half, tops,' replied Toi-mun, as he laid out his bedroll.

'I wish for us to be there by tomorrow. All this smoke hanging in the air is making me nervous.'

They awoke well before the dawn was upon them and set out while there was still a noticeable chill in the air.

Only a few hours later, Atiol stumbled and fell to the ground. Shi-liarne helped him to his feet and felt that his skin was drenched in sweat. She placed her hand upon his brow.

'You are hot with fever, Atiol. The corruption in your shoulder is spreading,' she informed him.

'Then I shall just have to put up with it,' he snapped, resuming his pace.

Shi-liarne slipped back to walk beside Toi-mun. 'He cannot keep up this pace. It will kill him. You are his protector. Is there nothing that you can do to at least make him rest a little?' she pleaded.

'No, not when he is in this mood. We can only be there to help him if he should fall, unless we tie him up,' he replied.

Shi-liarne looked at him hopefully. 'Despite his fever, he is still rather strong. We would not have a chance.'

The smoke was thicker now, and it blew directly toward them, stinging their eyes and making them cough. Finally, as the sun was threatening to set, Galteone came into view.

'There is no army here,' stated Toi-mun, scanning the area.

'No, not anymore, but there was an army here,' replied Atiol, pointing out the rubbish heaps and piles of broken and discarded equipment just visible in the fading light.

'It is too risky to enter the city by night,' advised Shi-liarne.

'It is just as risky to stay out in the open,' retorted Atiol.

'She is right, Atiol. We do not know who is waiting for us in the city, but at least, out here, we can detect anyone trying to sneak up on us.'

Atiol was not hearing the validity of the point Toi-mun was making, as he was staring at Galteone. Something was missing from the skyline above the city – and then it came to him. 'The Tri Tower!' he exclaimed.

'It is still there, or at least half of it is,' stated Toi-mun sombrely.

Atiol fell heavily to his knees in despair. 'I have failed them,' he said quietly.

'That is not true. We will wait until the light of day, and then we will go to the city. There may be people there who need our assistance,' consoled Toi-mun.

Shi-liarne laid out Atiol's bedroll and helped him into it. Despite his condition, he protested strongly when Shi-liarne slipped in beside him. 'You need to keep warm, Atiol, and I do not think it would be a good idea to start a fire and alert everyone to our presence,' she explained.

Only Toi-mun saw the look of contentment on Shi-liarne's face as she snuggled deeper down into the covers, and it did not take Atiol long to fall asleep.

'Why do I feel as though I am a rabbit about to walk into a snare?' said Toi-mun to the night air.

Morning came as mornings usually do, and Atiol was visibly weaker now. 'We had better get this over with before you drop where you stand,' said Toi-mun.

'I will be fine, Toi-mun, so stop worrying yourself,' replied Atiol.

As they got closer to the walls, the first bodies became evident. Atiol looked at the carnage and couldn't help but think of the dream he had all those weeks ago. He stole a worried glance at Toi-mun, fearing that the rest of the dream might come to be as had everything else.

'That is not one of ours,' reported Toi-mun as he studied a corpse with several arrows protruding from it. They had to pick the way around the bodies of the fallen as they entered the city via a collapsed section of wall, and gasped in horror as they came across the carnage resulting from hand-to-hand combat.

'Why do men do this to one another?' asked Shi-liarne, who was clearly appalled.

'It is in our nature,' replied Toi-mun bluntly.

The smell of thousands of bodies ripening in the sun turned their stomachs, and they were forced to breathe through their mouths to try and stop themselves from dry retching.

'There is naught but death here, Atiol. We should cut our losses and make for Weolm,' advised Toi-mun. Then a flutter of movement in his peripheral vision caused him to automatically turn his head toward it. 'I stand corrected. We are not alone here,' alerted Toi-mun.

'I know,' said Atiol, indicating with his eyes a man who was barely visible on a nearby roof.

'Keep walking, and do not let them know we are on to them,' advised Toi-mun.

'Where to now? It is clearly devoid of life,' asked Atiol.

'To the front gate, of course,' replied Toi-mun.

The men above them were becoming bolder in their appraisal of the trio, and were now not even bothering to hide.

'I think our ploy is not proving as useful as we first planned,' said Toi-mun, as they were approached.

'Well, well, it looks like we have ourselves some late-comers to the party,' sniggered one of the men as he openly appraised Shi-liarne's body.

'And by the looks of that one, we got just one of the sort we were fishing for,' said another, pointing at Atiol.

'I think it's time to run,' said Toi-mun.

They needed no coaxing and sprinted for the front gates, dodging the fallen rubble and jumping over the corpses of friends and foes alike. They made it to the front gate, which was propped open by a large timber beam, but were stopped in their tracks when ten men appeared on the other side of it.

'Leaving so soon?' asked one of them, laughing. The other men caught up to them from behind and effectively boxed them in.

Toi-mun drew his weapons. 'Make for the ones at the entrance,' he commanded.

Atiol nodded in agreement and flung out an energy sphere that produced a hole in the stomach of one of the ambushers. The others turned to look as their comrade collapsed to the ground with a sigh. It was a mistake. Toi-mun was amongst them like a flash, and between his superior skill and Atiol's energy spheres they dispensed with them rather efficiently, but only had a moment of reprieve before the others joined the party.

Atiol looked around and was thankful that Shi-liarne had done her disappearing trick and was not sticking around in the thick of the violence. Toi-mun herded Atiol protectively behind him as they attacked. They all came at him, except for one, who was staying out of harm's way and was blowing frantically on a shrill whistle. Even as skilled with the blade as he was, Toi-mun could not block everything and was frequently nicked. Neither he nor Atiol noticed the figure sneaking up behind them. Atiol received a clumsy glancing blow to the head from a mace and went down with a cry. Toi-mun spun deftly, blocked a killing blow with one of his war sickles, and sliced open the throat of the attacker. His preoccupation in saving Atiol's life had cost him several seconds of keeping the other attackers in sight, and he leant back just in time as he turned, in an attempt to avoid a swinging blade. But he was not fast enough, and the blade bit deeply and sliced a huge gash from his forehead to his chin, blinding him in one eye. He roared in pain, and desperation drove him to fight like a banshee. He did not even notice that he had been receiving help for a good twenty seconds. Then two, three, four of his Iron Shadow brothers at arms joined the fray and dispensed with the attackers.

'Come, brother,' beckoned one of them, gesturing to a raft where Crawley stood with two other Iron Shadows.

Then they heard them well before they could see them – the hair-raising braying and barking of Delrain's enormous war hounds reverberated in their ears.

'You need to get him on that raft quickly,' demanded Toi-mun, urging the two Iron Shadow who had just picked up the unconscious Atiol. They doubled their speed and had him aboard the raft in a snap.

'Brother, come with us,' said one of them.

'Nay, brother, you and I both know that they would only follow you to the ford further down the river, where not even all of us would be able to kill them before they killed us. They will not smell you once you are on the river. I only need to distract them long enough so that you will be out of sight before they can think of what to do next. They are strong, but they are not smart,' Toi-mun explained patiently.

'Your words are the truth, but it does not make this any easier. I wish you the best of luck,' replied the other Iron Shadow, clasping Toi-mun on the forearm.

Toi-mun returned the gesture. 'Now go. They are almost upon us,' he ordered.

The remaining Iron Shadow sprinted for the raft and had to jump for it as it had already been launched into the river. The rocking brought Atiol around to a semi-conscious state, and he stared at the rapidly shrinking figure waiting patiently in the fighter's stance, dripping with his blood and the blood of his fallen enemies, and he saw several impossibly large war hounds leaping at the figure before the darkness took him again.

**Here ends the first book.**
**Rejoin the story in the second instalment.**

Printed in Dunstable, United Kingdom